i

"Best Friends: Beth Keeps Her Promise, 1861-1865" is the continued story of the adventures of the friends in "Best Friends: Southern Indiana, 1860."

Follow Beth as she helps a number of slaves reach freedom in the North. She shows us not only that she is a southern lady but that she has a sly side as well.

Written by Sandy Andrews
Copyright 2011 Sandy Andrews
All rights reserved.
Cover Design: Sara Schapker
Cover Photo: Straub's Photography
Edited by: Amanda Merkley
Model: Scott Schapker
        Elizabeth Schapker
Union uniform courtesy of: Crescent City Sutler, Evansville, IN
Layout by Barbara E. Zwickel - Aztec Printing,Inc.

PUBLISHED BY

731 C. Erie Ave.
Evansville, Indiana 47715
www.cordonpublications.com
Cora@cordonpublications.com
(812) 303-9070

First printing: September 2011.
Printed in the United States of America
Manuscript ISBN: 978-0-9839858-1-5
e-book ISBN 978-0-9839858-2-2

BEST FRIENDS

Beth Keeps Her Promise

1861 - 1865

By

Sandy Andrews

2011

This book is dedicated to

all the young adults who have given

their all to our country.

Civil War
1861-1865

Indiana

The Edgewood Family

Rae (14-17)

Anna (mother)

Andrew (father)

Lee (brother 8-11)

Alan (brother 9-13)

Bessie (Housekeeper)

Gerald (Farmhand)

The Jefferson Family

A free family of color

Dawn (14-17, code name: Indiana)

Dolly (mother)

Thomas (father)

Bree (sister 4-9)

Doris (sister 9-12)

Granny Bella

Grampa Teddy

The Brown Family

Zane Avery (17-20, code name: Wabash)

Grant (father)

Abby (free slave)

Dew (Abby's son)

Indians

Night Hawk

Moon Beam

Lone Star

Little Dove

Georgia

The Taylor Family

Beth (15-19, code name: The Boy)

Denise (mother)

Eugene (father)

Robert (brother 21-24)

Rosa Mae (sister 18-22)

Momma Jo (house slave and nanny)

Bow and Sunny (Momma Jo's grandsons

Duke (Beth's beagle dog and protector)

Friends

Stella (17-21, code name: Smoky)

J.B. (20-23, code name: Slick)

FACTS

From the Times

Mail was very difficult to deliver in the 1800s. It often took weeks for a letter to be delivered and many times a letter would be lost and never delivered at all. It was quite common for letters to cross in the mail so that one might receive a second letter before the first.

During the Civil War this problem became much worse, because army camps on the move at all times made it very hard to locate a soldier to deliver his mail. Delivering mail across enemy lines was even harder and sometimes took months. When a soldier received a letter from home it was a treasure.

Underground Railroad

The Underground Railroad was a network of people, both black and white that worked in secret to help runaway slaves reach freedom in the north. When fugitives reached a safe place, they were hidden in caves, cellars, attics or barns and supplied with food and other items needed for their trip.

There were hundreds of these safe places, or stations, many of which were located in Southern Indiana. It is known that there were safe places in Newburgh, Evansville, Mount Vernon and New Harmony, as well as many other places along the Ohio and Wabash Rivers.

Those who worked for the Underground Railroad put their lives and their families' lives in danger many times. But these Conductors, as they were called, were a dedicated group of people. They did not believe in slavery and were willing to do whatever it took to abolish this cruel way of life.

CHAPTER ONE

Spring of 1861

It was April and Beth and her beagle, Duke, were waiting on the front veranda of her family's plantation home, Rivers View, located on the Savannah River north of Savannah, Georgia. Everyone knew that when they saw Beth, they were likely to see Duke as well. Duke had been a surprise gift from her cousin Rae. Rae had given Duke to Beth last summer when Beth had left for home after spending the summer with Rae and her family in Indiana. Right now he was sound asleep and every once in awhile his front legs would move as if he were running. Beth liked to think that he was chasing rabbits.

Beth was waiting for her father, Eugene. He had gone to Savannah to check on his mercantile store in which he had half ownership. He had also checked on their summer house and picked up the mail. He was due back home today, and Beth was hoping there would be a letter from her cousin Rae or her friends Dawn and Zane who all lived in Indiana. It would be one year next week since she had visited Rae and her family.

On that visit Beth had had the best time of her life. She

had met Rae's friends, Dawn, who was a free black girl, and Zane, a boy who was nearly a year older than Beth. Beth still couldn't believe she had a best friend who was a free black person. Dawn was Rae's neighbor and they had been best friends since they were babies. When Rae had told her about Dawn, Beth just couldn't believe that any black person would want to be free. Why should they when their masters gave them everything they needed?

That was an important lesson she had learned last summer. Until then she had believed with all her heart that black people were meant to be slaves and were happy serving their masters.

Now, after all the things she had seen last summer and the things that had happened since she had returned home, she knew that no one should be owned by another. Dawn had told her the story of what her grandparents had gone through to be free, of how they had wanted to be married but their masters would not allow it. They had run away to the north where they could get married and live as free persons.

The first time Rae had taken Beth to Dawn's home, Beth had no idea what to expect. She was sure it would be a small, rundown log cabin. She was shocked to find a nice size house painted white with a lovely front yard full of flowers. Dawn's family had welcomed her to their home. It didn't take long before she felt right at home and comfortable with all of Dawn's family. After that Beth had gone to Dawn's home and been a guest there many times during the summer. Dawn's parents and grandparents were so nice to her that it didn't take long for her to forget they were black.

And then when she and her friends had found Stella and her two brothers, orphaned runaways from Kentucky, hiding in some bushes, dirty, hungry and scared, her heart just went out to them. The friends had hidden the fugitives in Rae's family barn. When the adults had found out about Stella and the boys they had gotten together and, with the help of Lone Star, ensured that the family got far enough north that they would be safe from slave hunters.

These experiences changed something inside Beth so that before she left Indiana to return home she had promised her new friends that she would help free as many slaves as she could. To show that she was keeping her promise, she would send a red ribbon with each one that she helped. So far she had been able to help three to escape: a mother, father and their one-year-old little girl from a neighboring plantation, Pine Haven, which was about four miles from Rivers View

✳✳✳✳✳✳✳✳✳✳✳✳✳✳✳✳✳✳✳✳✳

Beth and her family had been visiting Pine Haven for a few days to help celebrate the marriage of one of the daughters of the plantation owner. Early one day Beth was walking to her guest room when she overheard some house slaves whispering about another house slave and also heard one of them crying. When Beth walked into her room, they all fell silent, bowed their heads and made their way out of the room as quickly as they could; except for one young girl. She was sitting in the corner behind the door and using her apron to dry her eyes. She had tried to follow the others out, but Beth had stopped her and asked her why she was crying. She told the girl not to be afraid, that she wouldn't tell anyone what she told her.

The girl started crying again, so Beth led her over to a set of white wicker chairs. She motioned for her to sit in one while she sat in the other. She handed the girl her lace handkerchief so she could dry her tears. The girl looked at Beth with her big brown eyes. Beth could tell that she was still scared half out of her wits. No white person had ever been this kind to her. And to ask her to sit in a white man's chair was unheard of. The girl decided she would be safer to just stand.

Beth looked at her, "Please sit down and tell me your name and why you are so upset."

The girl hung her head down. She remembered this was what was expected of her when she talked to a white person. She had been taught never to look a white person in the eye because that would be disrespectful. Beth reached over and put her hand under the girl's chin and lifted her face so she could look her in the eyes. The girl was blinking back more tears. After a few minutes she told Beth that her name was Robin and that she was a helper in the kitchen.

Robin really didn't want to tell Beth why she was so upset and what was making her cry. She was afraid that telling would only make her problem worse, if that was possible. Beth looked at Robin and smiled. She took Robin's hands in hers and patted them, trying to give Robin the courage to tell her what had upset her so badly.

Robin couldn't help it. She started to cry again, but Beth shook her head and Robin took a deep breath, wiped her eyes and stopped crying. She looked at Beth and told her why she was so upset. "Me and Do jumped the broom about a year ago and now he's my husband. Do is the stable man, he take care of Mr. Joe's racehorses. We got a baby girl, Pansy. She about a year old."

"That is wonderful Robin, it sounds like you have a very nice family," Beth told Robin still holding her hands.

"Yes ma'am, I do. But, the master he be selling my Do to your father."

Beth squeezed Robin's hands, "That's great Robin now you will all be on our plantation where you will be safe and sound." Beth was sure her father had bought the whole family and she had heard that the overseer on this plantation didn't always treat the slaves kindly like her father's did.

Then Robin explained, "Mr. Joe he need some extra money to buy a new racehorse so only Do was being sold, not me and Pansy. We be staying here at Pine Haven." Beth was so shocked that her father would do such a thing. She was sure he didn't know Do was married. He would never separate a family. She told Robin to go on about her work and she would see what she could do about their problem.

It was that very evening after dinner that Beth's parents, Eugene and Denise, went for a stroll in the garden. They had decided to walk off the enormous dinner of roast beef, sweet potato pie, stewed okra with tomatoes, turnip greens and corn on the cob. There had even been a chocolate cake with chocolate icing, but everyone had decided to have dessert later. Beth had seen her parents leave the house and decided this would be a great time to talk to her father. She waited about fifteen minutes before she couldn't stand it any longer. She went flying out the door. Then she remembered that her mother and Momma Jo had told her that a lady never went flying anywhere, so she decided to slow down. She didn't want a lecture from her mother about what a lady should and shouldn't do.

It took Beth a few minutes to find her parents. They were in the rose garden resting on a bench in the gazebo. When they saw Beth approaching they wondered why she would be following them. She entered the gazebo and gave her parents both a big hug. Eugene asked her, "To what do we owe this unexpected visit? I thought you and Jo Ann were going to play cards?"

Beth knew she could talk to her parents about anything. But this was a whole new subject. They had never talked about slaves before. She had thought and thought about what she was going to say to her father about Robin and her family. Beth knew he wouldn't tell Robin's master and she was sure Eugene would help Robin and her family.

Beth took a seat next to her father and told him about Do and Robin. She was surprised when Eugene told her, "I've already tried to get Joe to let me have Robin and Pansy. He won't let them go. He says Bertha, his cook, can't run the kitchen without Robin. Bertha says she's just too old and tired to train a new helper. He told me Robin's too good of a cook to let her go. I'm sorry, Honey, but I've already tried. You know how your mother and I feel about breaking apart families."

"Well, I think that is very selfish of Bertha," Beth told

her parents. "Why would she not want to keep a family together?"

"I don't know the whole story," Eugene explained. "But there isn't anything else I can do. I wish there was. I don't like to see a family separated any more than you do, Beth."

"I don't understand why Mr. Joe would want to sell Do. I have been out to the stables and he is excellent with the horses." There just had to be something she could do, Beth thought as she started walking back to the house. Halfway there she changed her mind and went to the stables instead. She decided to talk with Do. Maybe they could come up with a plan to solve this mess.

Robin was with Do. They were talking in low voices so no one would overhear them. Robin had been telling Do that Beth wanted to help them but when they saw her they stopped talking and stood there looking at her. They were both hoping that she had some good news for them

Beth was not looking forward to giving them the bad news. She had wanted to tell only Do so that he could tell Robin. Now she had to tell them both. Knowing that this was as good a time as any she told them what her father had told her. When Robin started crying, Do wrapped his arms around her, patted her on the back, and whispered in her ear that they would figure out some way to stay together. Beth could see how much the two loved one another. She knew that all slaves had a heart and loved just like everyone else. It doesn't matter what color your skin is, love is all the same.

Then, Beth surprised herself and asked them, "Have you

ever thought of going north?"

Robin's and Do's eyes got as big as saucers. They looked around to be sure no one had heard what Beth had asked them. Do put his finger to his mouth and shook his head. Robin whispered in Beth's ear that they could be whipped, maybe even killed, if their master heard such talk, but Beth already knew that. She told them, "I don't know what I can do. Just don't lose hope. I'll think of something to keep your family together, but it might take a few days. I promise I'll figure something out."

When Beth got back to the house she told her mother she didn't feel well and that she needed a good night's sleep. What she really needed was to be alone so she could think. She wished Rae, Dawn and Zane were here to help her. She knew that together they could come up with an answer to this problem, just like they had worked together to get Stella and her brothers north last summer.

North. That was what she needed, a way to get Robin and her family north where they could be together and free. But how could she do this? Beth knew she was on her own with this one. No one here in the south was going to help her free slaves. "I guess it's time I start keeping that promise I made to my friends last summer," she said to herself.

That night Beth prayed for help. She knew in her heart that God could not approve of slavery and that he would help her.

When Beth awoke the next morning she lay awake for some time before she decided to get up. When she finally got out of bed she had to hurry so she wouldn't be late for breakfast. She knew her mother would be upset with her if she was late. A lady was always on time for meals, especially when she was a guest. Beth had too much on her mind to be scolded that day.

She quickly washed her face with the warm water that her maid Honey had left in a small white water pitcher that had purple violets painted on the sides. With Honey's help she dressed in a burgundy riding skirt and vest with a pink blouse. As she went out the bedroom door she picked up her matching burgundy hat with a pink feather tucked in the black ribbon that wrapped around its crown. She and Jo Ann were going riding after breakfast. Beth was hoping this trip through the woods would show her a way to help Robin and her family, although she had no idea how.

Beth made it to the breakfast table just in time and sat down to find fresh baked biscuits, red eyed gravy, sugar cured ham and fried eggs. All of these were Beth's favorites and she knew that if she didn't eat a good breakfast her mother would think she was still sick and wouldn't let her go riding.

Jo Ann had instructed Bertha to pack a picnic lunch that they could take with them so that they wouldn't have to return until late in the day. They could take their time and enjoy themselves, maybe even go wading in Fern Grove Creek. The creek was about three miles behind the house and ran from Pine Haven to Rivers View. The large groves of lush green ferns growing all along the bank mixed with bunches of wild flowers created the perfect place for a picnic.

After excusing themselves from the table, the girls went to the stables for their horses. Beth rode her own horse, Maiden, a quarter horse mare. Jo Ann had her own mare, a black named Pretty Lady. Then they walked to the summer kitchen to pick-up their lunch. Bertha told them she had packed ham sandwiches, hard boiled eggs, sweet pickles, and a sweet surprise. She said, "You girls be careful and remember you best be home in time to get cleaned up for supper."

In the south, girls and young ladies weren't allowed to ride alone. They had to be accompanied by an adult or a stable boy. That day, a stable boy rode along with Beth and Jo Ann. He was expected to ride a short distance behind them and not to let them out of his sight. His job was to make sure that the girls didn't run into any kind of trouble. He was not allowed to talk to them or to share their picnic no matter how long they were gone. He could eat when he got home.

Beth didn't treat her stable boys that way, at least not since last summer. Now she always took extra food for them and talked to them as they rode. That day when the stable boy rode up behind them Beth halted Maiden and politely asked him, "What's your name?" The boy looked with surprise from Beth to Jo Ann. He wasn't accustomed to white people asking him questions this way. They usually only gave orders.

"Why, Beth Taylor! Whatever do you want to know his name for? He's just a stable boy and you know he's not allowed to talk to us," Jo Ann said.

"I just want to know," Beth said. "If I have a problem and need his help I'm not going to just call him boy."

The boy turned toward Beth with his head still down, "My name be Marty, Miss."

"How old are you, Marty?" Beth asked.

Marty again looked at both girls with a shocked look on his face. "Don't rightly no. My Ma thinks I'm fifteen, but don't nobody know for sure."

Jo Ann looked at Beth and shook her head. "Really, Beth why ever do you care how old a slave is anyway?"

Beth didn't answer Jo Ann; she just rode off towards the woods. She was thinking about how terrible it must be not to know how old you were. Her father kept records of the births and deaths of all of his slaves. All of the slaves at Rivers View knew how old they were and were given the special treat of a day off on their birthday.

During their ride, Beth kept asking Jo Ann to take her to places where she thought that Robin and her family could possibly hide or conceal their tracks. She knew that she only had two more days at Pine Haven and she needed to have a plan before she went home.

That night after dinner, Beth took an apple off the side board in the dining room and went to the barn to give Maiden her treat. Maiden heard Beth coming across the barnyard and started to neigh. When she saw the apple in Beth's hand she knew she was in for a treat. She moved her head up and down as if she were nodding. Beth laughed at her, "You are one spoiled horse. Yes you are," Beth told Maiden, while rubbing her between the ears. Maiden tried to eat the apple in one big bite, but Beth made her take small bites so the apple would last longer.

After Maiden finished off the apple, Beth found a brush and began grooming her horse. All horses loved to be brushed, especially Maiden, and Beth was waiting for the stable boys to finish their work and go to their cabins so she could talk to Do alone. Beth had a plan for Do and Robin. She wanted to talk it over with Do to see what he thought. When she finished brushing Maiden, she sat on a bale of straw and waited for Do to finish his work. She could tell that Do was nervous to be in the barn alone with her. He would get in big trouble if someone found them.

Just as he had finished his last chore and was approaching Beth, they heard someone walking across the barnyard. Beth didn't want to cause Do any trouble, so she quickly hid behind some bales of straw next to the one she had been sitting on. When the barn door opened, Do let out a sigh. "Oh, thank the Lord! It's just Robin," he told Beth.

"Good," Beth said as she came out of hiding. "I need to talk to both of you. I have a plan and I want to know if you think it will work and if you are willing to try what I have in mind. My family and I will be leaving for home the day after tomorrow. As we know, Do will be taken with us." Beth almost cried when she saw the look Do and Robin gave one another. But she continued, "When we get home, we will begin getting the racehorses ready to take them to the spring races in Savannah. The rest of the family will leave about three days before I do. I always stay and travel with the horses when they are taken a few days later. Father does not like to keep our racehorses stabled in the city before a race. He believes they do not get enough fresh air and exercise.

"Do will be expected to stay at home and take care of the horses. Also, the whole family here at Pine Haven will be going to Savannah at the same time as my family. With everyone gone there will be less chance of either of you being missed. So, on the night after everyone has left, Do and I will bring a boat to the Pine Haven wharf where we will pick-up Robin and Pansy. There should only be a quarter moon that night so you should not be seen. But remember, you will still need to be very careful. We will meet you at ten, after the remaining slaves are in bed. Robin, if you tie some rags around your feet it might help to throw the dogs off your scent.

"Momma Jo will help me to gather supplies that you will need for your trip. I will go with you as far up the river as I can and still get home before daylight. From there you will need to go west, then north. You might want to go back and forth for a few days. Do, do you know how to tell directions, east from west?"

"Yes, Miss Beth. I can tell by the sun when it comes up in the mornings."

"Great, that will be a big help for you. It will take you days to get north on foot. I will try to find a faster way for you to travel. I know this plan is dangerous, but it is all I can think of now. You both know how dangerous this is for you. So tell me, would you rather wait to see if we can find another way?"

Do looked at Robin and she gave him a nod. "We'll go now, Miss Beth."

CHAPTER TWO

The First Time

The first thing Beth did when she got home from Pine Haven was to tell Momma Jo all about Robin and Do and her plans for them. Momma Jo had been a nanny to Beth's family for two generations. Beth didn't know for sure how old Momma Jo was, but she guessed that she was in her late seventies. She was a big woman with a heart of gold who wore her gray hair in a knot on the top of her head and always had on her red apron. Beth hoped that Momma Jo would agree to help her. When she told her what she planned to do, Momma Jo gave her the biggest hug she had ever had. Then Beth looked at Momma Jo and saw her using her apron to wipe away the tears that had come to her eyes.

"I'm so proud of ya child. I knew you had a heart as big as the moon. But, child what if ya gets your self caught or someone sees you and tells?"

"I guess I will just cross that bridge if and when I come to it," Beth replied. Then she told Momma Jo about how she and her friends had helped Stella and her brothers get north to a safe place last summer and about the promise she had made to her friends before she left Indiana, that she would help more slaves when she got home.

By the time Beth had finished telling the whole story, the nanny was sitting on the side of the bed with big tears running down her face. "You know child I'll do what ever I can. If you need them, my grandsons Bow and Sunny will help. You just tell us what you need us to do?" Bow and Sunny were eighteen-year-old twins. They were orphaned at age six and had lived with Momma Jo ever since. They both worked in the stables; Bow trained and Sunny rode the racehorses.

"That's great, Momma Jo. I'm sure I'll need all the help I can get." Beth was so happy she was smiling from ear to ear. It was great to know that she was going to have some help.

The Taylor plantation had belonged to Beth's great-grandparents on her mother's side. Grandfather Jefferson had died four year ago in a riding accident when his horse had stepped into a rabbit hole and broke its leg. Grandfather had been thrown to the ground and hit his head on a rock. He never knew what had happened. Now, Eugene ran the plantation and Beth's family lived there with Grandmother Becca, her mother's mother, in the large eleven room plantation home with its own summer kitchen. On the main floor were the living room, library, parlor, dining room and Eugene's office. The second floor consisted of six bedrooms. Beth felt lucky because her bedroom was a corner room on the front side of the house. From her enormous windows she could always see who was coming up the drive. A balcony went all the way across the front of the house and Beth often went out the double glass doors to sit and enjoy the early mornings or late evenings.

Beth had finally gotten her wish this year. She had been granted permission to transform her bedroom from a little girl's room to a young lady's room. Denise and Rosa Mae had helped her, and they had just finished the room a few weeks ago. As in most plantation homes, the walls of Beth's bedroom were ten feet high. The bottom half of each wall was now painted a light rose pink while the top half was covered with rose pink silk wallpaper embellished with white tubular roses. At the place where paint and wallpaper met, a white crown molding ran all the way around the room.

Eugene had given Beth permission to order a bedroom suit from Dawn's father, Thomas, last summer. She had ordered a four poster bed with a canopy, a dressing table and two night tables all to be made of mahogany. The new furniture had arrived just last week. Thomas had even sent along a matching rocker and round accent table. Most girls had only one armoire for their clothes, but Beth had two, one had belonged to her mother and one to Aunt Anna, Rae's mother. The canopy over the bed matched the wall paper and the comforter was a pale pink with a white lace dust ruffle. Beth had chosen ruby red glass lanterns for each of the tables. She had also selected one of Dawn's mother's beautiful paintings to hang over her fireplace. The painting portrayed an apple orchard in full bloom. It reminded Beth of one of the adventures she and the girls had enjoyed when they had shown her the apple orchard behind Dawn's house. But Beth's favorite piece in the whole room was a full length oval mirror. It stood on the floor in a wooden frame that could be tilted at different angles. The mirror was special because it had been the last Christmas gift her grandfather Jefferson had given her.

After talking to Momma Jo, Beth decided to go downstairs to the library. She needed to relax and do some more thinking. Beth especially loved this room and it always helped to calm her when she had a problem. She spent many hours in this beautiful room thinking and reading her favorite books. Denise had decorated the library in shades of blue from the palest sky blue to deep royal blue. The chairs and settee were covered in baby blue silk embroidered with yellow rose buds. The drapes were a midnight blue, the same color as the sky at night. They were dark to help keep the sun out on hot days but today were held back with fabric that matched the chairs. The floor was covered with oriental rugs in many shades of blue and there were green ferns scattered all around the room. Denise loved ferns.

Book cases of floor to ceiling shelves full of books covered two walls of the room. You had to use a ladder to get to the top shelves. The third wall consisted of double glass doors that opened onto the front veranda. Along the last wall was a large oak fireplace. The oak had come from the woods behind the house. Hanging above the fireplace was a painting of the family. A traveling artist had stopped at Rivers View last spring and Eugene had paid him to paint the portrait.

Latto had done a marvelous job. Each family member looked so real. He had used the gazebo with Denise's rose garden as the background. For the portrait, Denise had worn a bright yellow muslin gown with purple violets embroidered all over it. Her hair was piled on top of her head and the masses of curls were intertwined with real violets. Around her neck she wore her mother's string of pearls and in her ears, the matching earrings. Rosa Mae had chosen a pale peach cotton gown with tiny bright green leaves woven into the material. The dress was trimmed with pale green lace at the neck and at the ends of the three-quarter length sleeves. Rosa Mae had decided to wear her hair covered with a snood net in the current fashion. Because the neckline of her dress was cut low, she wore a gold chain with a heart-shaped pendent and matching heart earrings. Beth had been wearing a light blue Swiss cotton gown with navy blue dots. She didn't care for lace, so the neck and puffy sleeves were trimmed in narrow navy blue ruffles. Beth was wearing her beautiful blond hair loose and it hung down past her waist. She had a light blue satin ribbon around the top and had tied it in the back. She wore a small pearl necklace with matching earrings, a gift from her grandmother Becca on her last birthday. Her father and brother, Robert, both wore black suits and white shirts with ruffles at the cuffs. Each wore a different color vest; Eugene's was black with gray stripes and Robert's was red with white stripes. Both men wore a black bow tie.

Beth thought they made a very striking family and she was so proud to be a part of it. But she wondered how proud they would be of her if they ever found out what she was about to do. She just hoped they never found out.

Just as Beth knew they would, her parents, Grandmother Becca, Robert and Rosa Mae all left for Savannah three days after their return to Rivers View. Within minutes of the family's departure Beth and Momma Jo got busy. They put a knapsack of food together and in another sack they put clothes, candles and blankets. They had to be careful that none of these things could be recognized as coming from Rivers View. Then they went to the attic where Momma Jo had found some of Robert's old clothes and a pair of boots for Beth to wear. She was going to tie her hair up on top of her head and wear her grandfather's old straw hat. A little dirt on her face and hands and who would guess she was a girl? That afternoon Beth planned to take a nap; she knew she had a long night ahead of her.

Beth had already sent word to Do that there had been a change in their plans, a much better and safer one she hoped. When she had talked to Bow and Sunny they had surprised her by telling her about a white farmer who lived down the Savannah River. He and his wife were involved in the Underground Railroad. Beth and Bow had gone to find this man two days ago on the pretense of a fishing trip.

Bow was pretty sure that he knew where the man lived and how to make contact with him. Beth knew they needed to be very careful not to ask the wrong people. She also knew that they had to be back before dark, so they left early in the morning. After all, catfish bite best in the mornings. They had taken a small flat bottom boat and right away had thrown their lines into the river so that if anyone saw them it would look like they were fishing.

It took them about two hours to row down the river. There, they tied the boat up to a rickety old wharf and walked about a mile until they found an old log cabin. It was so old that Beth thought a strong wind would blow it down in minutes. There was laundry on the clothes line, but no children's clothes, just a man and his wife's. When they got closer to the cabin they could see a woman hoeing in a small garden and an old man sitting in a rocker on the front porch and smoking a corn cob pipe. There beside him was an old coon dog.

When they got within speaking distance, the old man asked them "What's you two doing here?"

Bow knew the secret words that would let both him and the old man know that they were dealing with Underground business. No one would introduce themselves. Bow had told Beth that names were never exchanged. He stepped up to the old man and spoke in a low voice, just loud enough for the three of them to hear. "Sir, have you seen a rather large black alligator?"

The old man looked from Bow to Beth. He didn't quite know what to make of this pair. He wasn't sure if he should trust them or not. He knew this could be a trick to catch him and his wife. He looked Beth in the eye and she smiled at him. No way could a young lady looking that innocent be up to no good. So he shook his head and answered, "Nope, but I expect to see one in a few days. I'll be watching for him."

"Yes," Bow said, "in two nights."

"We'll watch and be ready for him."

"Be really careful, he may have a small family with him," Bow added. The old man then got up, went into his cabin and shut the door. Beth and Bow looked at each other and smiled. Then they took off running to the river. They made it back home in plenty of time and had even caught a mess of catfish.

On the night previously agreed upon Beth, Bow and Do took the Taylor family raft to pick-up Robin and Pansy. It would be crowed on the raft, but anything larger would be too big for Beth and Bow to get back home by themselves. Just as they had discussed before there was hardly any moonlight, making it harder to see on the river but providing valuable cover. They planned to keep close to the bank where the trees would help conceal them.

Once everyone was on board and the men had paddled them away from Pine Haven, Beth quietly explained to Do and Robin about the promise she had made the previous summer. She then gave each of them a piece of red ribbon and asked them to give the ribbon to her friends if they came across them in Indiana.

Speaking in almost a whisper Beth asked, "Is Do the name your momma gave you?"

After thinking about it for a few minutes, Do told her, "No, Miss Beth, it ain't. My ma named me Dodley when I was born. Don't know where she got that from though. But, the master he say that name was too uppity for a slave. So I's been called Do all my life. I's forgotten that Do wasn't my real name."

"What about you, Robin? Is that what your momma named you?"

"Yes'um, Miss Beth, it surely is. My momma truly loves the birds, especially robins. And the Missus say she could name me whatever she wants."

"Do either of you know how old you are or when your birthdays are?"

"No ma'am, we surely don't, but Robin thinks she be about eighteen, I think I be twenty-four."

Beth looked at Do, Robin and Pansy. "Today is your first day of freedom. What do you say to this being your birthday?"

"We ain't never had a birthday before," Robin told Beth.

"I know you don't have a last name but you will need one now. What would you like that last name to be?"

Do looked at Robin and they both smiled. "Pine," they said at the same time. Robin explained, "That so we always remember the Georgia pine trees and where we were all born. This also be where our American roots started and where we started to be free."

"That sounds like a great idea," Beth told them. "Dodley and Robin Pine, parents of Miss Pansy Pine. I think that sounds really nice." When Beth said that, Robin had to put her hand to her mouth to stop the giggles from being heard.

"That do sound great, Miss Beth. It surely do," Dodley told her.

It took them a lot longer to get to the old wharf tonight than it had before. It was almost two o'clock before they reached their destination. Beth and Bow told Do and his family good-bye and wished them luck. They watched from the raft as the family made their way up the path to the cabin. When they reached the top of the knoll, Do and Robin turned around and waved before disappearing over the hill. Beth was saying a silent prayer for the runaways' safety, as well as for her's and Bow's.

Even though they were traveling upstream, it took Bow and Beth less time to get home than it had taken to get to the wharf because there were only two of them. They arrived home and were in bed before daylight. Momma Jo hid Beth's boy clothes in an old trunk in the attic where she was sure no one would find them. She knew that this was not going to be the last time Beth would need these old clothes.

CHAPTER THREE

A Letter from Indiana

A few weeks ago, Eugene had brought Beth a letter from Indiana. It was from her cousin Rae. Beth had read it numerous times, but this being a beautiful morning and her last day at Rivers View before joining her family in Savannah, she decided to enjoy the morning by sitting on the upstairs balcony and re-reading her letter. Although she had read it a least half a dozen times, she hadn't really studied it to see if Rae had written any hidden messages. After reading the letter over twice, Beth decided there was no message. She tucked the letter away in her top bureau drawer with the other letters she had received from Indiana. There were two from Dawn and one from Zane, as well as five from Rae. She had read each letter so many times she almost knew them all by heart. Reading the letters made her feel closer to all three of her friends. Oh, how she missed them!

She especially loved to read the one from Zane, except the part where he wrote that he was thinking about leaving the farm and going north. Beth knew that what he really planned was to join the war. She had known all along that Zane would be one of the first to volunteer. The north and south were just starting to have problems that were causing people to seriously want to fight and the war they had spoken about last summer seemed closer than ever. Oh! She so hoped Zane, her father and Robert would all be safe and that what she had heard in the past about this conflict lasting only a few months would be true. She sighed and closed her bureau drawer.

Beth, Bow and Sunny were to leave for Savannah early the next morning. They would ride to Metter where they would catch a train. The horses and the boys would ride in a box car while Beth and her maid, Honey, traveled in the passenger car. The family would be staying in Savannah until the end of June. Most of the plantation-owning families, like the Taylors, owned or rented a house in the city where they always spent the spring, early summer, and fall. July and August were just too hot and humid to stay in the crowded city and most families wanted to be back on their plantations for Christmas.

While in the city there were always a lot of fun things to do. The horse races were one of the first events every spring and were Beth's favorite. Then there were parties aboard the paddle boats that went up and down the Savannah River. From the boats it was not unusual to see a group of dolphins playing in the river. Also, families took turns enjoying picnics in the city's many parks. The forefathers had laid out the town in twenty-one wards, each with a park in the center, so there was a different park to picnic in every day. That is, if no one was hanging their wash up in the park that day. Then there were the balls. There was one almost every week. Here one would find the most extravagant dinners, each hostess trying to outdo the others. Here, also, one would find the ladies attempting to out-dress and out-style one another.

All of these activities were great fun, but next to the races Beth liked the outings to Tybee Island best of all. Tybee Island is about nine miles east of downtown Savannah. The Savannah River is on the north side of the island and the Atlantic Ocean is on the east and south sides. Eugene always made reservations for the family to spend a few days at the Marshall House Hotel. Sometimes when they stayed on the island they rented a sailboat and went out in the ocean where they could watch the dolphins up close. Beth loved to spend her time on the island's beach. She usually got up early in the morning before most people were up and going. She loved this quite time and spent it walking in the sand listening to the waves roll into shore. Sometimes she would walk out onto the wharf where she could watch the dolphins. It was always so much fun watching them jump in and out of the water and race each other. There were always plenty of seashells to pick-up early in the mornings. Beth liked the starfish shells best, but they were harder to find. Quite often she would find sea turtles sunning themselves on the beach. Some of them were so large Beth didn't know what kept them from sinking to the bottom of the ocean. On one of her early morning strolls she had found a large sea turtle stranded on its back. She knew he would die if he couldn't get back in the water, but the turtle was so large she couldn't turn him over by herself no matter how hard she struggled. Just as she had decided that she had to give up, an older lady and gentleman happened along. They, like Beth, were out enjoying the sunrise. With their help, Beth had been able to get the turtle turned over and headed back toward the water. Then she had stared in awe as the turtle swam out a short distance and turned around to nod his head as if to say thank you. Beth wondered if they would get to go to the island this summer with all the war talk.

While Beth was sitting there day dreaming, Honey walked up behind her and tapped her on the shoulder. "Miss Beth, Mr. Jim would like to talk to you."

Beth was not ready for this; she knew what Mr. Jim wanted. But the longer she waited the harder it was going to be. She stood up, took a deep breath and followed Honey to the front porch. "You wanted to see me, Mr. Jim?" Beth asked.

"I did indeed, Miss Beth." Mr. Jim seemed to be agitated. "I can't seem to find Do, that new horse trainer your father just bought. Nobody knows where he is. By any chance do you happen to know where he might be?"

"I can't say for sure, but I did hear father talking about taking him to Savannah with him. I believe his idea was that Do could get the stables ready for when we arrive with Glory and the other horses. Did he not say anything to you about this?" Beth replied in what she hoped was a calm voice.

"No, I can't say that he did. I've asked and none of the other stable boys know anything about it either."

"Well, you know how father sometimes makes snap decisions. Maybe this is one of them."

"Let's hope your right, Miss Beth, cause if not I'm afraid

Do might have taken off."

"Taken off?" Beth asked, trying to sound surprised.

"You know, a runaway," Mr. Jim explained.

"Now why ever would Do go and do a thing like that?" Beth reasoned.

"Can't rightly say, these blacks just don't know how good they got it. They seem to think being free is a better life. I sure hope Do's not one of them. I sure would hate to have to go chasing after him. I really was starting to like him." With that, Mr. Jim turned around and started down the front steps. He shook his head and wiped his bald scalp with his blue bandana before putting his old straw hat back on and walking to the barn.

Beth rolled her eyes and took another deep breath. She hadn't lied. She had asked her father about taking Do with him and he had said that he might. Beth went back into the house and found Momma Jo standing just inside and behind the door where nobody could see her but where she could hear every word Beth and the overseer had said. "Child, I's hopes that man believes you and he don't start asking no more questions."

"So do I," said Beth. "At least this gives Do and his family a few extra days. Let's just hope no one comes over from Pine Haven looking for Robin."

CHAPTER FOUR

Off To Savannah

"**O**h! This is a glorious day for a trip to Savannah," Beth declared the next morning after looking out her bedroom window. It had rained during the night, but the sun was shining now and the bright blue sky didn't have a cloud in sight. After dressing in a pink and black striped traveling dress that only required one petticoat (Beth hated wearing a lot of petticoats), she went down to breakfast. Tilley, the cook, had prepared some of Beth's favorites: grits, fried ham, biscuits and gravy.

When she had finished her breakfast, Beth asked Honey to go upstairs to fetch her pink and black striped parasol and black hat with the pink ostrich feathers. She had forgotten to bring them down earlier. When Honey returned she and Beth made their way to the carriage. Beth knew that Bow and Sunny would have the carriage and the three racehorses ready to go. They would have also loaded her trunks and baskets of food for the day into a small cart. Tilley would have packed one basket for Beth and Honey and another for the boys to have in the boxcar. They were going first to Metter to catch a train to Savannah. The trip would take most of the day, so the food would be welcome come dinner time.

With a spring in her step and a smile on her face Beth headed for the carriage. She really felt good about helping Do and his family. In fact, she was proud of herself and her helpers. She just hoped her new friends made it safely north.

Once they arrived at Metter they had to wait for the train and after it appeared it took a while to load the horses into the boxcar. Beth and Honey rode in a comfortable passenger car while Bow and Sunny rode with the horses. The boys really didn't mind because here no one would bother them. They knew there would be plenty of fresh straw to sleep on when it came time to take a nap. And they had even brought a checkers board with them so they could play a few games on the long ride.

When the train arrived in Savannah the group was met at the station by Eugene. He escorted the girls to a buggy where the driver, Jasper, was waiting for them. Jasper tipped his big black top hat to Beth, "Welcome back to Savannah, Miss Beth."

"Why, thank you Jasper! I'm glad to be back. Savannah is such a beautiful city and I'm looking forward to seeing all of my friends."

"I speck they be glad to see you to, Miss Beth. Especially them young men what's keeps asking for you," Jasper said with a wink. Beth just shook her head and smiled as Eugene helped her get into the carriage. She had the back seat all to herself because Honey was to sit in the front seat with Jasper. One of the house boys had loaded their things into a small wagon and had already left for home. After seeing Beth safely into the carriage and on her way, Eugene went to oversee the unloading of the horses.

The Taylor house was located on West State Street but the horses would be taken to the community stable which was located about a block behind the house. The family utilized a private section of the stables which also had a small room where the stable boys could sleep and keep an eye on the horses. The house on West State Street was known as the Jefferson House. It had been built in 1830 for Beth's grandparents, the Jeffersons. The house was built across from Telfair Square Park, one of the twenty-one parks that the city had been built around.

Beth loved this house. It was one of the prettiest homes on the block. It was said that the Jefferson house was one of the finest examples of domestic Gothic architecture in all of Savannah. To Beth, it was the one place she loved to be next to Rivers View. The exterior was made up of bright pink brick. There were two staircases with black wrought iron handrails each curving up to either side of the stoop which also had a wrought iron railing. All of the railings had been cast in a heart and ivy pattern. Beth felt much pride knowing the bricks and railing had been made right here in Savannah.

A small but lovely country garden was behind and around one side of the house. Even though it was small, the garden had an abundance pleasant flora. There were a number of scented trees including magnolia, feathery mimosas, pink and white dogwood, red bud and crepe myrtle. There was a flower bed in every corner as well as around the fountain shaped like a lion with water flowing out of his mouth. The flower beds were planted with seasonal plants so that there would be flowers in bloom all the time. It being spring now, the garden was full of a variety of tulips, daffodils, yellow jasmine, daisies, mountain laurel and, of course, roses. In the summer, one could sit in the garden and smell the different flowers all season. As a finishing touch, a number of large green ferns were hanging from light posts.

Near the very back wall of the garden, a whicker swing painted forest green was hanging from a large limb of an old oak tree. Behind the swing was a black wrought iron trellis with a Cherokee rose bush growing up it. The Cherokee rose is a hardy plant with white blooms around yellow centers. According to legend the rose was first planted by a young Indian girl. She had fled from her Cherokee home to marry a Seminole chieftain. The land that she fled to was later known as Georgia.

Beth loved to sit in the swing in the evenings. It was here, just a few days after she arrived in Savannah, that she got a very pleasant surprise. Her family had all gone out for the evening. Denise, Eugene and Grandmother Becca were visiting friends while Robert and Rosa Mae had gone to a party. Beth had been invited to join Rosa Mae and her friends but had decided to stay home to catch up on her reading. Was she ever surprised when Jasper came to tell her, "There's a gentleman caller asking for you, Miss Beth."

Her first thought was to have Jasper send him away. After all, there was no adult present to chaperon (servants didn't count) and Beth knew her parents would not approve of her having a male caller in the house while she was alone. But her curiosity got the best of her. "Jasper, did the gentleman give you his name?"

"He only said he was a friend from Indiana."

Jasper had hardly gotten the words out of his mouth when Beth was up and out of the swing, holding her skirt up above her ankles and running for the front parlor. Oh! Could it possibly be Zane? Just before she reached the parlor door she made herself stop and take a deep breath. She knew it was unladylike to be caught running anywhere, especially through the house. "Sorry, mother," she thought. "I just cannot wait to see if my visitor is Zane."

She threw open the parlor door and there, standing in front of the fireplace, was her Zane. Running into his open arms, she just couldn't help herself when the tears started flowing down her cheeks. Zane wiped them away with his thumb. When Beth stopped crying they took a step back from one another. Beth felt tongue tied. She had so many questions she didn't know where to begin. When she did start talking it was one question after another. "How did you get here? What are you doing here? Are you safe? Please tell you are!"

Zane was laughing as he took both of Beth's hands and led her over to a settee that was in front of a large window. After they had both gotten comfortable he smiled at her and started answering her questions. "I'm glad to see you too, Miss Beth." Beth's hands flew to her mouth. Where ever were her manners? Zane reached up and took her hands so he could hold both of them. "I arrived by train this morning. I'm here in Savannah to buy cotton for a mill up North. And yes, I'm safe; at least for now. I just had to see you and to make sure you were alright."

"How long will you be in Savannah?" Beth wanted to know.

"I plan on staying only three or four days, at least this time. I hope to be able to make trips here at least every few months."

"Oh! That's wonderful news!" Beth was so excited she could hardly sit still. "We're having a summer party tomorrow night to celebrate the first horse race of the season. You must come. I will introduce you to a lot of people. You might learn some things to help you with your job." Beth knew Zane was not here to buy cotton but to gather information for the North.

Before Zane could answer, there was a commotion in the front hall. Beth knew it must be her parents returning home. She jumped up from the settee and went to open the parlor door. But before she could get it open, her father had already entered the room with her mother right behind him.

"Young lady, what is this we hear of you having a gentleman caller here by yourself?" Eugene demanded.

"Yes, father. Just look who has come to pay us a visit! I have invited Zane to the party. I'm not sure where he is staying, but I know we have an extra room he could use. I'm sure Momma wouldn't care, would you Momma?"

"Well, I suppose that would be just fine," Denise said. All the while Denise was glancing at Eugene who looked as surprised as she felt. They had never seen Beth take over like this. Did this mean she was really growing up?

Eugene shook Zane's hand. "I'll have Jasper take you to your hotel to pick-up your belongings. Of course you are welcome here for as long as you are in the city."

Beth turned to Zane and grabbed his hand, "I need some fresh air, so I'll ride along with you." Out the parlor door and down the hall they went. Eugene and Denise stood looking at each other. They just didn't know what to make of their daughter.

When Beth and Zane were in the carriage, Zane turned to Beth and said, "I think you might have embarrassed your parents."

"They'll get over it," Beth replied. "Besides, you'll be close now so I can help you more. And we will have more time for you to tell me what has been happening in Indiana since I left."

"You'll get to hear everything. But first I guess I need to tell Jasper which hotel my things are at so he will know where to go."

"I suppose you're right. And which hotel would that be?"

"I'm staying at the Willard's Hotel," Zane told Jasper.

Beth waited in the carriage while Zane went to check out and collect his belongings. It only took a few minutes but to Beth it seemed like hours. Having Zane with her was like a dream come true and she wanted to make every minute count. All the way to the hotel and back they told each other what they had been doing for the past year. Zane told Beth as much as he could about Rae and Dawn, but he had been gone from home for the last nine months so he didn't have the latest news. Beth explained how she had been keeping her promise and told her story about Do and his family.

Then Zane told Beth that he was working for the Union army in the secret service and explained that he was really in Savannah to make a detailed map and to see just how strong the southern army was in this area. They both knew they were walking on thin ice and it could break at anytime. If that happened, they would be in a world of trouble. But Beth, being the optimist, decided not to worry about any of this for the next few days. Zane was here and she aimed to enjoy every minute they had together.

Beth turned to Zane, "Let's not talk about any of that anymore. I have a plan for tomorrow after breakfast. Before we go to the horse races we will have Jasper take us for a ride all over town. I will show you where the river is. The main one is the Savannah River. We can go down River Street and you can see the counting houses and the port. This is where the cotton, tobacco and rice are shipped in and then back out. And if we have time the next day, we'll go to Tybee Island. We'll pass Fort Pulaski and Cockspur Lighthouse. Who knows? All of this may be of help to you some day."

Zane agreed, "I believe you could be right. All of these are important places. This information could come in handy in the future. I have an appointment in three days with a merchant who still wants to ship cotton north for as long as he can. I'll need to keep this meeting so I don't blow my cover." So that is how they spent their days. Beth showed

Zane everything they thought would be important for him to know about.

On the second night they were to attend the Taylor summer party where Zane discovered that Beth's family knew how to host a party. For him it sure was a fancy party. He had never seen anything like it in his life. There was to be a banquet and dancing. All of the men will be wearing black suits with tails and white shirts with ruffles at the cuffs and even down the front for some. Zane didn't know much about fashion, but he knew enough to tell that the ladies were dressed like queens. It looked to him like each one was trying to outdo the others. Some of them had really overdone it with lace, ruffles, feathers and jewelry.

Zane was waiting at the bottom of the stairway for Beth. When he saw her, he could hardly believe that she was the same girl he had met a year ago in Indiana. She was wearing a pale yellow satin gown with a bright pink silk ribbon tied around the waist of the bell shaped skirt. The hem and off-the-shoulder cap sleeves were trimmed with bright yellow ruffles. With the help of Honey she had parted her hair down the middle, using two pearl combs to hold it back. Honey had used a curling rod to make ringlets that hung down both sides of her face. She was wearing pearl earrings and a tiny gold chain with a small pearl around her neck.

As Beth reached the bottom of the stairway Zane stepped in front of her and bowed. Beth curtsied back to him. They had eyes for no one else in the room. Zane finally shook his head. "My dear Beth, you take my breath away. I knew you were beautiful, but I never knew how grown-up you were.

You certainly do not look like the girl I meet last summer, the one who was going barefoot and playing with little piglets."

"And you, Mr. Zane, look dashing. Also not like the boy I remember backing away from a family of skunks. You look very handsome, sir." She then leaned down and whispered in his ear, "Where ever did you get those clothes?"

Zane smiled and whispered back, "Compliments of my boss," meaning the Union Army.

They looked at each other and it was all Beth could do not to laugh. Zane offered his arm so that he could escort her outside to where the party was. The garden was lit up with lots of bright, colorful paper lanterns hanging from tree branches. There were wrought iron tables and chairs in every nook and corner with a bouquet of flowers on each. As they strolled around the garden, Beth began introducing Zane to her friends and the other quests. The guest list included the families of plantation owners, local merchants, and a number of politicians. The first group they encountered was a gathering of young people.

"Zane Brown from Indiana, these are my friends: the Cox sisters, Miss Christena, Miss Nichole, everyone calls her Nickie, and Miss Dawn and their brother, Max. And these two gentlemen are the Morris brothers, Alan and Andrew. We have all been friends since forever." The whole time Beth was making the introduction she was also watching her friend Nickie who was giving Zane a look over from the top of his head to the bottom of his feet.

The men shook hands, and then Nickie coyly extended

her hand to Zane expecting him to kiss the back of it. To Beth's surprise, that is just what Zane did.

"Why, Mr. Brown, how nice to meet you. Beth dear, wherever did you find this one?" Nickie wanted to know.

"I will tell you, Nickie. This one is a very dear friend from Indiana, as I said. We met last summer when I visited my cousin. Zane just arrived yesterday and he is here to buy cotton. Now, does that answer all of your questions?" Beth said a bit coolly to Nickie while looking straight at her with a look that said, "Back off! He's mine."

"It's a pleasure to meet all of you," Zane told the group. "But you'll have to excuse us. I believe I see Mr. Taylor motioning for us to join him."

As they approached Eugene and a group of men, the first thing Zane noticed was that some of them were in uniform. As they got closer he could hear that the gentlemen were discussing the latest skirmishes with the North. When Eugene introduced his house quest to the group, Zane couldn't believe his luck. He was introduced to General Robert E. Lee; Jefferson Davis, the newly elected confederate president; as well as General Pierre G.T. Beauregard. General Beauregard, Zane knew, was the general who had fired upon and captured Fort Sumter, South Carolina just this past April.

General Lee asked Zane, "Well son, are you in the army or do you plan to join?"

Zane didn't want to lie, yet he couldn't tell the truth either. So instead, he decided to tell just a little white lie. "Well, sir, right now I'm just trying to help the South by purchasing their cotton and finding buyers in the North."

"Very good, young man, very good," General Lee said to Zane. The other gentlemen were nodding their heads in agreement.

Beth was starting to get a little worried. She needed to get Zane away from this group before they could suspect anything. "Please excuse us, gentlemen. I promised to show Zane the goldfish pond," she said as she led Zane off toward the pond.

"That was close," Beth said when they were out of earshot. "I never thought of what could happen when you were introduced to father's friends."

"I know," Zane said, "but what an opportunity to meet such distinguished men! I'll never forget meeting and talking with each one of them. My boss will never believe me.

"Now, Miss Beth, I was told that this was a party, and I believe I hear music coming from the ballroom. Shall we join the others and take a turn around the dance floor?"

"You can dance?" Beth asked turning to Zane with a look of amazement on her face.

"You can decide that for yourself." Zane took her arm and guided her into the house.

After waltzing a few turns around the dance floor, Beth just shook her head. "However did you learn all this? No, don't tell me. The boss," she said causing both of them to laugh and lots of heads to turn their way. After finishing their waltz, Beth suggested they go to the dining room for supper. She knew it would be improper for her to dance two dances in a row with Zane and she didn't want to dance with anyone else.

When they reached the dining room Zane got another surprise. There was enough food to feed an army. "Wow!" he said. "I've never seen so much food. How do you decide what to eat first?" Beth laughed at him as she handed him a plate.

The cooks had been busy for days. There were six kinds of meat: a juicy roast beef, slices of smoked ham, fried chicken, shrimp cooked in a bourbon sauce, sea turtle cooked in a mixture of vegetables and a large roasted turkey. As for side dishes, the choices were unreal. Zane didn't know where to start. There were mashed potatoes, baked sweet potatoes, sweet corn on the cob, fried okra, stewed okra with tomatoes, green peas with pearl onions, green beans with hunks of bacon, dandelion salad and stewed butternut squash. As if all that wasn't enough there were pickled eggs, pickled beets and pickled okra. When they had filled their plates and were looking for a place to sit, Zane saw another table full of desserts. "Oh!" he told Beth, "I feel a stomach ache coming on." They had their plates so full they never made it to the desserts. They enjoyed the rest of the party with a little discomfort around the waist.

A couple of days later it was time for Zane to leave. He had made a good deal with the local cotton growers and with Beth's help had checked out every interesting spot in Savannah he could without raising suspension. He knew all the information would be helpful when he reported to his boss.

Right after breakfast Zane bid the Taylor family good-bye

and thanked them for their hospitality. He hoped to be back in a few months and would see them then. Eugene told him he was welcome at their home anytime and if they weren't in Savannah he was just as welcome at Rivers View.

Jasper drove Beth and Zane to the railroad station. They had left early so Zane would have time to look around the station. He was really surprised when Beth pointed out the round house. Savannah being the end of the train line going east meant that this station was a special place where trains could come in from the North, South or West and, while still on the same track, could be turned around to leave the way they had come. This was a new sight for Zane and the whole concept really fascinated him.

When it was time for Zane to board the train he took both of Beth's hands in his and looked her in the eye. "Please be careful. I've fallen in love with you and I couldn't bear it if anything were to happen to you."

Beth leaned forward and gave Zane a kiss on his chin, "I feel the same about you, dear Zane. Please promise me you will also be careful."

But it was too late to say more because the train conductor was calling, "All aboard! Last call to Atlanta."

Beth stood on the platform and watched the train until it was out of sight. Duke had come along and was standing beside her all this time. She bent down and picked him up even though he was now a very big dog. She just needed something to hug and hold onto.

CHAPTER FIVE

The Last Days of Summer

1861

Even though there were a lot of parties and picnics, as well as the horse races, Beth just couldn't enjoy the rest of her summer. All she could do was worry about Zane. She was really glad when the end of June came and it was time to go back to Rivers View.

She hadn't mentioned anything about Do or Mr. Jim's questions to her parents. When they reached home the overseer was waiting for them on the front steps. When he saw Do wasn't with them he told Eugene that Do had been gone since the day they had left for Savannah. "Woulda gone lookin' for him, but figured he was with you," Mr. Jim told Eugene.

Eugene took a deep breath and shook his head. "Well, it's too late to track him now. Guess all we can do is put up a wanted poster and hope someone's seen him and wants to collect the bounty." Beth was so glad to hear this she had to hurry to her room before she started cheering.

They hadn't been home long when Mr. Joe rode up the front drive from Pine Haven. The family had all gathered in the parlor and were getting ready to go into supper when he was shown in, clearly upset.

"What is wrong?" asked Eugene.

"While we were gone I lost two slaves, a kitchen maid and her one-year-old daughter," Mr. Joe replied agitatedly. "The girl was married to the stable boy I sold to you."

"I guess you mean Do?" Eugene asked.

"That would be the one. I came to ask if I could talk to him."

"I'm afraid not. You see, Do is gone as well," Eugene told Mr. Joe.

Mr. Joe shook his head, "I sure didn't think either one of them was smart enough to plan something like that."

"I told Mr. Jim it was too late to track them. I figure the best we can do is put out a wanted poster."

Mr. Joe agreed, "Guess you're right. That's all we can do now." Mr. Joe shook Eugene's hand and left, and the family went into the dining room for supper. No one mentioned the runaways again.

Dilly, the cook, always fixed a special supper for the family when they returned home. She served fried ham steaks, mashed potatoes, gravy, black eyed peas, turnip greens and to-die-for hot rolls. For dessert there was fresh peach cobbler. The family all agreed that Dilly had outdone herself this time.

For the next few weeks Beth, Sunny and Bow spent most

of their time working with the racehorses to keep them in shape for the fall races. Then one day about the middle of August, Eugene brought home three letters for Beth, one from Rae, one from Dawn and one from Zane. Right away Beth took the letters to her room. She decided to read Zane's last, so she began with Rae's.

July 1861

Dear Beth,

It seems like forever since you were here. A lot has happened in the last few months. Granny Bella has been very ill. She passed away a few days ago. I was so sorry that Dawn was not here. My family and I did what we could to help in her place. As far as I know, Dawn still does not know about her granny. I guess you are wondering why Dawn is not here and where she is.

Dawn left about a month ago to help wherever she can up north. I have not heard from her and I am very worried about her. Her plans were to try to find Stella and Zane. Her parents are very proud of her but are worried sick.

I guess you know about Zane. I got a letter yesterday from him. He said he had been to visit you. He told me about how you were keeping your promise. But I already knew that. My three new red ribbons are hanging on my dressing table mirror. I smile every time I see them. I would love to hear the story behind them sometime.

Night Hawk brought us a new friend just before Dawn left. Right now she and her new baby are staying with Zane's father.

All of my family send their love to you and yours. I hope this fighting is over real soon. I want my friends back where they belong, safe and sound.

Your cousin,

Rae

After reading the part about the three ribbons Beth knew that Do and his family were safe. She couldn't wait to tell Momma Jo and the boys. Then she opened Dawn's letter.

July 1861

To my friend Beth,

I have no idea if you will get this letter or not. I am hoping so. But I guess if you are reading it, you got it, right?

I do not know if you know about my leaving home or where I went. I am trying to do the same as you are. As of today I am in Tennessee. If I get to Georgia, I will try to come see you. So far I have had no trouble, just a few close calls. I hope to see Stella in a few days.

You were right last summer when you said we would all have to grow up sooner than we should. I am only fourteen, but I feel like I am a lot older. Some of the things I have already seen and done are just things I want to forget.

I guess you know what Zane is up to. When he left Indiana he planned to get to Savannah to see you. Knowing him, he will be there sooner or later, so you might watch for him.

Miss you friend!

Your friend,

Dawn

Next was the letter from Zane. Beth just held it for awhile feeling that it brought her closer to him.

My dear Beth,

I am writing to let you know that I am well. I have been very busy lately. You will never guess who was found sneaking around in the woods near our camp one night. It was Stella! Yes, our Stella. I would love to tell you more about that night, but I guess I will save that for later.

Things are getting out of control, so I do not know when I will get back to Savannah. I will keep trying. You never know when I will just stop in for another visit and surprise you. I know how much you like surprises.

I know they said this war would only last a few months, but I think everyone realizes now that it is not going to happen. I believe those months are going to turn into years. If this is so, God help us all. I cannot imagine what this country will be like when this is all over. I know that it will take many years to put it back together so that everyone can live in peace again.

My boss is calling, so I have to go. I will write again as soon as I can.

Your very best friend,

Zane

By the time Beth had read all three letters through twice, she couldn't stop crying. She was so worried about all of her friends.

CHAPTER SIX

October in Indiana 1860

Beth had been gone only a few months, but it seemed more like years. It was early fall and the weather was growing cooler each day. Rae and her friends, Dawn and Zane, had decided to go down to the Wabash River to do a little fishing. Rae wanted to share her latest letter from Beth with them. Zane also had something to share with the girls. He had just turned seventeen and had been talking to his dad, Grant, about joining the fight to help free slaves. He was going to tell the girls today. He knew this was a big decision, but he felt he had to do his part. He just hoped the girls would be proud of him and wish him well.

The morning had started off cool but now the sun was bright and there wasn't a cloud in the sky. The friends saw a pair of young robins flying from tree to tree and singing to each other. They could also hear squirrels jumping from branch to branch chasing each other up and down the pecan trees.

The girls began talking about Beth's letter and how she was keeping her promise to help runaways. Rae was saying that she was going to send a letter to Beth in a few days so either one of them could include their own letter if they wanted to, when they noticed that Zane was gone. He had gotten up to pick them each a small bouquet of flowers. When he gave them to the girls, they looked at each other and at the same time said, "Zane, what's going on?"

He sat down between them and told them what he thought was good news. "I'm leaving in a week to join the Indiana Calvary. I just can't sit here any longer not doing my part."

Rae and Dawn threw their arms around Zane trying not to cry. They knew that his leaving meant they might never see him again after next week, but they both felt in their hearts that he would be home again as soon as the war was over. He just had to be.

Rae told Zane, "I'm so proud of you, but what are we going to do without you?"

Dawn looked at him and asked, "What made you decide to do this?"

Zane looked at Rae, "Well, I guess you'll just have to take care of each other until I get home." Then he looked at Dawn and with a smile on his face told her, "I think the North needs someone that's good with a gun and knows how to handle a horse. And that someone would be me. I think that with my help the war will be over a lot faster. But I'm not sure fighting is what I want to do. I really want to help with the Underground Railroad."

"Oh, we see," said Rae. "You just want to find a way to see Beth, don't you?"

"That would be OK by me," Zane told them.

"Tell your father we'll all help him with the farm as much as we can," Dawn told Zane.

"I will. He'll really appreciate that. Thank you," Zane replied.

During the conversation they still had been watching their fishing poles, but not one had had a bite. At least they hadn't seen any. "I say we give up on the fish," Dawn announced. Rae and Zane nodded their heads in agreement. No one was in the mood to fish now anyway.

Just as they began to take their fishing poles out of the water, Rae looked up and saw an Indian canoe heading straight toward them. There were three people aboard. One was their friend Night Hawk. He had taken over the job of helping slaves get farther North by taking them up the Wabash River from his brother, Lone Star. With him were a black man and woman.

Night Hawk waved to them as he paddled to the shore. When he got close enough, he threw Zane a rope which Zane used to pull the canoe to the bank. Night Hawk and the man climbed out. Then the woman handed the man a large bundle that was all wrapped up in a blanket and Night Hawk carried her to the bank. When the man unwrapped the bundle, the friends were surprised that he held a small girl.

Night Hawk introduced the man and woman to them. "This is Dodley, Robin and Pansy. I think they have something for you."

"For us?" asked Rae. "What ever could they have for us?"

Dodley reached into his jacket pocket and pulled out three red ribbons. "Miss Beth asked us to give these to you if we by chance meet you. She helped us to get free and we'll never, never forget her."

These were the first slaves, now free persons of color, that Beth had sent their way. Rae took the ribbons, held them close to her heart and prayed that Beth was safe. Zane shook both Night Hawk's and Dodley's hands and invited them all to spend the night at the Brown farm. Night Hawk thanked Zane and told him that they would gratefully accept his hospitality. The men pulled the canoe further up the bank and hid it in some bushes. They didn't want to risk trackers finding it or anyone else stealing it.

Dawn's family were also free people of color, so Dawn was really glad to see Dodley and Robin. She could hardly wait to tell her family all that had happened today. As they were all walking to the Brown farm, Dawn asked Dodley and Robin about their journey, and, of course, Zane asked about Beth. No one noticed that Rae and Night Hawk were trailing behind and walking very slowly so that the others couldn't hear their conversation. Rae had no idea why she was doing this, but for some reason she just wanted to be with Night Hawk. She was still wearing the necklace that he had given her when they first met last summer. She had seen him going up and down the Wabash River from time to time, but he always seemed to be in a hurry and hadn't stopped to talk. He just waved and kept on going. Zane had talked to him a few times but Rae and Dawn had not.

Now that they were together again, Rae was the first to

say something. She stopped in the middle of the path, looked Night Hawk in the eye and said, "When we met, you said that I had been in your vision and that we would meet many times. You also told me that I was your woman and to wait for you. What did you mean by all of that? And just so you know, I'm my own woman."

Night Hawk looked at Rae and started laughing so hard that he doubled over and put his hands on his knees. The others even stopped and looked back to see what the commotion was about. When they didn't see anything out of the ordinary, they continued up the path and with their own conversation. Night Hawk finally stopped laughing and just stood there staring at Rae. Then he reached up to run his fingers through her bright red hair.

Still smiling he asked her, "Do you always ask so many questions all at once? Come, sit on this log with me and I will answer all of them. A vision is like what you call a dream, but my people usually have only one vision. That occurs when we reach early manhood. In my vision, I saw a young woman. She had the most beautiful red hair, just like yours. She looked just like you. My vision told me that you are to be my woman. That is why I looked so surprised when I first saw you. Lone Star told me later he knew all along that it was you I had seen in my vision."

"Why would you believe anything like that?" Rae asked. "You know I can never be your woman. You are an Indian and I am a white woman. It would never work. And besides, what makes you think I want to be your woman?"She put her hands on her hips and stamped her foot. "Just who do you think you are trying to tell me what I'm going to do?"

Looking very serious, Night Hawk reached over and took both of Rae's hands in his. "We will wait a while longer, Little One. I know it will take time for you to accept all of this. We will find a way to join our two worlds." Then he did a strange thing. He lowered his head and kissed Rae's forehead. Then turning loose of one hand, he began guiding her down the path toward the others.

Rae was so dazed she just followed him. "What is happening to me?" she wondered.

The next morning, Night Hawk left to take Dodley and his family farther North. He had told Rae and the others that he would be stopping more often from now on.

A few days later everyone told Zane good-bye. They all promised to pray for his safe return, and the sooner that was, the better. He was planning on joining the Indiana Calvary, so he took his favorite horse, a black stallion named Puddles. If only he and Puddles knew that ahead of them lay adventures they would never forget.

CHAPTER SEVEN

November 1861

Andrew, Grant and Thomas had just returned from a trading trip to Mt. Vernon. All of the families were together and sharing the latest news. Andrew was doing most of the talking. "Remember the rumor that several southern states had seceded from the Union to make their own little country? Well, it's true. As of now there are at least seven states that no longer consider themselves part of the United State of America." Looking at Anna he added, "Yes, dear, I'm afraid that Georgia is one of them. They now call themselves the Confederate States. They have even elected their own president, a man by the name of Jefferson Davis from Mississippi, and they now have their own state capital in Richmond, Virginia."

This was very upsetting news for Anna. "My poor sister and her family, right in the middle of all this mess! I just can't imagine what she's feeling. I'm so worried about all of them. Oh, I wish they would come stay with us, but I know they won't. I would not leave my home and I know they won't either. What a mess these men in our government have made for all of us! Let's hope everyone is right that this will only last a few months at the most."

"We all know that Aunt Denise wouldn't leave her home," Rae told her mother. "Remember, Rosa Mae is getting married sometime this summer. Knowing Rosa Mae, I bet she hates all of us by now, especially if this conflict messes up her wedding plans. As for Beth, she's not about to leave the cause she's involved in. So, mother, I would say your wish is not going to come true."

"I suppose you're right, Rae," Anna agreed.

"Just before we left for home there was a message received at the telegraph office," Thomas told them.

"Is it good news or bad news?" Rae was eager to know.

"I'm afraid it's more bad news," Andrew told her. "Early in the morning on April 12, an army of South Carolina men fired on Fort Sumter. A day later, the Union army surrendered the fort. Then on April 19, President Lincoln proclaimed a blockade of all southern ports, stopping all trade with the South. But southerners say Lincoln's not going to stop them from trading. They already have privateers, former pirates, smuggling merchandise in and their crops out. Personally, I don't think they'll get by with this smuggling for very long. Then I can't imagine how the South will survive. So much of what they use comes from the North or Europe. We all know they manufacture very little for themselves." As he was saying this, Andrew was pacing back and forth. He, too, was worried about their family in the South.

✱✱✱✱✱✱✱✱✱✱✱✱✱✱✱✱✱✱✱

In the south at Rivers View there was also a lot of unrest. Early one afternoon Beth was sitting on the front porch with her mother and Rosa Mae. Denise was sitting in a wicker rocker darning socks while Beth and Rosa Mae sat in very uncomfortable straight back chairs working on their samplers. Beth was helping Rosa Mae monogram napkins for her new home. Beth called this busy work, something that she hated to do but that her mother insisted all young ladies were meant to do.

They had been working there for nearly an hour when they heard horses running up the drive and looked up to see Eugene and Robert riding at breakneck speed. "I wonder what is wrong with those two," Denise said with alarm. "If they don't slow down they will surely break their necks."

"It must be something quite important for them to ride that fast," Beth said, her worry clear in her voice.

When Eugene and Robert reached the house they jumped from their horses, throwing the reins to two small slave boys who had run out to meet them when they heard the master coming up the drive. "Whatever is the matter with you two?" Denise demanded.

"Well, they did it," Eugene exclaimed while coming up the porch steps.

"Who did what?" Beth asked anxiously.

"In March they inaugurated that abolitionist country farmer from Illinois to be President of the United States. Now you can be sure that there will be a war. The talk in Savannah is that more southern states are going to be seceding from the Union."

"Do you really believe all this will happen, Eugene?" Denise asked.

"I can guarantee it, my dear."

Beth and Rosa Mae just sat there listening to their parents not knowing what to think. Rosa Mae was hoping that all this talk about a war was not going to postpone her wedding. She and her childhood friend, William, were to be married in September. And what of William? Would he go off to war?

"Oh, Momma! Please tell me this is not going to interfere with my wedding," Rosa Mae pleaded.

"Child, I don't know. We'll just have to wait and see," Denise told her.

"Well, I just won't have it!" Rosa Mae declared defiantly. "I will have my wedding no matter what!"

"Rosa, you are a selfish girl," Beth scolded her older sister. "Think of what a war means! William will probably be going away to fight like all the other men in Georgia, even our father and Robert."

"Momma, tell me Beth is just being mean to me. My William is not a fighter and neither are Robert and father."

"Rosa, calm down," Eugene told her. "As much as I hate to agree with Beth she's probably right, not only about William and Robert but about myself as well." With that Denise looked at her husband. Clutching her lace handkerchief to her mouth she ran into the house and up the stairs to her bedroom, slamming the door behind her. She fell across the big four poster bed and began crying. This is how Eugene found her a few minutes later.

Sitting down beside her and rubbing her back, Eugene reminded his wife that they had talked about all of this many times in the past. "We have been sure that something like this was going to happen ever since I returned from Virginia. Just remember that it will be over in a few weeks or months at the most, just as soon as we teach those Yankees who's boss. Then we'll all be home."

"Are you sure, Eugene? A few weeks? I so hope you are right."

While Robert had gone to the stables, Rosa was pacing the veranda lost in her thoughts. Beth, too, was lost in her own thoughts. She was really worried about Zane as well as her own family. She decided that she needed to take a walk down to the riverbank where she was hoping the sound of the water lapping on the shore would help calm her and clear her head. It always seemed to help when she went to the river, took her shoes and stocking off and dangled her feet in the cool water. But when she got to the wharf she had a surprise. Already sitting on the dock was Honey, doing just what Beth had intended to do. Except Honey didn't have to worry about removing stocking and shoes; she didn't have any.

"What are you doing here?" Beth asked her.

"I's know you, Miss Beth, and I was sure this is where you would end up. And I wanted to talk to you about this here war and being free."

"Well, you were right, Miss Smarty Pants," Beth said laughing as she sat down beside Honey and took off her shoes. "What's on your mind?"

"I'd be worried, Miss Beth. What's gonna happen to all of us slaves? That Mr. Lincoln he say we gonna be free! I's not sure what he means 'bout us being free. I's know we been helping others to go north. But I's not sure how I feel about all that."

"Honey, being free means that you can go wherever and whenever you want to," Beth explained.

"Buts I's wouldn't know where to go if you didn't tell me," Honey told her.

"Let's not worry about that now, Honey. I will help you to understand a little at a time," Beth promised.

"Thank you, Miss Beth."

As Beth slipped her feet into the water she was remembering how last summer she and her friends had gone barefooted most of the time. "My, but that feels good, doesn't it Honey?"

"Yes'um it do, it surly do," was Honey's reply.

Beth decided to rest and laid back on the wharf using her shawl for a pillow. Above her, the sky was bright blue with a scattering of white fluffy clouds. After a few minutes, Beth drifted off to sleep, and it wasn't long before she was dreaming.

First in her dream she could see her father and Robert mounted on horses in a battle. Then her father was falling off his horse. He had been shot and there was blood all over the front of his gray uniform. Robert also saw this and rode as quickly as he could to help his father. Just as he reached his side, Beth's dream ended. She drifted out of sleep for just a few seconds but was soon dreaming again, this time of Zane. The horrible picture she saw was of Zane chained to a tree, bleeding, and men laughing at him.

Beth woke up startled. She was crying and could hardly breathe. When her tears stopped and she caught her breath she looked around. At first she didn't know where she was. Then she remembered she was on the bank of the Savannah River. She remembered Honey was there with her, but when she looked around Honey was gone. She looked up at the sky and realized the sun was setting. She had been sleeping for a long time, but it seemed like only seconds. She sat there for a few more minutes to clear her head before going to the house for dinner. She prayed these dreams would never, ever come true.

CHAPTER EIGHT

More Red Ribbons Going North

The first of September came and the Taylor family was preparing to go back to Savannah to stay until mid-December. Beth knew that Rosa Mae would not be returning with them. Her wedding was planned for the third week in September, after which she would be moving to William's family home. Beth was hoping that she, her mother and grandmother would not be the only ones returning to Rivers View for Christmas. She was afraid that once her father and Robert arrived in Savannah they would become more involved in the war and go off to join the fight.

Again, the family was taking the racehorses to the city. Even with a war being fought in parts of the state there were still races planned for the fall. As she had in the spring, Beth was to follow with the horses a few days after the rest of the family's departure. As it so happened, this arrangement turned out to be a great opportunity. A few days before the family left, Bow told Beth about a young slave girl and her brother who were being cruelly mistreated at a plantation just up the river. The word had passed from plantation to plantation that they wanted to go north.

After Bow told Beth about the pair he asked, "Can we help them, Miss Beth?"

"How far away are they?" she wanted to know.

"Bout five miles upriver on that plantation nobody likes to visit," Bow answered.

"I know the one. It's called Dogwood Plantation. Let me think about this and I'll talk to you tomorrow about what we can possibly do." Beth then went to the house to find Momma Jo who was helping Denise pack for her trip. Beth told Momma Jo that she wanted to talk to her later. Momma Jo knew what she wanted to talk about. Bow had already told her about the brother and sister on Dogwood Plantation.

After everyone had retired for the night, Momma Jo made her way to Beth's room. "I's specs I know what you want to talk bout," Momma Jo told her.

"Yes. Bow told me about the brother and sister," Beth replied.

Momma Jo nodded her head, "What is you planning, child?"

"I think I've got everything figured out except how to get them here at the right time," Beth told Momma Jo.

"Well child, you think on it tonight. I know something will come to you."

Beth hugged Momma Jo tight. "I hope you are right. Come to my room again tomorrow night and we'll put a plan together."

The next night Beth asked Momma Jo if she thought Bow could get a message to the brother or sister, hopefully the next day.

"He have to have a reason to go there. Can't think what that could be. That overseer is plum crazy. And the owner is never home so he don't know what's happening on his own plantation. Last I's heard he was in England. Hear tell he been gone over a year this time," Momma Jo informed Beth.

"I suppose I will go for a long ride tomorrow," Beth planned. "Of course, Bow will need to go with me. Who knows, we might just end up at Dogwood Plantation. If one of our horses was to go lame, I'm certain someone there would help us. Surely one of us could then make contact with the brother or sister. Bow told me the brother worked in the stables and the sister in the house." Momma Jo agreed that this was an ingenious idea. She told Beth good night then went to find Bow to tell him the scheme.

The next morning after breakfast, Beth told her mother she was going for a ride and would be taking Bow with her. It was Beth's job to exercise the horses, so she knew that being gone all day would not look suspicious. Denise was used to Beth and Bow, and sometime Sunny, riding all day.

"Be careful, and make sure you are home in time for dinner," was all Denise said to her.

"We will. I think we'll ride upriver a ways today." Beth always told someone where she planned to go, just in case she didn't make it back when she should.

Once they were on their way, Beth explained her escape plan to Bow so that if he got the chance he could tell the brother. If she could, Beth would tell the sister. She hoped that at least one of their messages would get through. "We have to make our move in two days, the day after my family leaves for Savannah. Late at night, after everyone had gone to sleep, they will need to cross the river and stay in the water as long as they can to throw the dogs off their trail. We'll pick them up as soon as possible and bring them here to hide in the attic until I leave for the city. Then we'll take them to Savannah with us."

"Savannah? Are you sure, Miss Beth? That sounds awful dangerous to me." Bow didn't know if he liked this plan or not, but he trusted Miss Beth, so he didn't say anything else.

"Bow, how will we know who we're looking for? I know we don't know their names; that would have been too dangerous. All I know is where to find them, but I'm sure that there are a lot of slaves at Dogwood."

"If it's the two I think it is they be twins and real fair skinned. Heard tell that the owner or the overseer be their pappy," Bow told her.

"If you're right that should make our job a lot easier. Yes sir, a lot easier," Beth was thinking aloud.

They had been trotting the horses along a road that ran beside the river. After passing two lanes that led to other plantations, they finally came across the lane that would take them to Dogwood. They knew they were in the right place because an old, faded wooden sign that read "Dogwood Plantation" was leaning up against an even older crumbling stone post.

"This place gives me a bad feeling," Beth said. "Makes

me worry already."

The house couldn't be seen from the road, which was good because this is where Beth dismounted and motioned for Bow to do the same.

"What we gone a do now, Miss Beth?"

"As much as I hate to, we're going to put a small pebble in Glory's back hoof. Help me find one. It needs to be just large enough to make him limp but not large enough to hurt him."

"Very smart, Miss Beth. And I guess that when the pebble is removed you'll need to let him rest for a bit?"

"That's the plan. Smart or not that's the best I can think of for now."

Bow and Beth looked around until they found a small round pebble. A round one would cause Glory less pain. "I'm sorry, Glory, but it's for a good cause," Beth told her horse as Bow carefully placed the pebble so that it would look accidental. Then, the pair remounted and directed their horses up the lane. As they approached the plantation house they could see a small group of slaves working around the stables supervised by a middle-aged white man.

"That man must be the overseer," Bow told Beth. "Look, one of those boys is almost as white and he is. You think that be the one we're looking for?"

"I hope so. Let's head toward the stables," Beth directed. As she headed that way, Bow fell back a few feet behind her, the proper position for a slave accompanying his mistress. When they arrived, the white man took off his hat and went to assist Beth from her horse. "Well now, who might you be?" he inquired.

"Good day to you, sir. I'm Beth Taylor from Rivers View. My stable boy and I have been out exercising my horse but it seems that my Glory has picked up a rock in his hind hoof. And wouldn't you know my boy forgot to bring a pick! I would be forever thankful if one of your boys could help us out. That is, if it wouldn't be too much trouble."

"No trouble at all, Miss Taylor," the man smiled. Then he turned and yelled gruffly, "Bear, you get yourself over here right now and help this boy with this pretty little lady's horse," The whole time the man was yelling at Bear he was smiling at Beth with a look in his eyes that Beth didn't much care for. "Now, Miss Taylor, while them boys take care of your horse, why don't we go up to the porch and have us a nice cool glass of lemonade. I believe the cook has just baked a chocolate cake this very morning."

"Lemonade would be very nice, Mr.--. I'm sorry; I don't believe you told me your name," Beth was saying as she walked away from the stables toward the house. She needed to get this man as far away from the stables as she could so Bow could talk to Bear.

"Sorry bout that, Miss Taylor. You caught me off guard. We don't have many visitors here at Dogwood, you see. I'm Mr. Mayflower, the overseer for Mr. Scott, the owner, who is in Europe getting his self married. I don't expect him back for months, maybe a year. Until then, I'm in charge around here."

"How nice for you, Mr. Mayflower. It's almost like having your own plantations, isn't it?" Beth was thinking to herself,

"He sure likes to blow his own horn."

"You come right on up here and have a seat on the front porch and I'll get Willow to bring us that lemonade. Wouldn't you care for a slice of cake as well?"

"No thank you, Mr. Mayflower. You know how we ladies are about sweets," Beth told him in her sweetest voice.

Mr. Mayflower disappeared into the house. A few minutes later a young slave girl came out the front door caring a tray with a pitcher of lemonade and two glasses. Beth looked at the tray and thought, "So, Mr. Mayflower intends to sit and have lemonade with me. He must really think highly of himself." Entertaining guests was something an overseer never did.

Then Beth looked at the girl. Her skin was so fair that her curly black hair was the only hint that she was a Negro. Beth realized that this had to be Bear's twin sister. She looked just like him. Willow set the tray on a small wooden table between two old rockers. "Mr. Mayflower say he be out in a few minutes. He needs to wash up a bit," the girl told Beth before turning to go back inside.

Beth knew she only had a few minutes to talk to Willow before the overseer returned. "Thank you," she said. Before the girl could leave, Beth walked to the far end of the porch. Looking out over the yard, Beth asked her, "Willow, do you know the name of the flowers that are growing over by that giant cypress tree?"

Willow didn't quite know what to think. A white lady had never asked her a question about flowers before, or anything else for that matter, and she was rarely addressed by name.

She walked over to where Beth was standing, but before she could even open her mouth to say that she didn't know, Beth began whispering to her. "My name is Beth Taylor. I'm from Rivers View, a plantation down river from here, and I'm here to help you and your brother. My stable boy, Bow, is talking to Bear right now. Just follow his instructions and you'll both be safe." After relaying her message, Beth turned around and walked back to her seat. She had just picked up her glass to fill it when Mr. Mayflower returned.

Before he sat down, Mr. Mayflower yelled for Willow to get herself back in the house and back to work. "All them Negroes are so uppity and lazy any more. Especially since some fool went and told them they could all be free someday soon. Whoever heard of a free Negro?"

"I understand there are a lot of free black people up north, but I believe there are very few here in the South. I guess you know that we have men at war right now to keep them in their place," Beth said. "By the way, Mr. Mayflower, if you feel so strongly about this why are you not one of these men?"

"Yes, ma'am, I feel real strong about keeping them slaves in their place. I would gladly be one of them fighting men but, you see, someone has to stay and oversee this plantation," Mr. Mayflower said with a smug look on his face.

It was at this time that Bow and Bear came in front of the house leading Glory and Bow's horse. "I believe Glory be OK now, Miss Beth, so when you be ready we can start home." After telling this to Beth, Bow turned around and started talking to Bear.

"Well then, Mr. Mayflower, I'll be on my way. I thank you for your help and hospitality. If I can ever return the favor, just stop in at Rivers View." With that, Beth left Mr. Mayflower standing on the porch. Bow helped her to mount and they rode off down the lane.

When they had ridden a ways up the main road they found a cool place on the river to water their horses. "Oh! Bow, that Mr. Mayflower is such a smug mean old man. And so full of himself, don't you think?" Beth asked. Bow nodded his head. "Now spill it!" she said impatiently. "Was Bear the right one? Did you get to talk to him? What did he say? Did you tell him our plan? I talked to his sister, Willow. Or at least I hoped it was his sister."

"Yes, Miss Beth, them are the right ones. I told Bear your plan and he says he and his sister will meet us as planned."

"Then we had better get ourselves home. We have a lot of work to do," Beth told Bow.

When they arrived home, Denise and Rosa Mae were supervising the last of the packing. Early the next morning the rest of the family would be off to Savannah. Beth realized how fortunate it was that they would be out of the way for her to help two more slaves to freedom.

As soon as the family was out of sight the next day, Beth and Momma Jo got to work. Beth knew that Honey would take care of her packing, so all she needed to worry about was her plan for Bear and Willow. They had to get her boy's clothes from the attic and pack supplies for Bear and Willow, extra clothes, blankets, etc. Momma Jo helped her find and alter clothes for Willow and Bear to wear on the train. Dilly prepared food for their trip to Savannah, as well as extra to last the runaways at least a few a days.

Beth had originally planned to hide the siblings in the attic of the house, but after thinking it through she knew that wouldn't work. Mr. Jim would be there when they left in two days, so there would be no way to get the pair out of the house. To solve this dilemma, Beth decided to hide them in the stables. That way, Bow and Sunny could hide Bear in the luggage wagon and Willow in the boot of the buggy that Beth and Honey would be riding in to Metter. Mr. Jim never checked any of these places.

On the night she and Bow went to meet Bear and Willow, Beth again dressed as a boy. This time they didn't have as far to go, but as before they took the raft so there would be enough room. Beth had decided to bring Duke along on this trip. She always felt safer when he was with her, and if they were to run into Mr. Mayflower, she knew she would need Duke's help.

Bow and Beth were able to sneak away from Rivers View and board the raft without trouble. The moon was high tonight so they had to be extremely careful. Wanting to get back to safety as soon as possible, they moved quickly up the river keeping a sharp eye out for the fugitives. About a mile downstream from Dogwood Plantation, they came across the pair holding onto a log for dear life. Beth could see that Willow was terrified by the look in her eyes. Bow helped them aboard the raft and he and Bear began poling it back to Rivers View. Willow was shivering with fear and cold, making Beth glad she had brought a blanket to wrap around her.

Once they reached the shore near Rivers View, Bow and Bear pulled the raft onto the bank. Bear picked up his sister to carry her so they would make only one set of tracks. Being sure to stay in the shadows of the trees and building as much as he could, Bow led the way to the stables while Beth followed with Duke, trying as best she could to cover Bear's tracks. She had wrapped his feet in rags hoping to throw any tracking dogs off his scent. After making sure Bear and Willow were settled and Bow and Sunny were there to get anything they needed, Beth went straight to her room for bed. Momma Jo instructed Honey to hide Beth's disguise in a secret compartment in the lid of her trunk, just in case she needed them in Savannah.

Everyone was up before dawn the next morning. After a light breakfast, Beth was ready to go. When she went outside to get into the buggy she looked at Bow and Sunny who both simply nodded their heads, signaling that everything was under control. Then the boys each climbed into a driver's seat and Honey joined Beth in the buggy. Once everyone was settled, they waved good-bye to Momma Jo and Dilly and were on their way.

When the travelers were about halfway to Metter they pulled off the main road and drove a short distance up a deserted lane where Bear and Willow were helped out of their hiding places. Beth handed Willow a light brown and white cotton dress with a matching bonnet and a light brown scarf with which to tie up her hair. Willow had never had such a fine dress, but she needed one because she was to ride on the train as a second maid to Beth. Bear was given a clean pair of pants and shirt. He was going to help Sunny and Bow with the horses. Once the fugitives were dressed, Willow joined Beth and Honey in the buggy while Bear climbed onto the luggage wagon next to Bow.

They reached the train station in Metter and the boys began by unloading the luggage. Then, Bow and Bear settled the horses in a private box car while Sunny took the buggy and then the wagon to the town stables where they would be left until their return. Meanwhile, Willow and Honey accompanied Beth as she made herself comfortable in a passenger car of the train. Both servant girls sat in the seat opposite Beth. All three were very quiet, trying not to attract attention so that no one would remember they had ever been aboard. Beth had even worn a rather plain pink dress and had tucked her hair up under a bonnet. She was hoping that if anyone noticed her they would think she was from one of the poorer plantations or farms.

Fortunately, there was a new conductor working their car that day. He was so preoccupied learning his new job that he didn't have time to pay any attention to who his passengers were. The train ride began and ended without incident.

Eugene had already told Beth he wouldn't be meeting her at the station this time. He planned to be in Atlanta at a military meeting on the day of her arrival. Lamar would be picking her and Honey up. Beth was so glad for this because it would make her plan go a lot more smoothly. On the way to Metter she had spelled out the plan to Bear and Willow. She told them what they were to do when they arrived in Savannah and explained that they would have to be on their own but she would try to think of a way to be close by. As soon as the train stopped the two were to head off. Bear was to follow about a block behind Willow. She would be carrying a basket of clothes and Bear a basket of fruit so that it would look like they had been out tending to their master's business.

Beth had asked if either of them knew how to count or to read. Neither of them did, so she had taught Willow how to make a fist and release one finger each time she crossed a street. They were going to have to walk one block from the train station and then turn left. Beth told Willow to hold her basket in her left hand so she would remember which way to turn. After the left turn they would have to walk until they came to the sixth street then turn right and walk one block to Bryan Street where there would be a church on their right. They needed to go around to the back of the church and ask for Mr. Angel. From here on, Mr. Angel would take care of them. Beth had given Bear and Willow each a red ribbon hoping that someday Rae would get these also.

Honey had been the one who told Beth about the church. The First African Baptist Church was a church exclusively for blacks and was a station along the Underground Railroad. "The church has a hiding place in the cellar under the main floor," Honey had explained. "There's a large diamond shape in the middle of the center isle made from holes drilled into the floor. The white leaders think it's a church symbol, but it's not. It was put there to help the slaves get fresh air."

"Whoever said that black people are stupid?" Beth had asked and they had both laughed.

When Beth got off the train and into the carriage she told

Lamar that she wanted to take a slow ride through town to see the sights before going home to the Jefferson House. She directed him so that they would be following Willow and Bear. She wanted to make sure they made all of the turns as she had directed and made it to the church without trouble. She was anxious the whole ride, and as Bear went around to the back of the church she let out a sigh of relief. She hadn't realized she had been holding her breath. "I'm ready to go home now," she told Lamar.

It was then that her face lit up with a big smile. "Honey, I have the most wonderful idea!" Beth exclaimed.

Honey, who was sitting across from Beth in the carriage, saw the look and knew that it usually meant trouble. "Oh, Miss Beth, what now?" she groaned. "Isn't one adventure at a time enough for you? It surely is for me."

Beth started laughing, "Not that kind of idea. How would you like to learn to read and write and even count?"

"Miss Beth, you know I can't do that. It's against the law. We could both get in big trouble just talking about such a thing."

"We both know you can already read some," Beth continued, ignoring Honey's warning. "I say we go all the way. In fact, when we get back to Rivers View, I'm going to teach not only you, but Bow and Sunny as well. I want all of you to be prepared when this war is over. What do you think, Honey?"

"I think it's one of the best ideas you ever had, Miss Beth. Maybe I should tell you; I've already been teaching what I know to Bow and Sunny as well as some of the children at

Rivers View," Honey confessed.

Reaching over and taking Honey's hands, Beth said "Honey, why didn't you tell me about what you've been doing? You should have known I would have helped you anyway that I could. From now on we'll do this together. That is, if it's OK with you."

"I was afraid to tell you. I didn't want to cause you any trouble. You're right, Miss Beth. Now with your help, we can all learn a lot more and a lot faster. But what will your parents say about all this?"

"You know that they are hardly ever home. When I tell them what I plan to do, I'm sure they'll think it's as great an idea as we do."

Later that day when Beth told her parents about her new idea, they supported her even though it was against the law. Eugene cautioned her to keep it as quite as possible and not to tell any of her friends. He even went so far as to tell her she could make one of the barn stalls into a classroom. Denise reminded her that there were boxes of old textbooks in the attic, both in Savannah and at Rivers View. Beth and Honey spent the next few weeks making plans for their new school. They got the books out of the attic and, after dusting them off, went through each one to see what they could use. Beth made a trip to the general store to purchase slates and chalk. When they left for Rivers View in December they would be ready to start teaching. They were both so excited they could hardly wait.

CHAPTER NINE

1862

Blue Ridge Mountains, Georgia

Zane had been assigned to an intelligent - secret service-spy unit. His unit, under the command of Major Jess Odell, was camped in a remote area in the woods of the Blue Ridge Mountains in Georgia near four different Confederate state lines: Tennessee, South Carolina, North Carolina and Alabama. Major Odell had assigned Zane to be partners with a free black man around twenty-years old named J.B. The two had become friends right away. They balanced one another's weaknesses and strengths. What one couldn't do or figure out, the other one could.

All of the men in this unit had code names. Zane's was Wabash, and J.B. was known as Slick. Zane had chosen his name but J.B. had just kind of earned his because he could sneak in and out of places that nobody else could and no one would even know he had been there. Everyone said he was as slick as an eel.

Both Zane and J.B. loved their jobs and Major Odell knew it. He also knew he could always depend on these two young men. That is why he had called them into his tent one night. He had a special assignment for them in southern Georgia.

The three men were sitting in Major Odell's tent drinking strong black coffee; strong was the only way the army knew how to make coffee. Major Odell had given Zane and J.B. their orders. Then he asked them about their families and where they were from. Zane told him that he lived on a farm along the Wabash River in southern Indiana. He explained that his mother had died from a snake bite years ago and that he and his father, Grant, had lived alone ever since.

J.B. told the major his story. "I was born a slave on a tobacco plantation in Alabama. My sister and I were sold when I was twelve-years-old and she was ten. Our master needed the money to impress his new bride. He wanted to take her to Europe for their honeymoon. Our Ma and Pa had both died the year before of sickness. When we were fourteen and twelve we ran away to Detroit, Michigan. I got a job in an iron mill and my sister, Effie, she got a job as a maid in a big house for the mill owner. When I was seventeen I got involved with the Underground Railroad. My boss sent me along with two white men to Virginia to talk a ship builder into buying our iron for his anchors. While there I met a black couple who were helping runaways. They asked me to help them get a young girl north. Her master was abusing her and they were afraid for her life. I helped smuggle the girl north when we went back to Michigan. That's when I decided to come south and do what I could for others."

After they had finished talking with the major and

drinking their coffee, Zane and J.B. went back to their own tent. They needed a good night's sleep because they were to leave bright and early the next morning. While on their mission, Zane was hoping to get to Savannah or Rivers View, wherever Beth was. He hadn't seen her for months.

✳✳✳✳✳✳✳✳✳✳✳✳✳✳✳✳✳✳✳✳

After the young men had left his tent, Major Odell poured himself another cup of coffee. He had some paperwork to do before he could get any rest. He also needed to write a letter to his family in Ohio as well as to the families of the three young men who had been lost in a skirmish the day before. One of them had been so young he had never even gotten to shave. "What do I say to the families of these young men?" Odell thought. This war was already full of so many tragedies.

He began reading a report he had just received from up North, but listening to Zane and J.B. talk about their families caused him to think about his own. The night was so still he could hear the sounds of crickets chirping in the nearby woods and of the small brook behind the camp as it cascaded over rocks on its way down the mountainside. Odell was listening to this serenade as he sat on his camp stool with his elbows on his desk and his overlapped hands holding up his chin. He was so tired that he laid his head down on top of his papers and drifted off to sleep.

It wasn't long before he began dreaming about his sixteenth birthday and the letter his great-great-grandmother had given him on that special day, a letter that had changed his life forever. His Granny Jane had written the letter the day Jess was born and addressed it to him to be opened on his sixteenth birthday. She knew that if she didn't live to see Jess turn sixteen, no one would open the letter except him. His father would want to, but his southern honesty would never let him do such a thing.

On the evening of that birthday when Granny was ready to go to her room she asked Jess to help her up the stairs. No one thought much about this. After all, Granny had turned eighty-eight the day before, and because of her arthritis she often had trouble climbing the stairs. When Granny and Jess reached her door, Jess moved to give Granny a hug and to thank her again for his new pocket knife, but Granny took his hand in hers and led him into her bedroom. She went to her dresser and pulled out an envelope which she handed to Jess.

Jess looked at the envelope with surprise. "What's this, Granny?" he asked. "You don't need to give me another present. The knife was wonderful. I love it and will keep it with me always." Just dreaming of that knife caused the sleeping major to reach down to make sure Granny's knife was in his pocket.

Granny looked at him and said, "No, Jess, this is not another present. I wrote this letter just for you on the day you were born. Since you are an only child you will need to destroy it when you have finished reading it. Now, take it to your room and put it away until you go to bed. If you have any questions, we'll talk about them in the morning. Remember, you'll want to destroy it. There is information in here that you won't want to share. No other living person knows what this letter will tell you."

Even though Jess was curious, he did as Granny had told him. He hid the letter in his room until later, wondering all the time what could be such a big secret. When he returned to his room that night he locked the door pulled the letter out of its hiding place. He walked over to the old rocker that sat beside the terrace window and turned up the wick of the oil lamp. Opening the envelope, he took out the letter and began reading.

My dearest Jess,

I hope you have had a great birthday. Now that you are sixteen and a young man I want to tell you a true story about myself and your great-great-grandpa.

When I was five-years-old my poppa bought a new stable boy named Ben. Ben was only eight-years-old at the time. When Poppa drug Ben into the barn, I was in one of the horse stalls petting my mare, so Poppa didn't know I was there. Ben was crying and I had no idea why. I heard Poppa tell him to be quite or else he would go without supper and every meal after until he quit. I had no idea Poppa treated our slaves in such a way. Poppa then told the head stableman, Mo, to chain Ben in one of the stalls until he stopped crying.

"Boy's your responsibility now. He's to be your new helper. I expect you to train him well. His Pa was the head groomsman on a plantation in South Carolina. I paid a lot of money for this here boy so you see that you take good care of him"

"Yes, sir," Mo told Poppa. "I'll teach him all I know. And I's make sure he don't miss behave."

I knew Mo was very smart. He knew all there was to know about horses, from training to doctoring them. After Poppa left the stable, Mo knelt in front of Ben, put his hands on his shoulders and looked him right in the eye. "You stop that crying and tell old Mo when was the last time you ate?"

Ben looked at Mo and wiped his tears on the back of his hand. "Yesterday morning before daylight, and I'm right hungry."

"I know you be sad for leaving your family. But, there's nothing anyone can do to change what's happened to you. You know it happens all the time, so you might as well make the best of it. You want to learn to be the best stableman I can teach you to be, then the master won't want to sell you again. I gonna put you in that stall over there for the night. I don't want to chain you in but if the master comes back we'll both be in trouble if I don't. I'll be leaving the stall door open and there's new straw in there. You get some rest, you look plum tuckered out. I be bringing you some supper and a quilt in a little while."

Ben nodded his head and walked to the stall that Mo had pointed to. It was right next to the one I was in. After Mo left, I crawled around to get a closer look at this new boy. I sat there for a long time watching him. His eyes were closed and I thought he was asleep. After awhile I decided I had better things to do than watch some slave boy sleep. I got up and was leaving the stall when Ben said to me, "You tired of staring at me? Who's you be anyway?"

"I am the master's daughter so you better be nice to me."

Ben just laughed at that, so I marched right over to his stall and put my hands on my hips and asked him, "Just what are you laughing at? "We both stared at each other for a few minutes. Then we both started laughing. We knew we were going to be friends from then on.

From that day on I spent every minute I could in the stables. I watched and listened to everything Mo was teaching Ben. My parents were gone a lot, they liked to travel and visit other countries. Since I was so young I was left at home. It really didn't bother me much. I liked it on the plantation and I could come and go as I wanted. By the time I was sixteen and Ben nineteen we were together almost all the time. We both loved to be around horses.

One sunny day that summer I decided I wanted to go for a ride. I had a beautiful palomino mare that I had named Babe. I loved Babe more than anything. Even though Ben and I were together a lot we had never been alone. Mo or one of the other stable boys had always been close. I knew that a white girl was not allowed to be alone with a black man except when he was escorting her on a ride, and Ben knew that he would be in big trouble if this ever happened. On this particular day all the stables boys and the overseer were working in the hay field and Ben was the only one who could ride with me, so I went to the summer kitchen and I asked cook to make a picnic for two. I told her I was going riding and I was really hungry. We both knew I was not allowed to share with a slave. Then I went to the stables to get Babe.

Ben asked me, "Where do you think you going girl?" I told him I was going on a picnic and I knew everyone else was busy, so he would just have to go with me to protect me.

"You just asking for us both to get in trouble," Ben told me.

"You know my parents are in New York now visiting my Aunt Gracie, mother's sister. So who's to know?" I asked him.

I didn't leave Ben any choice. He knew I couldn't go by myself, and I would if he didn't go. What was he to do? So while I went to the kitchen to get the picnic Ben went and threw a blanket on old Two Feet, a mule with two white feet.

We rode for an hour until we got to a stream that ran through our property. At this place in the stream was a big hole deep enough to swim in. My friends and I had been here many times. There were lots of wild flowers, violet, honeysuckle and a large old oak tree for shade and a swing hung from one of the limbs for us to swing on. Ben tied up Babe and old Two Feet then took the picnic basket off Babe's back and asked me where I wanted him to put it. I could tell he still was not happy with me. I had put both of us in a very dangerous situation. I spread out a blanket and told him to put the basket there. When he had put the basket down he started to walk off toward the stream.

"Aren't you hungry?" I asked him. "I had cook pack a lunch for two. I told her I was really hungry."

Ben looked at me like I was crazy. "You know I can't do that Miss Jane."

I smiled right back at him. I turned around and looked at him again and asked, "Just who is there to tell us what we can and can't do, Mr. Ben? Now come on over here and let's see what cook packed for us to eat."Ben came over but he wouldn't sit on the blanket with me. He had his pride and was not going to break all the rules. Cook had sent us a very nice lunch. I remember we had fried chicken, baked yams, biscuits, sliced tomatoes and two pieces of my favorite orange cake with white sticky icing.

The day had gotten really hot, so after lunch I told Ben to do whatever he wanted to do, I was going wading to cool off. He could take a nap or he could go wadding with me. I took off my shoes and stockings. Then I went behind a bush and took off my petticoats. They were just too heavy to have to hold up and I didn't want to get them wet. It looked like Ben had decided to just sit on the bank and take a nap. I hadn't been wadding very long before a black snake went swimming by, scaring me half to death. Of course, I screamed and lost my balance causing me to fall face down in the water. When I tried to get up I fell again. Even though I had removed my petticoats my dress was very heavy when it got wet. As I was trying to get up the second time I felt Ben's strong hands lift me up and carry me back to the blanket. I had not been scared so much by the snake, but when I fell I had hit my head on a rock. I was really lucky I wasn't hurt.

Ben looked at me, "You crazy girl. You coulda been killed. When you ever gonna grow up?"

And then something happened that neither of us could explain. He wrapped his arms around me and just held me tight. At the same time I wrapped my arms around him. We stood there for what seemed like forever. And then it dawned on us what was happening. We jumped apart. I turned my back to him because I didn't want him to see I was crying. I knew at that moment I loved Ben and I would never love anyone else as much or quite the same way. When I turned around and looked at him I could see in his eyes that he felt the same.

"Oh! Ben I've fallen in love with you and I think you feel the same way about me."

Ben just looked at me shaking his head, "You know this can't be, Miss Jane. It's against the law for me to even touch you."

"I know Ben, but we'll figure something out. I can't lose you." I held my hands out to him and he took them and pulled me back into his arms. It was then that I had my first kiss.

Jess, I know this is a long story, but you will soon see why I'm telling you all of this. I hope this is not upsetting you and that you will not think less of your old Granny. But love holds no bounds, color or otherwise. One kiss led to our getting very, very close. Before either one of us knew it we were as close as a woman and man can get. We were both so happy to have at last shown the other how we felt. We lay there for a long time wrapped in each other's arms.

It was getting late in the afternoon when Ben said, "We need to go home. We must never, ever speak of this afternoon to anyone." We agreed to keep our secret. I knew I would never forget this day and that it would probably be the only time we would have together.

About two months later I knew I was pregnant. I didn't know what to do or who to tell, but I did know I couldn't keep it a secret for long. First I had to tell Ben. He had a right to know about our baby. When I told him, he was just as scared as I was. We both knew that my reputation and family name would be ruined and that if it was discovered that he was the father he would be killed, probably beat and then hung.

I could not let this happen to the man I loved. I told Ben I had a plan. My parents had sailed to Europe the week before, so I would just leave them a note telling them I had gone to visit my Aunt Gracie in New York, that I was not sure how long I would be gone, and that I would see them in a few months. I told them I took Ben for protection and of course Nan, my maid, went along with us. I knew Aunt Gracie would help us.

Ten days later we left for New York. I knew that when I returned my life would be very different. On the way to New York I told Nan our story, making her promise not to tell anyone else. I knew I was going to need her help from now on.

I had sent a letter to Aunt Gracie so that she would be expecting us. I hadn't seen her since three years before when she had been to see us.

Aunt Gracie had received my letter and was happy to see me. She knew something was wrong but waited until after dinner to talk to me about my problem. The first evening we were there she sat me down in her parlor and asked me, "What's wrong child? As glad as I am to see you I can tell you have a problem. I know you are not missing your parents.

Lord knows they are never there for you. I look at your eyes and can tell you are worried about something. So tell me, why this unexpected visit? You wouldn't have come to your Aunt Gracie's if you didn't think she could help you, now would you?"

I told Aunt Gracie my story and then we both had a good cry. After we cried ourselves out she hugged me and sent me off to my bed, promising to help find a solution for both Ben and me.

The next morning after breakfast she asked me to join her in the parlor again. She asked me, "How much do you love Ben? Enough to let him go so that he can be safe?" I couldn't speak so I just nodded my head. I knew we had to do whatever it took to keep him safe.

The following spring your great-grandfather Benjamin was born. That was the happiest day of my life and the saddest. I held my beautiful baby boy in my arms and cried. I was happy because Benny was healthy and had no traces of Negro. He looked just like my father, blue eyes and all. I was sad because I knew that in a few months Ben would be walking out of my life forever, never to see me or his son again. I had decided to name my baby Benjamin as a way of keeping Ben close to me. When he was four months old I would return home. I made up a lie that I had fallen in love with a young man in New York and we had gotten married. A few days after we were married he had been killed in a boating accident. After his death I had discovered I was pregnant. Even though Benny was four months old I was going to tell everyone he was big for his age because his father had been a tall and muscular man.

The day Aunt Gracie and Ben took us to the train station was very hard on all of us. Ben held his son for the last time. Knowing we couldn't touch each other at the station we had said our good-byes before we left the house. The last I saw of my Ben he and Aunt Gracie were standing on the station platform waving to me. We knew that Nan and I would be safe on our trip home. No one would bother a young woman with a new baby. The next morning Ben was to leave for Canada where he was to start a new life with a new name.

Everyone believed my story. It had helped that Aunt Gracie had also written a letter to my parents telling them about my problems, my make believe problems.

When Benny was a year old I married your great-great-grandfather, Felix Stall. As I am sure you remember he was a widower with two children, a daughter and a son. We raised these three children as a family, never having any children together.

When Benny got married and I was told they were expecting a baby I was so happy for them. But at night I prayed the child would be white. I have done the same for every baby born in our family since. So far we have been very lucky. You know that if color ever shows up, the child will be made a slave and the family will not be able to claim it as one of their own. That is why I have told you this story. Ben had told me that he had an ancestor who was white, so hopefully this will never be a problem.

Remember I love you,

Granny Jane

By the time Jess had finished reading his letter he had tears running down his checks. He put the letter back in hiding for the night, blew out the lamp and went to bed. It was a long time before he was able to go to sleep.

The next morning Jess had gone straight to Granny's room. He wanted to tell her how proud he was of her for raising his grandfather Benny. He had only one question. How did one give up somebody that they loved as much and she and Ben had loved each other? Jess had knocked on Granny's door, but there had been no answer. After knocking a few times he opened the door and stuck his head in. Granny was still sitting in her rocking chair wearing the clothes she had worn the night before. During the night she had passed away in her sleep. Jess remembered kissing her on the forehead and promising that no one would ever know her secret. Later, Jess had reread the letter and then thrown it in the fireplace to burn.

Back in the Georgian mountains, Major Jess Odell was now awake and sitting alone in his tent. Remembering Granny Jane inspired him as to what to write to the families of his fallen men. When he finished the letters he blew out his small candle and went to his cot. He knew that tonight, like the night he turned sixteen, sleep would be a long time coming.

While lying awake he thought of a free Negro girl from Illinois he had met a few days ago. Her name was Stella and she was seventeen. She had told him a story about four friends and an Indian named Lone Star who had helped her and her two brothers get to freedom. For some reason, Jess couldn't get Stella off his mind. He hoped he would see her again sometime soon. He knew Stella was helping with the Underground Railroad, and he had decided to help her any way he could.

CHAPTER TEN

Stella

A few weeks later Major Odell was again sitting in his tent at a camp not five miles from Vicksburg, Mississippi. Sergeant Wayne had brought his dinner an hour ago. Now he was writing a letter to his family telling them only the good things, like the story J.B. had told him and how highly he thought of both J.B. and Zane. His daughter April would enjoy the story about how he had ridden a mule for two days because his horse had injured its foot. He had just signed his name and was finishing up his last cup of coffee when Sergeant Wayne asked permission to enter his tent.

"Yes, sergeant what is it this time?" Major Odell asked.

"Sir, the night patrol has found a young Negro boy just outside of camp. He says he's with the Underground Railroad. What would you like us to do with him?"

"Where is he now, Sergeant?"

"He's waiting just outside your tent, sir."

"Well, bring him in and let's have a look." Sergeant Wayne stepped outside the tent and returned with the young boy. Major Odell thought he looked to be about eighteen, the same age as his daughter April, or maybe even younger. "Well, young man, Sergeant Wayne tells me you're here helping the Underground Railroad. Now why should I believe you? How do I know you're not a spy?"

"No, sir, I'm not a spy," the young man answered.

"Tell me your name and what you were doing outside our camp," the major requested.

"My name is–," But before the boy could finish there was another appeal to enter the major's tent.

"Sir, permission to enter." The major didn't have to ask who it was. He recognized the voice of his number one spy, Zane, who had just returned days ago from an uneventful but successful mission to Georgia.

"Enter young man. Can't you see I'm busy?"

"Yes, sir, but Private Dole told me we might have a spy on our hands. I thought I might be of help," Zane replied.

"Who knows? You might be right," the major told him.

By then the young boy couldn't keep his laugh back any longer. He laughed as he removed the hat and bandana that covered his head. Major Odell and Zane stopped talking to take a really good look at the boy.

"Stella, is that you?" Zane and the major exclaimed at the same time.

"Yes, it's me. My disguise must be better than I thought. Neither one of you could tell who I was or even suspected that I was a girl," Stella said between laughs.

"Stella, what in the world are you doing here?" Zane

wanted to know. Major Odell already knew.

"Well, it looks like the two of you are already acquainted, so I guess there is no need for introductions," Major Odell observed. "But I would like to know how you two know each other."

Zane explained, "Remember me telling you about the girl and her two brothers my friends and I found in some bushes back in Indiana a couple of summers ago before I left to join the army? Well, this is that girl."

"It's a small world, isn't it? You see, Stella and I met a few weeks ago while you were gone on a mission. Our Miss Stella is working for the Underground Railroad. What brings you to our neck of the woods again, young lady?" Odell wanted to know.

Stella had never expected to see any of her Indiana friends again, especially here in Mississippi. When she realized that the major was now talking to her, she had to shake her head to clear her thoughts so she could hear his question. "I'm sorry, sir; I was so surprised to see Zane I didn't hear your question."

"I asked what you are doing back here in my camp."

Stella explained to both her friends, "It's my job to meet runaway slaves near here and take them to the next station. In fact, that is why I was sneaking around your camp. I was making sure it wasn't a rebel camp. I was just leaving when your patrol found me. You see, I'm expecting a party tonight, and I had to be sure we would be safe."

"Aren't you awful young for such a job? Just how old are

you anyway?" the major asked. He was already worrying about this young girl.

"I'm seventeen, sir. At least I think so. But I've been doing this for months," Stella told him. "I'm very careful and so far very lucky."

"Well, I'm going to send Zane with you on this trip. You look like you could use a little help," Major Odell informed her.

"Thank you, sir. I think you might be right. I understand this party tonight is larger than usual."

The major looked at Zane, "Get this young lady something to eat. Then be on your way to meet her party. When your mission is completed I want both of you back here." He then looked at Stella. "Do you know how long you might be gone?"

"Ten to fifteen days. I never know for sure. It depends on the weather and whether we run into any rebels along the way."

"OK, I'll see you both in a number of days. Now off with you two, and be careful. And Zane, you take good care of this young lady."

"Yes, sir. I'll do my best," Zane replied as he saluted before going out.

After Zane and Stella had left his tent, the major smiled and thought to himself that with the help of courageous young people like those two, this war might end on a good note after all.

Zane took Stella straight to the cook's tent where he told

him that Major Odell had sent him to get some food for a new member of his team. It was after supper time and the cook had already cleaned up for the night, but he just nodded his head and rustled up some grub. He found some warm beans, a couple of biscuits and a sweet potato. Just as Zane began to leave, the cook stopped him to hand him a plate of pecan pie. When Zane came out of the cook's tent he motioned for Stella to follow him to his own tent. He knew they would be alone there and could talk. His tent-mate, J.B., was on night patrol until midnight.

Stella hadn't eaten a real meal in three days. She had been eating only hardtack and wild berries, so this modest meal was a small feast to her. Once she had finished her meal, Zane began asking questions. "What are you doing in the south again? Aren't you afraid you'll get caught?"

Stella looked at Zane and smiled. She thought it was so sweet of him to worry about her, so she told him what had been happening in her life. "After Lone Star left us in Illinois, my brothers and I lived with a very nice white family. They treated us like we were part of their family. They even taught us to read and write. Just think, I can read and write now. Isn't that great?

"About a year ago a black family showed up in our area. You'll never believe it, but they were from Beth's plantation in Georgia. They told me about how she had helped them escape to freedom. I knew right then that I needed to do my part, too. So I talked to my family and explained what I needed to do."

"And what was that?" asked Zane.

"I headed south and joined the Underground Railroad. My job is to help runaways on one leg of their journey north. I meet them about a mile from here and take them another twenty miles to the next station."

Zane was still full of questions. "How many have you helped so far? Are you sure you're safe? How often do you make these trips?"

"So far I think I've helped over fifty. And I'm as safe as I can be. As I told you and the major, it takes about ten to fifteen days round trip. We spend a lot of time finding hiding places and staying hidden for hours."

"How often do you make these trips?"

Stella thought a minute. "Two, sometimes three, times a month."

"What do you do in between trips out here all by yourself? And where do you live?"

Stella could tell Zane was really worried about her. "There isn't much time between trips, but I scout for new trails and hiding places whenever I can. I live in the woods. I've found a couple nice caves to keep me dry and warm. I've never showed either of them to anybody. They're my secret places. I can hide in either one and no one can find me. After all, a girl in my line of business can't be too careful, now can she?"

Zane looked at her and shook his head, "I guess that's why you're dressed like a boy? I sure didn't recognize you at first wearing those old ragged pants and jacket and work boots. It wasn't 'til you took off that old straw hat and uncovered your hair that I knew who you were. I guess you don't want anyone to know you're a girl, do you? Does the Underground Railroad even know you're a girl?"

"No way. I don't think they would let me stay out here by myself if they did," Stella told him.

"So, I guess that means you have a code name, right?"

"Yes, they call me Smoky. I think that's because I mostly work in the Smoky Mountains." Stella wanted to change the subject, so she said, "Guess who I saw on my way South."

"Well, if you came through Indiana I'll have to guess Rae and Dawn."

"You're right. I even spent a few days with them. I saw your Pa the day I left. He's doing just fine. But he misses you and worries about you, just like all parents do, you know? Night Hawk picked me up at the usual spot on the Wabash and brought me down the river as far south as Memphis, Tennessee.

"Oh, and you'll never guess what they've all done to help the Underground Railroad! In the woods between your house and Rae's they've built a cellar big enough to hide ten people. You would never find it if you didn't know where it was. On the inside it looks as nice as any log cabin. It was so nice and cozy I almost stayed there. Dawn told me they have already used it a lot. In fact, if they hadn't of had it she said they might have lost a young sister and brother. The trackers were right behind them.

"Now it's your turn to tell me what you've been doing, Mr. Zane."

"I'm working for the North as a secret service agent," Zane explained.

"What do you do? It sounds more dangerous than what I'm doing."

"Maybe about the same," Zane thought. Then he explained what he did to help with the war. "It's the same as being a spy. I go south often and mingle with different people to find out what they're planning, when and where, how big their army camps are and things like that. Then I bring that information back to Major Odell. Did you know that Beth is helping the Railroad, too?"

"Remember I told you about the family she helped, her father's stable man and his family?" Stella said. "Isn't it great how all of us are helping with this war?"

"I don't think any of us will have to help much longer. I heard Major Odell talking about President Lincoln making a new law to free all slaves. I can't imagine what that will be like, can you?" Zane asked.

"Only that it will be one of the greatest things to ever happen. Have you had a chance to see Beth?" Stella wanted to know.

"On one of my missions I was sent to Savannah and was a guest at her home. I even attended a garden party with her. Can you imagine me all dressed up in a suit and fancy shoes? We even danced. It was really something. You should have seen Beth. Was she ever beautiful? After this trip maybe we can find a way for you to see her. What do you think? Would you like that?"

"Like that? I would love to see her and thank her for what she's been doing. I know it's not been easy for her."

"Speaking of this trip, we need to leave. Let me change out of my uniform and we'll be on our way."

Fifteen minutes later they were making their way through the woods, neither one making a sound. When Stella motioned for Zane to stop he looked around for a log to sit on while they waited for the group to show up. Stella sat down beside him and they waited, watching and listing for any noise that might alert them of company.

CHAPTER ELEVEN

An Underground Mission

They were meeting the party in southern Mississippi and Zane was wondering where the next station was. In a quiet voice he asked Stella, "Where are we taking this party?"

"Halfway through Tennessee," Stella whispered. "We go as far as the Smoky Mountains where we'll meet another guide. From there they'll go across the mountains, meeting a third guide on the other side. It will take at least five, maybe six, guides to get them to a free state. Some will end up staying in Indiana or Illinois and some will not feel safe there so will go on even farther north. Some will even end up as far north as Canada."

"It sounds like a lot of organizing to me. Looks like you guides sometimes have to be ready at a minute's notice," Zane commented.

"You're right, Zane, but it's so exciting. And I love the end results."

"Don't we all," Zane agreed.

As he said this they heard a racket in the woods just a few yards away. They both ducked down behind the log they had been sitting on. Then Stella heard what sounded like a squirrel chattering. She knew this was the signal she had been waiting for. Her party had arrived. She echoed the signal back and then stood up so she could be seen. When the party came out of the woods she saw that there were fifteen of them.

Emerging from his hiding place Zane was shocked. "I thought you said there would be ten. How are we going to sneak fifteen fugitives through enemy lines?" he wanted to know.

"Guess they must have picked up a few extras on the way," Stella told him. "And to answer your question, very carefully. Wait here. I have to talk to their guide and reassure them that you're alright, being that you're white." Stella then walked off in the direction of her party. After a brief conversation she returned with the fugitives close behind her. "It's alright now, they trust you. They've been traveling for hours and will need to rest for awhile. I told them we would move out in half an hour. We'll need to be at our first hide out before dawn."

Although the party still looked tired after their half-hour break was over, they couldn't wait any longer to move on because there were only about five hours left before dawn. Stella led the way and Zane followed in the rear. Both vigilantly kept their eyes open for any kind of danger. They knew that there could be four-legged as well as two-legged predators in these woods and that they could encounter an enemy at any time of the day or night.

Fortunately that night was an easy journey. Just before

dawn Stella called a halt for the day. They had reached their first hiding place. She explained, "We need to walk downstream for about half a mile. We'll come out on the other side, walk around on some rocks and then get back in the water and walk upstream. This will hopefully throw the dogs off our scent." She then explained that this stream ran into a small river and that the loud noise they were hearing was coming from a waterfall that was around the bend. "We'll be hiding under that waterfall. Once we get to the edge of the stream I'll need all of you men to pick-up a woman or child and carry them until we get back in the water. That should help fool the tracker as to how many of us there are. Any questions?" Stella asked. Everyone shook their heads. Zane was thinking that Stella was one smart woman.

They spent the day under the falls. The adults took turns watching for trouble and sleeping. There was food stored in the cave and they had plenty of water. There were also blankets and a few extra clothes for anyone who needed them. Stella tried to keep plenty of supplies in her usual hiding places. She was glad she had managed extra this time since she had more guests than she had anticipated.

Just before dusk Stella made sure everyone had eaten and had an apple to take with them. She cautioned them not to throw the core on the ground or to leave it anywhere. If the trackers found one they would know that they were on the right trail. As soon as everyone was ready to leave, Zane headed for the front of the cave, but Stella stopped him and pointed to the back of the cave. "There's a back entrance at the other end of this cave. It will be safer and save us a lot of miles."

"Well I'll be. Who would have thought about another entrance?" Zane smiled.

This is how it went for the next seven days, Stella leading and Zane bringing up the rear. They traveled at night and slept during the day. At each stop they found much needed supplies. On the seventh night, just after midnight, they rendezvoused with the next guide. Thankfully this had been a very uneventful trip.

Everyone in the party was sad to see Stella and Zane leave them. They had learned to trust both with their lives. Their guides had made their trip a safe one. Stella reassured the runaways that the next guide would take just as good care of them.

Zane and Stella waited until everyone was out of sight. Then Stella turned to Zane and said, "One of my secret caves is real close to here. We'll go there to rest for the day and start back tonight."

"I thought you didn't let anybody know where your secret caves were. You make me feel special by sharing them with me."

"You're a special friend and I know I can trust you," Stella said as she started walking away.

They walked for about an hour, again doing whatever they could to throw the trackers and their dogs off their scent.

Once they even climbed a tree and traveled above the forest floor by climbing from limb to limb. When they reached their destination Stella stooped down and started crawling under some bushes. Zane followed her and just a few feet into the bushes they found a small cave. In fact, Zane wouldn't call it a real cave. It was more like a space the weather had carved out on the side of a hill. It was so small Stella could hardly stand up straight and Zane couldn't stand up at all.

Again Stella had plenty of supplies. After a breakfast of dried meat and fruit they both crawled into a corner, rolled themselves up in blankets and were soon sound asleep. When Zane awoke it was almost noon. He stretched and then looked around for Stella. She was nowhere in the cave. Zane jumped up from his pallet, hitting his head on the low ceiling. He had forgotten how small the cave was. Right away he began looking for Stella. A few minutes later he found her fishing in a small creek. She had already caught enough small catfish to feed both of them. In fact, she was preparing to go back to the cave when she turned around and saw Zane watching her.

"I must be slipping. I didn't hear you come up behind me," she confessed.

Zane laughed, "A trick I've learned in the past few months. I'm glad all the practice and time I've spent learning to walk like an Indian was worth it."

Stella agreed, "I believe you've got that trick down pretty good. Now let's go cook these fish Indian style with a small fire and no smoke."

For their noon meal they made fresh fish, canned beans and hoecakes. Zane started the fire and cleaned the fish while Stella went back into the cave to get the other supplies they would need: a small pan, forks, cups, a can of beans and the ingredients for the hoecakes. Stella cooked the fish the Indian way by weaving a small green stick in and out of each fish. She hung the fish over a tripod made of more green sticks which she then placed over some very low burning coals so that the fish would cook slowly and not burn. She used green sticks, green tree limbs with the bark removed, because they would not catch on fire. The sticks would also double as a way of rotating the fish. Stella had a small saucepan that she carried in her knapsack. She used it to cook a can of beans that she kept stored in her cave. She also mixed up some hoecakes and cooked them on hot rocks. Both she and Zane decided this was a meal fit for any queen or king.

While they were eating they caught up on some more news of the last several months. Stella told Zane more about her visit with Rae and Dawn. "I guess you know that Night Hawk considers Rae his woman. Rae has no idea how to handle all this. They look at each other all the time. They like each other a lot but have no idea what they're going to do. They really feel confused."

"I knew they were attracted to each other before I left, but I didn't know it was serious," Zane told her.

"How about you and Beth?" Stella asked. "The girls think you like each other a lot."

"They're right. In fact, I think we love each other. We're just waiting for this war to be over and see what happens."

"I hope all of you will solve your problems and find happiness," Stella told him.

"I hope you're right, Stella, and I hope it's soon, very,

very soon," was all Zane could say. They could not have known that it would be months and months before that would happen.

They spent the rest of the day talking, bathing in the stream and taking a nap. They knew they had a long night ahead of them because they planned to make much better time traveling back to camp by themselves. Just after dusk they left the cave to head back to Mississippi. The return journey was much quicker. It only took them three nights to get back to Major Odell.

When they arrived back at the major's tent they gave him a full report of everything that had happened. It was a rather boring account since nothing unusual had transpired. Then Major Odell asked Stella, "Do you know when you'll leave on your next mission?"

"I won't know until my contact gets in touch with me," Stella told the Major.

"Our orders are to stay camped here as an information unit, so if you need anything, anything at all, you just let us know and we'll help you," the Major told her as he accompanied them out of his tent. Stella thanked him and said she would keep in contact. She then turned to Zane to say good bye.

"Remember what the Major said. We'll help you anyway we can," Zane repeated. "Let's try to meet up in a few weeks. Maybe we can find a way for you to see Beth."

"That would be great. I'll look forward to that day," Stella replied

"Stella, please be careful. I wouldn't want anything to

happen to you. You know that we all think of you as one of our dear friends."

"I'm thinking the same about you, Mr. Zane." With that, Stella walked toward the woods and was soon out of sight. Zane turned and went back to his tent. Waiting there for him was his trusted partner, J.B. J.B. knew how to get in and out of places that Zane would never be able to manage on his own. Zane knew he could never do what he did without J.B.'s help.

CHAPTER TWELVE

Spying From a Hot Air Balloon

Late fall 1862

A few days later Major Odell sent for Zane and J.B. He had a very important mission for the two of them, one he was sure they were going to like. This assignment had come straight from President Lincoln. When their commander told them where the order had come from, the two spies knew it had to be important. The major explained that they were to meet a balloonist, a Mr. Bower, in New Madrid, Mississippi in three days. They could ride their horses on this mission and therefore wouldn't have any trouble making the trip in three days. They were to report to Sergeant Cowles, General Pope's aid. He would take them to Mr. Bower. The major cautioned them, "There will be little tree cover this time of the year, but they tell me Mr. Bower is quite good at maneuvering his hot air balloon, so you should be safe and not run into any complications. Besides, little tree cover should make your job easier. Your mission is to count Confederate patrols and camps as well as horses, cannons and anything else you see."

"Excuse me, sir," J.B. asked, "what exactly is a hot air balloon?"

"Well, J.B., they've been around for years, but using them is something very new to the war effort. I believe this just might be the first time they've been used in helping with the war. To the best of my knowledge, a hot air balloon is a very large balloon that is not enclosed at the bottom and is attached to a straw basket that is large enough to hold two to four people. The balloon is controlled by using a hot air pump to blow hot air into the bottom of it. Apparently the pump has to be pumped by hand. I understand that the more hot air that is pumped into the balloon, the higher it goes, and when you're ready to come down, you decrease the amount of hot air."

"You're sending us up in the sky in a straw basket with a big balloon to hold it up?" J.B. asked incredulously. Judging by the look on his face, J.B. was not thrilled with this new assignment.

"Oh, come on, J.B. It'll be fun. We'll be just like a big bird flying through the sky," Zane told J.B. while laughing the whole time.

"But what if some Rebel shoots that balloon?" J.B. wanted to know.

Zane was still laughing. "Then we'll really be a big bird, and we'll be flying on our own."

"That don't sound too funny to me," J.B. told him.

Major Odell was laughing as the boys left his tent. "It'll be OK, J.B. I promise," the major told him.

Zane and J.B went to get their saddle bags ready and to check their rifles and side arms. When they had finished packing they went to get their horses. Both rode black geldings. They had chosen black so they would be harder to see at night. They left as soon as they were ready and headed for New Madrid.

When they arrived at the designated meeting place they were greeted by Sergeant Cowles. Straight away he took them to a tent and introduced them to Mr. Bower. They were surprised when he also introduced them to Mr. Roberts. He explained that Mr. Roberts was a newspaper photographer. "Mr. Roberts is also going up in the balloon with you. He will be taking photographs to send back to the President as well as to his newspaper. In order for him to take clear photographs you will have to fly closer to the ground than usual. We believe his photographs will be the first ones of a war taken from the air to appear in a newspaper,"

"Wow! Guess I better start learning how to fly," J.B. said while flapping his arms.

Mr. Bower chuckled and told him, "Well, young man, you have until morning to practice."

Early the next morning the group met outside of camp where Mr. Bower had the balloon ready for flight. He explained how he could keep the balloon in the air with the help of hot air. He would need J.B. to help with the pumps while Zane recorded the information for the mission and Mr. Roberts took his photographs.

When they were airborne it really felt like they were flying. It was a free feeling, one Zane and J.B. didn't think they could ever explain to anyone. Zane looked at J.B., "Not so scary after all, is it?"

"No. In fact, this is great. Look, we're flying with the birds. They don't know what to make of us. I think they're more scared than I was before we got up here."

When they first went up they were flying over Union camps. It was forty-five minutes before they saw their first Confederate camp. Zane started taking notes right away. He counted troopers, wagons, artillery, horses and even mules and made note whether they were on the move and in what direction they were headed. All the while Mr. Roberts was taking photographs as quickly as he could. He knew these would be helpful to the Union Army and later he could sell them to newspapers up north. All of this information was vital to General Pope. His troops were trying to stop the South from using the Mississippi River as a means of shipping supplies.

When they started their mission the sun had been behind the clouds, making it harder for them to be seen. Then all of a sudden the sun peeked out from behind a large cloud, casting a shadow of the balloon over a Confederate camp below. It didn't take but a few seconds for the balloon to be spotted. The soldiers on the ground immediately picked-up their rifles and started shooting. Everyone in the balloon except Mr. Bower thought they were done for. He explained, "We're too high for the rifles to hit us."

But a large gust of unexpected wind blew them off track. The balloon took a sudden drop and a stray bullet went right through the bottom of the basket, barely missing J.B.

"That was a little too close," Mr. Bower told them. "I think we need to head back to camp. Maybe we can try again tomorrow."

"That's OK by me," J.B. told him. He was breathing so hard he could hardly speak. Zane and Mr. Roberts looked at each other and nodded their heads in agreement.

Early the next morning they tried again. This time when they got above the Confederate camps they were in for a big surprise. Some of the camps were already gone and the rest were on the move. They were all headed east.

"We have to get back to camp and fast. We need to pass this information on. I'm sure General Pope will want to send a dispatch to the other camps and a telegraph to the President."

They didn't linger but got back to camp in record time. Before they even landed Zane was yelling for a dispatch rider. When the rider showed up Zane threw him a saddle bag containing all his notes. He knew the general would receive this information right away. By the time they had landed Sergeant Cowles was there to meet them. He told them how grateful General Pope was for their information. He instructed Zane and J.B. to return to Major Odell's camp at will. Both were ready to head back to Vicksburg. They knew a big battle was in the making. It probably wouldn't take place for a few months, maybe not even until after the first of the year, but one thing was for sure. A battle was coming. Major Odell had told them before that Vicksburg needed to be taken because it was keeping Union troops from going up and down the Mississippi River to deliver supplies and stop Confederate troop movements.

Zane and J.B. had been in the town of Vicksburg just a few days before their latest mission disguised as a farmer and his slave. The town and military leaders were telling the citizens to begin preparing for an attack on their town in the near future. As far as the two spies could tell, very few people were paying any attention to this warning. They had seen evidence of parties and balls occurring almost every night.

All of the military personnel on both sides knew this battle would come, and soon. The Union leaders knew that the South was not going to give up control of this important port without a major fight.

CHAPTER THIRTEEN

A New Baby

Indiana, Fall 1862

As Rae walked out the back door of her family home she let out a big sigh and then smiled. Very early that morning it had been raining, but now the sun was shining bright and warming this early September morning. It was so good to see the sun after three days of rain. Rae was headed to the barn to do her morning chores. She had to feed and water the horses, pigs, chickens and cats as well as her favorite beagle Dottie and her five puppies. Rae patted the pocket of her apron to make sure she still had her latest letter from her cousin, Beth. Just touching the letter made her think of the summer Beth had spent with her and her family and of how she, Beth and their friends Dawn and Zane had had such a great summer of adventures. Rae planned to climb up to the loft to read her letter again just as soon as she got her chores done. She would have to hurry because she needed to help her mother, Anna, and the housekeeper, Bessie, can apples and bake pies for the church social that Sunday.

Just as she began to enter the barn, she heard a horse

coming up the lane. It was Zane's father, Grant. Rae and Dawn had missed Zane very much since he had joined the Union Secret Service. It had been over a year since they had seen him, and Rae's first thought was that Grant had heard from Zane and something awful had happened to him. As soon as Grant jumped off his horse Rae could see by his face that there really was something serious going on. "Oh, Grant! Please tell me nothing's happened to Zane!" Rae pleaded. She was extremely worried because Zane was one of her very best friends.

"No, no, it's not Zane," Grant told her

"Then what is wrong?" Rae asked.

"It's Night Hawk," Grant told Rae.

"Night Hawk?" Rae's heart gave a surprising jump at just the sound of his name. It was a feeling she didn't understand. "Grant, tell me he's OK also."

"He's fine, but we have a very big problem. He just showed up at my doorstep on his way north with a young Negro girl. She went into labor early this morning. It looks like she's going to have a baby sometime today. I need you and your mother to come help us. Night Hawk and I don't have any idea what to do to help her."

"I'll go get mother and tell her what's happening. Harness up Babe to the cart for us. Pa, Gerald and the boys are all in the field," Rae shouted over her shoulder as she ran toward the house.

"It'll be ready when you get back," Grant promised.

When Rae explained the problem to her mother and

Bessie, the two women looked at each other and went right to work getting supplies together for Anna and Rae to take with them. Rae got a large straw basket off the back porch and it was soon full of extra quilts, food and a few medical supplies. Then Rae and Anna rushed out the back door, grabbing their shawls and bonnets on the way. As promised, Grant had the cart ready for the two mile ride to his farm. Rae jumped up on the cart and then turned to help her mother. Anna was holding the basket so Rae grabbed the reins and flicked them so that Babe was off at a very fast pace.

During this short ride all Rae could think about was seeing Night Hawk again. It had been at least a month since she had seen him, and he hadn't seen her that time. She and Dawn had just happened to be at the river fishing one day when he went by in his canoe with what looked like three Negroes, two boys and an older woman. She hadn't tried to stop them because she knew he was trying to get them to their next stop on the Underground Railroad. That was what he was doing with this girl also. He had taken over the job of transporting runaways north via the Wabash River from his brother Lone Star two years ago. Lone Star had to stop helping the runaways when his father, the chief, had died and Lone Star had to take his place. Rae and Night Hawk had met on the same day that Beth and her parents had left for Georgia. Beth had never met Night Hawk, but Rae knew she would like him. Maybe someday the two would meet.

Rae didn't have long to think about all of this. It only took them a few minutes to get to Grant's farm. Night Hawk heard them arrive and came out of the barn to greet them and see if they needed any help. Rae had hardly stopped the cart when she and Anna jumped down and headed for the house. Grant was a little embarrassed, but he stopped them and told them the girl was in the barn.

"In the barn?" Anna asked in shock. "Why is she in the barn? Grant, I can't believe you put her in the barn!"

Grant and Night Hawk looked at each other and Night Hawk answered, "I feel she will be safer there if anyone comes looking for her. There are more places to hide her or we can get her out the back barn door faster."

"Well, I guess you're right about that," Anna told him. She looked toward the barn while shaking her head and saying to herself, "In the barn! Who would have thought of that but a man?"

When Night Hawk saw that Rae was with her mother a smile lit up his face. He was hoping they would have some time to talk and be alone later, but right now he knew that Abby and her baby were most important. Abby was scared and needed Anna's help.

"Well, let's go to the barn and see what we can do for this girl." Anna looked at Night Hawk and asked, "What is her name?"

"Her name is Abby and she's from Alabama. She ran away because her master is the baby's father. He told her he would sell the child as soon as it was old enough because he didn't want his wife to know the child was his. Abby loved her master and wants to keep her baby, so she ran off about a month ago. She had her brother and his wife with her when they left Alabama, but she got separated from them about a week ago. She has no idea where the rest of her family is or even if they're alive. She's scared to death."

Just as they were entering the barn Abby yelled for Night Hawk. She was afraid he had left her and she didn't know what to do. Night Hawk ran to her side with Rae, Anna and Grant right behind him. Anna took one look at the young girl and her heart went out to her. She bent down and laid her hand on Abby's forehead and then her stomach. She introduced herself and Rae to her and explained that they were there to help her. "Abby, you don't need to be scared anymore," Anna reassured the girl.

Night Hawk was standing behind Anna all this time. Abby looked up at him and saw him smile at her and nod his head. Immediately Abby relaxed knowing everything was going to be alright.

Anna asked, "Abby, is it time for your baby or are you early? How long have you been having pains? Is this your first baby?"

Abby told her, "It be my time, Miss Anna. My pains started just a while before the sun comes up this morning. This be my first baby, but I's helped with birthing before."

Anna was relieved to know that the baby was fully grown and that Abby knew what to expect. She said to everyone, "This is probably going to be a long day. Grant, you might as well go about your business as usual. Night Hawk will come get you if we need anything."

Grant nodded and left the barn. He was glad to get away from it all. It brought back sad memories of when his wife had had such a hard time during Zane's birth. He would worry until it was all over and Abby and her baby were both safe.

Night Hawk moved to a corner of the stall where Abby lay. He made a pallet of fresh straw and was soon asleep. When Rae saw this she walked over and covered him with a quilt. He opened his eyes for just a second and smiled at her. Then she returned to where Abby was resting and sat down on one side of her while Anna sat on the other. They each reached down and took one of Abby's hands, hoping to reassure the girl and give her some comfort.

After awhile Abby nodded off to sleep and Rae decided to go outside to get some fresh air and stretch her legs. She had just walked over to look at Grant's piglets when she heard a wagon coming up the lane. Night Hawk must have heard the wagon also because he came out of the barn and met Rae halfway across the barnyard. Rae was really surprised to see that it was her father, Andrew. With him was her best friend Dawn and Dawn's mother, Dolly. Rae and Night Hawk went to help Dolly and Dawn out of the wagon. Then Night Hawk greeted Andrew. The men shook hands and patted each other on the shoulder.

"What are you all doing here?" Rae asked.

"Well, I think in all your haste this morning you and your mother forgot that Dolly and Dawn were coming over to help with the canning," Andrew told her.

"Oh, my goodness!" Rae said. "We did forget." She looked at Dolly and told her how sorry she was that they had forgotten them and that she was sure her mother was sorry as well.

Dolly put her arm around Rae's shoulder and gave her a hug. "We understand .You two are not to worry yourselves. Dawn and I have come to see if we can help. Bessie has sent sausage sandwiches and spice cookies. She was afraid you might not have time to think about food."

Grant heard all of this as he came around the barn where he had been chopping wood. "I've got a pot of beans cooking for later, but they won't be done for awhile. Sausage sandwiches sound real good to me. How about the rest of you?" he asked. "I have a pot of coffee on the stove, if anyone wants a cup."

Everyone eagerly accepted the offer. While Dawn and Dolly set the food out on the tailgate of the wagon, Rae went back inside the barn to see if Abby was still sleeping. When she saw that she was indeed asleep, she motioned her mother over to one side and told her what was going on. She knew Anna needed a break and some fresh air.

"Mother, please go outside and eat. Ask Dawn to bring in two sandwiches. She and I will eat in here so if Abby wakes up she won't be afraid again." Anna nodded her head and went out to talk to Dawn. It was just a few minutes later when not only Dawn but Night Hawk, also, came into the barn with food for all of them. Rae didn't know how long Dawn and Dolly were going to stay, but she hoped they would be there until after the baby was born. She knew Abby would feel even better when she woke up and saw two women of color there to help her.

Rae was right. A few minutes later when Abby was awakened by another pain, her eyes lit up when she saw

Dawn sitting beside her. And later when Dolly and Anna came into the stall she reached both arms up to Dolly and began to cry. Dolly explained to Abby that she and Dawn lived a few miles down the road with their family.

"But I thought this be a free state," Abby protested.

"Yes, dear, this is a free state," Dolly assured her. "My family and I are all free. We have our own farm and live there in peace."

"Oh, that must be wonderful," Abby said longingly.

"Well, you're not to worry anymore. We're all here to help you and your baby. Remember, you're free now as well." Dolly had already told Anna that she and Dawn would stay as long as they were needed.

After lunch Andrew prepared to head home. Before he left he offered to ride over to tell Dolly's family where she and Dawn were and that it would probably be morning before they came home. For the rest of the day the girls and their mothers took turns sitting and talking with Abby and doing whatever they could to make her comfortable. Night Hawk helped Grant chop wood, make repairs to the split-rail fence in which he kept his hogs, and whatever else they could find to keep busy.

By dusk Abby's pains were coming closer and closer together. Everyone knew it wouldn't be long before a new baby was born. And they were right; about an hour after sunset Abby gave birth to a healthy baby boy. He was small but had a set of lungs on him that could be heard yards away. There was no mistake that his father was a white man. The baby had blue eyes and it looked like he would have light colored hair. Dolly wrapped him in a small quilt and put him in his mother's arms. Abby hugged her baby to her heart and kissed the top of his head.

Rae went out to tell Grant and Night Hawk that a baby boy had been born and that they could come see him now. She knew they were anxious to see this new miracle. When they entered the stall Night Hawk knelt down beside Abby and asked her, "What are you going to name this fine young man?"

Abby looked at him and then at the others, but before she could say anything tears started running down her cheeks.

"What wrong?" Rae asked her.

"I want to name him Dew. That was my baby brother's name. He was killed when he was two, and I want to name my baby after him. That's be alright, ain't it, to name him Dew?" Abby asked and looked around at everyone. "We be free now and I don't have to ask. I can name him anything I wants?"

"Yes," Anna told her. "You and your son are free now and can do whatever you want. No one is going to tell you what you can or cannot do ever again."

Abby smiled and, still holding Dew in her arms, slipped off to sleep.

CHAPTER FOURTEEN

A New Home for Abby and Dew

While Abby was asleep, everyone except Dolly went to the house to eat the meal Grant had cooked for them. Besides the beans with ham, he had cooked a large skillet of fried potatoes, baked some cornbread and made a fresh pot of coffee. Bessie had sent a couple of the apple pies she had made over with Rae's brother Alan.

Rae was finished first, so she told everyone she would go sit with Abby and send Dolly in to eat. When she got up to leave the house Night Hawk was right behind her. Rae looked at him and smiled. She was hoping they would get a chance to talk, just the two of them. Night Hawk was hoping the same thing. When they got to the barn they sent Dolly to the house and checked to make sure Abby and Dew were still asleep. Finding Abby still resting peacefully, Night Hawk took Rae's hand and led her off to a far corner of the barn where Grant stored bales of fresh hay. The hay smelled like sunshine and was very refreshing. Rae sat down on one of the bales and Night Hawk sat across from her.

"This has been quite a day," Rae said. "I'm so glad Abby and Dew are OK."

"Yes," said Night Hawk. "Everyone has been so good to Abby. I thought all of you were wonderful with her. She was incredibly lucky to have all of your help. But the best part of this day is being with you."

With a puzzled look on her face Rae told Night Hawk, "I really don't understand any of this, but I feel the same way."

Night Hawk smiled at Rae. He, having seen eighteen summers and Rae only fourteen, knew what it was they were feeling. But how to explain this to Rae without upsetting her was the problem. Night Hawk moved to sit closer to her. He reached over and took both her hands in his, then leaned forward and kissed her on the forehead. Rae was so surprised she tried to pull her hands free, but Night Hawk wouldn't let go. He started to speak in a low, soft voice. "Rae, do you remember when we first met I told you that my vision had spoken to me about you and how we were meant to be together?"

"Yes, we've talked about this before, but I still have no idea what your vision has to do with me."

"I'll try to explain," Night Hawk told her. "A vision is like a dream, except our visions come true. In my tribe, when a young man reaches his sixteenth summer he goes off in the wilderness by himself for a few days to seek his future. While there he hopes to have a vision to help answer some questions about the tribe and his own future. Just before my brother brought me to meet you I had gone on my vision quest. My vision told me I would soon meet a girl with red hair and that she was to be my soul mate. That is why I was so shocked to see you that first day. In my heart I know that somehow you and I will one day be as one. Do you understand what I'm telling you, Little One?"

All this time Rae had been looking down at their interlocked hands. When Night Hawk finished speaking she sat silently for a few minutes trying to absorb everything he had just told her. Then she looked up and smiled at him. "Yes, I do believe I understand all you have said. I have no idea how this will change our lives, but for some reason I feel very close to you."

Night Hawk reached over and lifted her beautiful red hair off her shoulders and put his arm around her. He then moved close enough to put her head on his shoulder. They sat like this for some time. When finally Night Hawk broke the silence, he told Rae, "We'll work out our issues a little at a time. In the end, we will be together."

Suddenly the stillness was broken by the sharp wailing of a baby. Startled, Rae exclaimed, "Oh, we forgot about Dew and Abby!" She jumped up and went quickly to their stall. "Abby, are you OK?"

"Yes," Abby replied as she rocked Dew to soothe him. "I am so happy to find Dew beside me and to know he hadn't been a dream."

"Are you hungry?" Night Hawk asked.

"Yes, I'm very hungry," Abby told them.

"I'll stay with her," Rae said to Night Hawk, "if you'll go get her something to eat."

Anna and Dolly were cleaning up the supper dishes so

they sent Dawn back with Night Hawk to take Abby's food to the barn. Rae had just finished changing Dew's diaper when her friends returned. While Abby ate, the rest of them sat around on bales of straw and talked about what a miracle it was to see a baby born. Rae and Dawn had seen plenty of animals born before, but this had been their first time to see a woman give birth. While they talked they took turns holding Dew.

Rae looked at Abby and said to her, "You named Dew after your brother. We were wondering what had happened to him."

Abby closed her eyes and after a few minutes she cleared her throat and began telling them the story of how her brother had been killed. "It was three summers ago. Dew was two years old; he had just had his birthday. It was only a few months after he had started running without falling down all the time. One day he was playing on our front porch with a kitten. When the kitten ran into the path of a team of horses pulling a wagon full of logs, Dew ran after it. The boy that was driving the wagon saw Dew but just couldn't stop in time. My baby brother never knew what happened. My Ma never was quite the same in her head after that. She died just a few days before I ran away."

With tears running down her face Dawn told Abby, "I know your Ma would be so glad you named your baby after your brother." The adults had entered the barn just as Abby had started her story. They were all as sad as Rae and Dawn by the time Abby was finished.

"Now we want to help keep you and Dew safe. If it's

alright with you, in a few days we would like to move you to our home which is about four miles from here. Rae and Anna are going to take turns staying with you until then. You'll need to rest here for a few days before we can take you home," Dolly explained to Abby. "You can stay with us until you and Dew are strong enough and you decide where you want to go from here. Does that sound alright to you, dear?"

Abby looked around at everyone and really started to cry. In fact, she was sobbing. "I can't believe how much all of you care. Are you sure you wouldn't be in any danger yourselves?"

"We'll be fine," Dolly told her. "Remember, we're in a free state and my family has always been free. So, will you come and stay with us?"

"It sounds wonderful," Abby told her. "But I don't want to be a burden."

"A burden? Oh, my goodness!" Dolly exclaimed. "My mother-in-law will be beside herself with joy to have a new baby to fuss over."

"Well, now that that is all settled I think we all need some rest," Anna told everyone. Just thinking about sleep seemed to cause everyone to start yawning, so they all agreed and began making beds by throwing quilts over piles of clean straw. Anna and Dolly made their beds in the stall with Abby, but Rae and Dawn decided to sleep in the loft where they wouldn't disturb everyone else. They wanted to stay up and talk about everything that had happened that day. Rae especially wanted to tell Dawn about her conversation with

Night Hawk.

As the women got settled for the night, Grant bid them good night and headed for his house, inviting Night Hawk to sleep in Zane's bed.

"Thank you," Night Hawk told him, "but it's a beautiful, warm night so I'll sleep outside." He looked at Rae when he said this. "I'll spread my blankets under that big oak tree on the other side of the barn if anyone needs me."

When the girls reached the loft the first thing they did was open the loft door so they could see the beautiful night sky. Then they raked fresh straw into two piles and covered them with old quilts. Both girls curled up in a cover and then turned over onto their stomachs so they could look out the loft door.

After they were settled Dawn looked at Rae, "Now tell me what's on your mind, girl"

Rae told her all that Night Hawk had said. "I'm not sure about my feelings or what's happening to me. But I'm always the happiest when Night Hawk is close to me. What do you think it all means, Dawn?"

Dawn just leaned over and patted Rae on the shoulder. "I believe it's called young love, my dear. Now let's get some sleep and talk more tomorrow."

About an hour later everyone in the barn was asleep except Rae, or at least that's what she thought. She decided to take a walk to see if Night Hawk was asleep. As she climbed down the loft ladder Dawn was smiling to herself; she knew where Rae was going.

CHAPTER FIFTEEN

Time with Night Hawk

Rae was walking as quietly as she could. She didn't want to wake Night Hawk if he was asleep. But while she was tiptoeing up to the oak tree she heard Night Hawk whisper her name. She should have known she couldn't sneak up on an Indian. Night Hawk had built a small campfire and was laying there on his blankets looking at the heavens. The night was clear and the sky was full of stars. As Rae approached he sat up and motioned for her to sit beside him.

"The air is so refreshing and the night is beautiful. And look at the moon. It's so full and such a bright yellow. The perfect ending to an exciting day," Rae said while taking deep breaths of the night air. Then she turned to her companion.

"What will you do now, Night Hawk? You know that Abby should rest for several weeks before she and Dew continue their journey."

"I've been thinking about that. I plan to leave in the morning and go south again. I need to check on my mother and the rest of my family. I haven't been home in months. In three or four weeks I'll come back to take Abby farther north. That way

I can also see you again, and that is most important to me."
For a long time Rae and Night Hawk sat side by side, just
watching the fire and the stars, neither saying a word. They
could hear crickets chirping and a hoot owl in a nearby tree.
These soothing sounds were making it very difficult for Rae
to keep her eyes open. She finally had to give up. "I need to
go to bed. It's been a very long day. But first I want to tell you
to please be careful and come back as soon as you can."

"I will be very careful because I believe I have something
to be careful for. All the time I'm gone I'll be counting the
days until I see you again." Night Hawk stood up and reached
out to take both of Rae's hands and help her up. Still holding
her hands he walked with her to the barn door. After saying
goodnight, Rae slipped through the barn and back up to the
loft.

Despite her sleepiness, both Rae and Night Hawk lay
awake for a long time. Rae watched the same stars through
the loft door that Night Hawk was watching through the
tree limbs. Both were wondering what the future held for
them and if it truly would bring them together. Rae was also
thinking about the day she and Night Hawk had first met.
At that time Rae had thought he was a little strange. He had
hardly looked at Dawn and Zane but just kept staring at her.
He had walked up to her and touched her red hair as though it
was on fire. Then he had told her that she was his and to wait
and watch for him. He also had taken a beautiful turquoise
beaded necklace from around his neck and placed it around
hers before turning around and leaving with Lone Star in
their canoe. Rae didn't understand why, but she had never

taken the necklace off. To this day she was still trying to figure all this out.

The next morning everyone was up early knowing they all had a lot to do. First they told Night Hawk goodbye. He had explained his plan of returning in a few weeks to the rest of the group that morning. Rae and Dawn walked with him to the river and watched as he paddled his canoe south on his journey home. When they got back to the barn, Grant had hitched Babe to the cart. Anna and Rae were going home to get clean clothes and to tell their family about Dew and the plan for the next few days. When they returned to Grant's, Andrew was with them. He was going to drive Dolly and Dawn home. Before they left, Andrew told Anna he would be back in two days to pick up her and Rae and to take Abby and Dew to their temporary home.

Soon after the others had left Anna took Dew to the house to give him a bath. Rae stayed with Abby to help her clean up and refresh her bedding. While at home, Anna had gone through her things and found a couple of night gowns and an extra dress that she thought would fit Abby. Fortunately, Bessie was also expecting a baby in a few months so she, Anna and Rae had been sewing baby clothes for weeks. Bessie knew that Abby wouldn't have any, so she sent over an assortment of clothes for Dew along with a beautiful quilt with brightly colored appliquéd animals all over the top. Bessie had worked late into the night just to finish this very quilt. She wanted Dew to have something very special of his own. Bessie knew she had other quilts for her baby and that there would be time to make even more.

The evening before Abby was to go home to Dolly, Grant found her sitting on his front porch in an old rocker, the very one Zane's mother had used to rock him in years ago. She was nursing Dew and humming a song to him. Grant took a seat on the top step and lit his favorite pipe. He sat there for a few minutes listening to the crickets chirping in the woods. After awhile he turned around to look at Abby and said, "Abby, you know that you are now in free territory. There is no need to be worried about the trackers because they don't come this far north anymore, not since the war started. I've grown very fond of you and Dew in the last few days and I've come to think of you as the daughter I never had. So, I was wondering if you and Dew would like to live here instead of going farther north? I thought you might help me around the farm and the house. I can't pay you much, but if a roof over your heads and food is enough for now, then maybe we can help each other. I'll get a few of my neighbors to come and help me build you and Dew your own little house. I thought maybe over on the other side of the barn in that grove of pecan trees so you would have your privacy. We should be able to finish it in two or three weeks. In the mean time you can go ahead and stay with Dolly and her family.

"I've thought a lot about this. I know there might be some gossip but it won't bother me if it won't bother you. Of course, I'll understand if you had rather go on north. So don't you think you'll hurt my feelings if you decide not to stay. But maybe it's time to stop running, at least for awhile."

Abby didn't know what to think of Grant's generous offer. She didn't care at all about the gossip. She just knew that she and Dew were home where they belonged. She couldn't think of a better place to begin their life of freedom than right here where Dew had been born.

"Oh, Mr. Grant, are you sure? I'm a good cook and housekeeper. I never learned much about working outside but I'm a fast learner. Yes, we'll stay! Thank you very much, Mr. Grant, thank you," Abby told him with tears of happiness running down her cheeks. She could hardly wait to tell her new friends that she and Dew would be staying here in Indiana in a home of their very own. She was so excited she wanted to know if the house would have windows and a wooden door, not just a blanket to cover the doorway, and maybe even a fireplace and a front porch.

"Yes," Grant told her. "All of this and more."

So it was decided that all the men would begin building a new one-room home for Abby and Dew.

CHAPTER SIXTEEN

Dawn's Decision

Fall of 1862

It was a few weeks later when Dawn went over to Rae's and asked her to go for a walk in the woods. Although it was late fall, there were still a few trees with colorful leaves, especially bright yellow and rusty brown ones. The girls headed for one of their favorite places to talk, the bank of the Wabash River, which was just over a mile from Rae's house. On the way they talked about the latest letter Rae had received from Beth. They both hoped Beth was safe because she was still helping slaves get north. They also talked about Zane and his last letter and about Stella's visit when she had stopped by on her way south. They were both worried about her because they knew she was right in the middle of everything and could be captured and punished at any time.

They soon reached the riverbank and came across a large log which they sat on in silence for a few minutes as they watched a raft float by. "OK, Dawn," Rae finally said, "I know something's troubling you. You didn't ask me to come for a walk just to chat. Out with it, friend. Tell me what's troubling you."

"I don't know how to tell you this except just to say it," Dawn sighed. "When Night Hawk returns, I'm going south with him."

"What would you want to go and do a thing like that for? You know there's a war going on in the south," Rae said as she choked back the tears that were beginning to form. "Do you have any idea how dangerous that could be, especially for you?"

"Believe me, I've thought of all of that. I just can't sit here at home and do nothing any longer. I think I can do some good if I go south, at least for a few months. I'm sure the Underground Railroad won't be needed much longer and I want to help while it still exists."

"I can't believe your family agreed to this," Rae told Dawn.

"I've not told them yet. I wanted to tell you first. I so hoped for your support," Dawn told Rae. "And please don't tell your family. I want to tell them myself."

"Oh my, are they all in for a great big shock!" Rae exclaimed. She reached over and gave Dawn a big sisterly hug. "I know we're not going to be able to talk you out of this. You've already made up your mind to go. All I can say at this point is please be careful. I'll pray for you just like I've been praying for the others. When are you going to tell your family?"

"Tonight, I need to get it over with so they'll have time

to prepare for my leaving. Oh, Rae, I just have to go and do something, and this is the only thing I can think of right now. Who knows, I might run into Stella or Beth or even Zane, maybe even that friend of his, J.B., that he keeps writing about. He sounds like quite a man and a good friend to Zane."

Rae agreed and then the two friends sat in silence again for a long time, staring at the river as each reflected on her own private hopes and concerns.

That night while her whole family was still sitting at the supper table, Dawn announced that she had something important to tell them.

"Well, child, what's so important that would make you look so serious?" Grampa Teddy wanted to know.

"Honey, you do look sad. Come sit here next to Granny Bella and tell us what's troubling you."

Dawn did as Granny Bella said and moved to sit next to her. She took a deep breath and looked at all her family gathered around her; her parents, two sisters, Bree and Doris, and lastly her grandparents. "I've decided to go south and help with the Underground Railroad. I plan to go with Night Hawk when he returns in a few days," Dawn said all in one breath. She was afraid that if she breathed she might lose her nerve.

Standing up so suddenly that he knocked over his chair, Thomas asked, "You've decided to do what?"

"Now, Thomas, please calm down," Dolly told him.

"Calm down? Did you hear what your fifteen-year-old

daughter just told us she's planning on doing? I can't believe she just decided all this on her own, never bothering to talk to us about her plans."

"Pa, please understand. This is something I need to do. And before you ask, yes, I've thought of the dangers, of where I will stay and how I will get food. I hope you'll trust me. You and Grampa have taught me many things: how to track, to hunt, how to shoot a gun and how to survive in the woods. Now I want to use these teachings for the good of others." Dolly and Granny Bella were both crying. They were worried about Dawn as well as very proud of her.

"Dawn, are you sure you've thought this through?" Grampa asked.

"Yes, sir, I have, and I plan to leave as soon as Night Hawk returns," Dawn told him.

"I'm really proud of you, girl. And I know you'll use all those teaching to the best of your ability. We'll just have to count the days until you're safe at home," Grampa told her, giving her a big bear hug.

"Sounds like you've got your mind set on this. I guess we'll just have to pray for one more of our young ones," Dolly told her daughter while using her apron to wipe tears from her eyes.

Thomas was still in shock. He didn't know what to do or say. "Son, give your daughter your blessing," Grampa Teddy told him.

Thomas came around the table and put his arms around Dawn. "All I can say is God bless you and keep you safe, my child."

Dawn knew that Night Hawk could show up at any time during the next week, so the next morning she rode over to the Edgewood farm to tell Andrew and Anna about her plans. She hoped that after she talked to them, Rae would be able to go with her to talk to Grant. She had a message for him to give to Night Hawk. As she thought of this, Dawn stared laughing to herself. "I guess I could just give my message to Rae. If anyone is going to see Night Hawk, it'll be her. He never goes by anymore without stopping to see her."

Rae was coming out of the tool shed as Dawn rode up the lane. She had just finished hoeing weeds in the garden. "Dawn, did you tell your family your plans, yet?"

Dawn nodded her head. "Pa had a hard time accepting all of it, but he came around in the end."

When Dawn told Andrew and Anna her news they, like her family, were worried for her but also knew that she was following her heart, something that everyone has to do at one time or another. Anna looked at Dawn with tears in her eyes. "You know you're like a daughter to us. I am so proud of you. Remember that you'll be in my prayers just like Beth, Zane, Stella and even Night Hawk. All of you are walking such a dangerous path."

"I know, Miss Anna, but I know that it will be an adventure I'll never forget. Would it be alright if Rae and I went for a ride?"

"You two go right ahead. I'm going over to talk to Dolly and Granny Bella."

Andrew looked at Anna, "I think I'll tag along to see Thomas as well."

When Anna, Andrew and the boys reached the Jefferson farm, Dolly and Thomas were surprised but very happy to see them. They both needed someone to talk to about Dawn's future.

"Dawn stopped by and told us her news," Anna told them.

"We had to come over and make sure you all were alright. I can't imagine how you feel, but I know how I would feel if it was Rae."

"At first we were in shock," Thomas answered. "But now we're just proud of her. We were thinking of a get-together before she left. What do you think?"

"We were thinking the same thing," Anna told him.

"Oh, that sounds like a great idea. Think we can make it a surprise party?" Granny Bell asked.

Putting her arm around Anna's shoulder, Dolly began walking toward the house. "I say we all go into the kitchen and have some hot coffee and fresh ginger bread."

As the adults headed for the kitchen, Doris, Bree, Alan and Lee asked if they could play hide-and-seek in the woods. "Sure, go ahead, but be careful. Someone will come and get you when we're ready to go home," Andrew told them. But all four kids were gone before Andrew had finished answering them. "Guess they knew the answer to that question before they even asked," he said and everyone laughed.

When the adults reached the kitchen they each pulled a

chair up to the big round oak table. Like all of the furniture in the house, Thomas had made this special just for Dolly. The table was now covered with a blue and white checkered tablecloth, a glass spoon jar and a matching sugar bowl and creamer. Granny went to her favorite spot in the big kitchen, the china cabinet that housed the beautiful white china that had been a Christmas gift to her from her family a few years ago. She got out dessert plates and put slices of warm ginger bread on each. Dolly poured coffee into matching cups and placed them on saucers in front of her guests and family. Everyone enjoyed the refreshments as they discussed the upcoming party. They decided to have the party at the Edgewood farm so that Dawn wouldn't know what they were up to. It would be held the day after tomorrow. Nobody really knew how many days they had until Night Hawk returned and they didn't want to run out of time.

In the meantime, Rae and Dawn had headed over to give Grant the message for Night Hawk. When they arrived at his farm he was surprised to see them. As they rode up to the front porch Abby stepped out of Grant's house. The girls could tell she had been baking because she had flour on her hands and nose. "What's you girls up to?" she asked.

While the girls alighted from their horses Grant walked over from the barn to meet them. "What a surprise. We don't see you two enough anymore. To what do we owe the honor of this visit?"

"I've got some good news," Dawn told him. "I've decided to go south and help with the Underground Railroad. I know it's not going to be easy, but I hope to find Stella. Night Hawk might be able to help me or at least put me in contact with someone who can. I plan on going with him when he comes back in a few days. Will you give him a message for me?"

"I'll tell him just as soon as I see him," Grant assured Dawn. "And you're right. He should be by any day now."

The girls talked with Grant and Abby and played with Dew for awhile before they left. They both loved to hold and play with the baby. They each wondered if they would ever have a little one of their own.

When the girls got back to Rae's farm, Bessie told them that the family hadn't gotten back from Dawn's house yet, so Rae decided to ride over with Dawn and return with her family. She wanted to spend as much time with her best friend as she could. By the time the friends arrived, Rae's family was preparing to head home. Dawn had hardly dismounted when Bree ran up to her saying, "We're gone a have a party for you."

"Well, so much for surprises," Thomas chuckled.

"A party for me?" Dawn asked, not knowing what to say or think.

"That's right," Dolly told her. "Day after tomorrow. We hope Night Hawk will be here so he can join in the fun."

"Oh, you all are so good to me!" Dawn exclaimed.

"Sounds to me like we need to go fishing early in the morning. What do you think?" Rae asked Dawn.

"We can't have a party without some good old catfish, now can we? I'll be there as early as I can, just as soon as I get my chores done."

On the way home Andrew and Anna could tell that Rae was upset. She was leading Babe and walking between her parents. Andrew put his arm around Rae's shoulder and asked her, "What's bothering you, girl?"

"I feel bad that all my friends are helping with the war and I'm not," she told her parents. "I just don't know what to do."

In his heart, Andrew knew how Rae was feeling. He, too, felt the need to help with the war. But the Union Army had told him that supplying food for the soldiers was just as important as fighting, so he, Thomas and Grant were all raising beef and crops. The last thing Andrew wanted was for Rae to get mixed up in a crazy war. "Rae, I think what you're doing right here with the Underground Railroad is quite a large job in itself. Just think how many slaves you and Night Hawk have helped? And you're a very big help to me on the farm. I feel certain that you couldn't be of any more help anywhere else. Don't you agree, Anna?"

All this time Anna had been hoping that Andrew could convince Rae to stay. "Yes, Andrew, I do," she replied. "Please, don't ever think of going off to that war, Rae. It would just plum break our hearts."

"I guess you're both right. I'll stay, but I surely will miss all my best friends."

Early the next morning, Rae hurried to finish her chores before Dawn arrived. She no longer had to care for the small animals; Lee and Alan did that. Rae was now responsible for looking after the horses, milking the cows, and helping in the fields and the garden. She saw Dawn coming down the path just as she was leaving the barn after finishing her last task. Dawn had her fishing pole, two cans of worms and a basket full of food. "All you need is yourself and your pole. I've got everything else," she told Rae. So Rae went into the house to tell her mother where on the river they were going. Bessie had packed a lunch for the girls and although she knew that Dawn had brought plenty, Rae thanked Bessie and took the basket anyway. She didn't want to hurt Bessie's feelings and a second lunch would give them more variety.

The girls had decided to walk to the river instead of ride. It would take them longer to walk the couple of miles to their favorite place to fish, but they were not as interested in fishing as in spending the day with just the two of them. There were a lot of things they wanted to share with one another. It was a cool morning, and both girls knew that in a few days it would be freezing, maybe even snowing. As they walked over the light covering of frost that still lay on the ground, they thought of how they both loved to play in the snow but also that Dawn wouldn't be there this year to go sledding and make snow angels and enjoy snow ice cream.

After they reached their destination and got their fishing lines in the water, the girls found a log that had washed up on the bank the last time the river had flooded. They moved it over to a sunny spot near their lines which, lucky for them, was also covered in soft grass. Now they could use the log to lean back on as they sat in the warm sun on an old quilt they had brought to cover the cold wet grass.

Rae was the first to talk. "I feel bad about all of you going south, first Zane, then Stella and now you. I'm really confused. I feel like I should be going to help, too"

"You're going to stay right here and continue to help Night Hawk and our families and teach at the school," Dawn replied firmly.

"That's what mother and father said," Rae told her.

"Well, we can't all be wrong, now can we?" Dawn asked.

Rae shrugged and they both fell silent. Dawn laid her head back on the log and closed her eyes. She lay like that for so long that Rae thought she had fallen asleep. Then all at once Dawn started talking, "I know I can count on you to keep an eye on my family. They'll need to know that at least one of us is safe. And you'll know how to get in contact with me through Night Hawk if my family needs me. Night Hawk told me that his contacts have said that Stella is doing a fantastic job, but I just know she could use a couple of extra hands."

"I'm going to write letters to Stella, Zane and Beth," Rae said. "I'll mail Beth's, but will you deliver the other two if you get the chance?"

"I'll will," Dawn promised. Then after a pause she asked, "So, what about you and Night Hawk?"

Rae sighed. "We've decided to wait and see what happens. As they say, we'll just let nature take its course. I'm crazy about him, but I can't see how our lives together can ever be anything but one problem after another." She was doing her best not to cry.

They talked about other things after that, pausing only

periodically to check their lines. Rae told Dawn how excited she was to be able to teach the younger children this fall. They chatted about Grant, Abby and Dew. They even talked about the adventures they had had the summer of Beth's visit. The time flew by and before they knew it, a couple of hours had passed and their stomachs were beginning to growl.

"Um, I'm getting hungry," Rae said rubbing her tummy.

"Me too," Dawn agreed. "Let's see what Granny and Bessie packed for us."

Granny had packed many of Dawn's favorites: ham and biscuit sandwiches, sweet and dill pickles, hard boiled eggs and slices of cheese. For dessert she had packed slices of blackberry pie. Bessie had also packed some of Dawn's favorites: leftover fried chicken, cold sweet potatoes, corn salad and chocolate cake.

"Oh, do you think we've died and gone to heaven?" Rae asked when she saw all of this. " Both of these ladies deserve big hugs when we get home."The girls ate so much that when they were finished and the baskets were almost empty, they both laid their heads back on the log and sighed.

"What did you think of Beth's last letter?" Rae asked after a few minutes.

"Sounds like she's not going to that girls' school after all, doesn't it?" Dawn replied.

"I didn't think she was all that excited about going anyway. And with everything going on with the war, I'm sure that sending her to school is the last thing Aunt Denise and Uncle Eugene are worried about."

"Reading between the lines, it sounds like she has her hands full trying to stay out of trouble. Wonder when you'll get some more red ribbons from her. It's been awhile since those three young boys delivered the last ones. What was that, about two months ago?" Dawn asked.

"Knowing Beth, it won't be long before I get some more," Rae answered.

"Guess you haven't heard from Zane lately, huh?" Dawn wanted to know.

"It's been months since we've heard from him. Even Grant hasn't heard from him. He's starting to get worried. I'm so glad he has Abby helping him on his farm. It's nice for him to have someone to talk to. Hopefully that keeps him from worrying as much."

"Rae, would you mind if I took a walk up the river by myself?" Dawn asked quietly.

"Of course not. I'll be right here when you get back. Take as long as you like," Rae smiled at her best friend. She knew Dawn needed the time to say goodbye to the old times.

Dawn walked about a quarter of a mile up the riverbank to a path that led down to the river and a small sandy beach. The friends had all gone swimming here many times in the past. She walked to the water's edge. A short distance from the shore, a large bolder stuck partially out of the water, making a pleasant place for her to sit and think. Even though she knew the water would be cold, she took off her shoes and stockings and, holding up her dress, waded out to the boulder. Once seated there, she took a good look around. At the edge of the bank was a giant old birch tree. Dawn remembered how beautiful it had been only weeks ago, before it had lost all its leaves. Sitting there listening to the calming sound of the water as it lapped up against the boulder and the river bank, she took deep breaths of fresh air and looked up at a beautiful blue sky full of fluffy white clouds. She closed her eyes and said a silent prayer.

"God, I've prayed for days about my decision to go south. I think I've made the right choice. Now I pray you will be with my family while I'm away and that you will continue to guide me and keep me safe until I can return home. Amen."

Dawn sat there for a little while longer, kicking her feet in the cool water. When she looked up, she saw a canoe headed toward the bank where she had left Rae. "Could it be Night Hawk?" she wondered. She was so hoping that it was. She was ready to start her new journey. Eger to find out, she hastily put on her stocking and shoes and headed back to where they had been fishing. When Dawn came around the river bend she found Rae and Night Hawk holding hands and smiling at each other.

CHAPTER SEVENTEEN

Night Hawk Pays a Visit

"Night Hawk, I'm so glad to see you," Dawn told him. "I've decided to go South with you when you leave, if that's still OK."

"Rae was just telling me your news. I would like very much to take you south and help you any way I can."

"Uh, would it be alright if we wait two days?" Dawn asked. "My family is planning a party for tomorrow and they were so hoping that you would be here for it."

"Yes, of course. I need a rest and I wouldn't mind a few days to visit with Rae," Night Hawk told her. He was still holding Rae's hands.

Night Hawk would be staying with Grant, so the girls rode with him a little further down river where he could hide his canoe in some tall bushes. Then the three of them walked to Grant's together. The girls needed to go there anyway to invite Grant and Abby to the party.

Before the girls left for home, Rae invited Night Hawk to come over after supper that night. She told him, "We can sit on the front porch and talk some more about the future."

Night Hawk smiled, "I will see you then, Little One."

Dusk had just begun to fall when there was a knock on the back door of the Edgewood house. Lee went to answer it, and when he saw who was at the door he gave a shout. He was so glad to see Night Hawk. In fact, the whole family was crazy about him. Lee grabbed his hands and pulled him into the kitchen. "Look what I found on our back porch!" Lee exclaimed to the others.

Rae and Alan were just finishing up the supper dishes. Rae had been washing, Alan drying, and Lee putting things away. Anna and Andrew were sitting in the living room when they had heard Lee and knew that it had to be Night Hawk. Rae had told them he was coming over for a visit. They were both relaxing in rocking chairs facing the fireplace where a small fire was burning. It was just big enough to take the evening chill off.

Andrew had been reading the latest newspaper he had picked up in Mount Vernon a few days ago. He was catching up on the war news of the last several months. There was a detailed article from March about the battle between two ironclad ships, the Confederate Merrimac and the Union Monitor. They were some of the first of a new type of ship that was covered in iron and almost completely submerged in the water. The paper stated that the battle had taken place in a large and sheltered harbor near Norfolk, Virginia and had lasted nearly five hours. Huge crowds of spectators had watched the battle from the shore. The article reported that neither ship had sunk the other, but both had retreated with sustained damage.

There was also an article about the Union forces' efforts to stop the South from smuggling supplies by way of the Mississippi River. Following that was a short article describing how Horace Greeley, editor of the New York Tribune, was pushing for a bill to legally free all slaves. President Lincoln's reply was, "My paramount object in the struggle is to save the Union, and is not either to save or destroy slavery."

Just before they heard Lee's announcement, Andrew had just finished an article about a traveling theater group. The Cincinnati Dramatic Company was going to be performing in Harmony the following Tuesday night. They would be presenting their old but still enjoyable plays "The Inn-Keeper of Abbeville," "The Oslter and Robber" and a laughable farce of "The Village Lawyer." Tickets were forty cents or viewers could sit in the pit for thirty cents. The famous Mr. George D. Chaplin and Miss Bella Llewellyn Golden would be the main attraction. Everyone had heard of Miss Bella; she was a great soprano. She and her family spent a great deal of their time in the Harmony area.

Andrew had been thinking that a trip to the theatre would be a great way to take Rae's mind off her friends, when he heard Lee yell. Anna had been altering one of Alan's shirts to fit Lee while listening to Andrew read the paper out loud. Right away they both left what they had been doing and headed to the kitchen. They were both anxious to see Night Hawk. It had been awhile since either one of them had talked to him. They knew he would have the latest news, and they wanted to hear what was happening in the east. When

153

they saw him, Anna gave him a hug and Andrew shook his hand.

"We're glad to see you, young man, and to see that you're OK," Andrew told him.

They sat down around the table and talked while Rae and the boys did the last of the dishes. Night Hawk told them that things had gotten a lot worse since the last time he had been by. "There are many more big battles and a lot of killing on both sides. I'm afraid a lot of people are going to die before this war is all over, not just soldiers but women and children as well."

Night Hawk enjoyed talking with Andrew and Anna, but the first chance he got he reached for Rae's hand and they slipped out the back door. Anna and Andrew smiled at each other. They knew how Rae and Night Hawk felt about one another. They had no idea what the future held, but for now they were OK with the two and their feelings for each other.

Lee and Alan started to run to the living room where they could eavesdrop on their sister's conversation, but as they passed their parents they were both grabbed by their suspenders. "I believe it's your bedtime, so up the stairs with both of you. And don't be sneaking back down. Leave your sister and Night Hawk alone," Andrew told the two boys.

"Oh, father, we never get to have any fun," Lee groaned on his way up the stairs.

Once the young couple had settled themselves on the front porch steps, Night Hawk looked at Rae and said, "Your eyes are sad, Little One. You are worried about Dawn?"

Rae nodded. "My heart is breaking. Everyone will be off on an adventure and I'll be stuck here worrying about all of you."

"You need not worry about us, Little One. I will keep you updated on everyone," Night Hawk assured her as he picked up Rae's hands. "Besides, you are needed here. Someone needs to stay and help the adults. They all will need you in many different ways. They will need help with their farms. Remember, your families are helping to feed the Union Army, a very important job. And you are a big help to the Underground Railroad. Without you, I would not have a safe place to shelter runaways. But I believe that Dawn's family will need you most of all. When they see you, they will feel more hopeful that Dawn will return to them soon. And you realize that if any of the men here join the war your share of responsibility will be even greater?" While saying all of this Night Hawk had pulled Rae closer and she was resting her head on his shoulder.

"I know that you are right. Let's just hope that doesn't happen," Rae told him. She was having a hard time fighting back her tears. She really was worried about so many things.

"Now, I say we talk about happy things," Night Hawk suggested. "Don't you think that would be best?"

Rae was anxious to change the subject as well. "What of Lone Star and Little Dove? You told me they were to marry. Has that happened yet?"

"Yes, my brother has at last taken Little Dove as his bride. It happened the day after I arrived at our camp. Little

155

Dove made a beautiful bride. You would have loved her wedding dress and the feast that was held after the ceremony. You should have seen Lone Star when he thought no one was watching. He and Little Dove stole away to their bride tepee."

"Please, Night Hawk, tell me about Little Dove's dress. And what is a bride tepee?" Rae asked.

"Little Dove's dress was made of deer skin. She had worked on it for many weeks with the help of her mother and grandmother. To make the skin soft, first they had to scrape all the hair off the hide and work the skin in their hands and chew it until it was as soft as a baby's bottom. Then they stretched it out in the sun to bleach it white. They added fringe along the hem, down the sides, and around the neck of the dress with lots of Indian beads tied to the narrow strips. If I remember correctly, she also had a beaded belt around her waist and a matching head band to hold her long black hair in place."

"She must have been beautiful. I wish I had been there to see her. Now tell me what Lone Star wore. Surely he had on more than just his usual loin cloth," Rae said with a big smile on her face.

"Let me think. Oh yes, you're right. He didn't wear his loin cloth. Instead he wore a new set of buckskins that our mother, Moon Beam, had made for him. They were just as soft as Little Dove's dress but they hadn't been bleached out, so they were still brown. He also had fringe on his sleeves and down his pant legs. He wore a beaded head bonnet with lots of eagle feathers in the back as a sign that he was a brave warrior."

"How handsome he must have been," Rae sighed. "Now you must tell me what your people serve at a wedding feast."

"All of the women in our tribe helped with the feast. They made roasted deer, rabbit stew, and squirrel and fish cooked on hot rocks. There was also squash, corn, sweet potatoes, wild greens and a variety of fruits and nuts."

Rae was really surprised. "I would never have thought that your feast would be so much like our own gatherings."

"Do you think it would be alright if we took a little walk?" Night Hawk asked.

"Only if you tell me about the bride tepee," Rae told him. "You thought I would forget about it, didn't you? Now tell me, please."

"I can see you're not going to leave me alone until I do. I never should have mentioned it," Night Hawk laughed and Rae joined in. "A bridal tepee is a special tepee set up a mile or so from the rest of the camp by the bride and her female relatives. It has a supply of food and blankets and everything else the newly married couple will need for a few days and is usually close to a stream or creek. The couple will go there to stay for a few days, sometimes a week or more. This is a special place for them to get to know each other a lot better."

Night Hawk was explaining this to Rae as they walked down the lane toward the main road. Stopping in the middle of the lane, Rae looked at Night Hawk and asked, "Does all this make you think about when you will take a wife?"

Night Hawk looked at Rae, "Yes, Little One, but not until you are ready to be that wife." Rae felt a large lump form in her throat. She couldn't say a word, so she just put an arm around Night Hawk's waist and they kept on walking.

CHAPTER EIGHTEEN

Dawn Leaves Home

Night Hawk escorted Dawn as far as the foothills of the Smoky Mountains. When they reached the Kentucky-Tennessee boarder, he told her that this was as far south as he had ever been, but that he did know where to meet up with a local Underground conductor. When they reached the farm he was looking for, Night Hawk explained to the farmer that the young boy with him needed to make contact with "Smoky," referring to Stella by her code name. Dawn was wearing some of Alan's old clothes. She and Night Hawk felt that she would be safer disguised as a boy.

"I've heard of this Smoky. I believe he works farther south of here, mostly in Georgia and the Carolinas. The best I can do is send this young man south with the next runner that comes this way. Never know for sure when that will be. I'm a looking for a runner in a few days though," the conductor told Night Hawk and Dawn.

"Do you have a place I can stay until this runner gets here?" Dawn asked the conductor. "I'll be glad to help you here on your farm anyway I can."

"It won't be no trouble a' tall for you to stay a few days. That is, if you don't mind sleepin' in the hay loft. We got no more room in the house. We've got four young'uns and my missus can always use help with the housework and the garden."

"That would be great," Dawn told him.

The farmer went into the house to assure his family that everything was OK. They all came out to meet Dawn, who of course was introduced as a boy by the name of Indiana, the code name she had chosen. Then it was time for Night Hawk to head north again. He had left a small family of fugitives at the last stop, promising to return in a few days to take them farther north. Dawn and Night Hawk looked at each other. Dawn knew that this was it. Once Night Hawk left she would be on her own and there would be no family or friends to turn to, at least not until she found Stella or Zane. And for all she knew, that might not ever happen.

Dawn took the few steps to reach Night Hawk and, although she knew it might look funny to the farmer and his family, put her arms around his waist and gave him a big hug. Night Hawk returned the hug. Resting his chin on her head he told her, "You take care. I will need to take you home safe and sound some day or my Little One will skin me alive."

"Oh, Night Hawk, I promise because I think you would look silly without any skin." By this time they were both laughing. Night Hawk knew this was a good time to leave, so he gave Dawn one more hug, turned around and walked into the woods.

That night as Dawn lay in the loft waiting for sleep to

come she thought about the trip she and Night Hawk had just made. She had grown very fond of him and he had treated her like a sister and friend. He had also taught her many new things about surviving in the woods. They had seen so many wonderful sights on their trip. The one that was the most memorable for her was the beautiful blue heron. They had been paddling down the Ohio River on a warm sunny afternoon without a cloud in sight when Night Hawk had pointed to a small outlet off to their right. There was the heron standing straight and tall and so still one could easily have missed seeing him. As they had paddled closer, the bird had taken flight and sailed away with his wings ever so wide. His flight had seemed effortless. Once in the air he had circled back and flown right over them so low that Dawn thought she could have reached up and touched him. The heron had been so beautiful and sleek. Just thinking of him and how peaceful he had seemed lulled Dawn off to sleep.

The next morning Dawn was up just before the sun rose. She was used to getting up early. In fact, she didn't remember a time when she had ever been asleep after the sun was completely up. She sat up in her makeshift bed of straw and old quilts. It had been a fine bed. Once she had stopped thinking about the future, she had slept very well. She had enjoyed watching the stars out the loft door and there had been a number of wild animals carrying on in the nearby woods. She was sure she had heard an owl and a bear. After stretching and rubbing her eyes she climbed down the ladder. She knew the farmer was already awake because she had heard him enter the barn. She had no idea what to call the farmer and his wife, but since they didn't exchange names in the Underground, she decided she would just have to ask him.

"Good morning, young man. Did you sleep OK?" the farmer asked when he saw Dawn coming down the ladder.

"Yes, thank you. I'll just hurry and wash up and go help your missus, unless you need me to help you. But first I need to ask a question. What should I call the two of you?"

"Our code names are Jake and Daisy. I'm sure your help in the house would be appreciated. Daisy's not been feeling like herself as of lately. She could use all the help you can give her," Jake explained.

"I'll do all I can to help until the next runner gets here," Dawn told him. When she had met Daisy the day before, Dawn had thought the woman didn't look too healthy. She probably worked from daylight until she dropped in bed at night. Dawn figured she hadn't had a day's rest in years.

After Night Hawk had left the day before, Dawn had gotten a chance to look around the farm. She had yet to figure out how these people existed here. They literally lived on the side of a mountain. There was no place to raise cattle or plant crops and hardly enough room for the undersized garden that Dawn had found on one side of the house. Actually it was more like three really small gardens because there wasn't a flat spot large enough for one large garden. None of the plots looked like they had been tended in awhile. Behind the barn Dawn had seen a small pen with one old sow and a litter of six sorry looking piglets. Hobbled in a little grassy spot was one horse, one milk cow and a pair of mules. A few chickens roamed free all over the yard.

When Dawn and Jake came out of the barn together that morning, she saw something she hadn't noticed the day before. A short distance down the mountain she saw a flat spot with something growing on it. She knew that it had to be a crop of some sort because all the plants were similar and growing in rows, but she had no idea what it could be. "What is that growing down there?" she asked Jake. "I've never seen a crop that looks like that before."

"That be my bacca crop," Jake told her. "It's about the only thing that will grow up here. I use some for myself and sell the rest."

"So what is that building down there with the narrow windows going up and down?"

"That be where I dry the bacca before I take it to Middlesboro to sell. The money buys a few extras for us that we can't make ourselves."

"Do you just hang the leaves to dry them?" Dawn wanted to know.

"Yap, that's how it's done, with the help of a few small smoky fires to help with the drying," Jake answered.

"How do you keep bugs and dirt out of the leaves?" was Dawns next question.

"That would be impossible, but they just adds taste to the bacca."

Dawn didn't think that sounded too good to her, but after learning that they had a crop she felt better about staying. "At least I'm not eating food they need," she thought.

When Dawn went into the cabin she could see why there

wasn't room for her there. The house was rather small. She knew this kind of cabin was called a dogtrot cabin, meaning the kitchen and living area was a separate building from the bedroom where Jake and Daisy slept with the infants. The older children slept in lofts above each room. The two parts of the house were separated by an open breezeway but connected by a single roof. Jake had also built a porch across the front and fashioned a couple of rockers and a small table out of tree limbs. Daisy had made cushions for the rockers out of old feed sacks by stuffing them with Spanish moss. The rockers gave the place a welcoming look. Dawn wondered if Daisy ever had time to sit down and enjoy any of this.

After a hot breakfast of biscuits, gravy and scrambled eggs everyone got to work. Dawn helped Daisy clean the cabin and then went outside to see what she could do in the gardens. Jake and the two oldest boys left to go squirrel hunting. He had told Dawn that sometimes they got lucky and brought home a bear.

"A bear?" Dawn had asked as her eyes got wide. Bear hunting sounded pretty scary to her. "What good comes from killing a bear?"

"Why, lots of things," Jake explained. "The meat is good to eat, and if it's a large one we can dry some of the meat to eat this winter. Bear meat makes for a good change in our diet. Daisy uses the skin for all kinds of things. She makes bedcovers to keeps us real warm on cold nights. The small ones we use for rugs."

Later while she and Daisy worked in the garden, Dawn asked her about the skins. "What do you have to do to make blankets and rugs out of bear skins?"

"We take the skin and scrape the back, just like the Indians taught us," Daisy described. "That makes them soft. My husband has even sold a few. People in the town like them for rugs and to hang on their walls. Like us, they hang them over their windows when it gets really cold to keep the wind and snow out." Dawn found the way of life here very interesting. She learned new ways of doing things every day she stayed with the farmer and his family.

A few days later, Dawn awoke to a number of voices in the barn. As quietly as she could she crawled to the edge of the loft and peeked over. There below her was Jake with a group of five Negroes. Dawn laid there on her stomach and listened to their whispered conversation. It was just loud enough for her to make out most of what was being said. They were telling Jake how happy they were to be here at his farm and asking him when the next runner would be coming.

There was a lot of dust rising up to the loft from all those people moving around and it caused Dawn to sneeze. Jake looked up at her. "Didn't aim to wake you, boy," he told Dawn. "You might as well come on down. I think this here be the runner you been waiting for."

When Dawn got to the bottom of the ladder and turned around she was as shocked to see the runner as the runner was to see her. Right there in front of her was Stella. The girls ran to each other laughing and crying at the same time. They wrapped their arms around each other and danced about in circles.

"Don't think I need to ask if this is the one you been

wanting to find," Jake observed as he looked on in amusement at what he thought was two boys. "Must be some strange northern tradition," he thought to himself.

"Yes, Jake, this is my friend," Dawn told him. "I never thought I would be so lucky as to find him this quickly."

Stella stepped back away from Dawn, "What are you doing here, g-- boy?" She almost said girl but had caught herself just in time. "Don't you know how much danger you're in?"

"Look who's talking," Dawn retorted.

"Will you answer my question? What are you doing here?"

By this time the girls had walked outside the barn and found an old stump to sit on, so Dawn was free to reply. "I just couldn't sit at home any longer. I had to come find you to see if I could help. I know there are more slaves running north than ever and I was hoping to help in some way."

"You be right there, girl. These people be more scared than ever. No one knows how this war is going to end and what going to happen to these black folk when it does. I guess since you're here I can find something for you to do," Stella told Dawn.

Jake and the runaways had come to the barn door and were watching the two girls. They enjoyed seeing how happy the friends were. When one of Jake's sons came out of the house to milk the cow, he was surprised to see that they had company. Jake said to him, "Boy, you go tell your Ma we have five extra guests for breakfast."

"I'll go, Jake," Dawn offered. "Daisy will need some extra help. We'll talk later," she added to Stella.

Soon after breakfast Dawn and Stella wished the runaways a safe journey north. They would be staying here until another runner came to take them on the next stretch of the Railroad. The two girls, on the other hand, were headed south. Daisy had filled a knapsack for the girls to take with them. She had put in a few biscuits left over from breakfast and fried squirrel from last night's supper as well as a few nuts and a couple of pears from the tree that grew at the back of their house.

Dawn had grown quite attached to the family and admired their compassion. Although they had little for themselves, they were willing to share their meager possessions with those in need and to risk their safety by helping with the Underground Railroad. Dawn thanked the couple sincerely for their help and hospitality and then followed Stella as she disappeared into the forest.

CHAPTER NINETEEN

The Girls Get Down To Business

As much as they wanted to, the girls didn't talk to each other while they traveled until they stopped to rest in a grove of pine trees that they found along a small stream. One of the trees had branches that were just high enough off the ground for them to crawl under to be out of the weather and out of sight. They each had a tin cup in their backpacks which they had filled at the stream. After they made sure they were well concealed by the pine branches, Dawn took out the food Daisy had sent with them.

They had been very quite on the trail because Stella had explained that they needed to be as silent as possible to be able to watch and listen for other people as well as all kinds of wild animals that lived in these mountains. She already had seen wild boar, bear and an assortment of snakes. Dawn had actually enjoyed the quite of their morning walk. It had given her a chance to enjoy the mountains and all their beauty. The mountainsides were covered in vast expanses of pine trees interrupted periodically by patches of mountain laurel, wild rose and even Dutchman's breeches. The forest floor was covered with pine cones of all sizes and shapes.

A variety of rodents were scurrying everywhere, including rabbits, squirrels, chipmunks and raccoons, while red birds and blue jays flew overhead from tree to tree. Early in their journey, Stella had pointed out a black bear and her two small cubs a safe distance away, so the girls had taken time to rest and watch the cubs at play. They had chased one another up and down the trees and across the forest floor. When one of them caught the other they would stand on their hind legs and wrestle, rolling all over the ground. Once they had even rolled down the side of the mountain until they came to a sudden stop against the trunk of a tree. The girls had smiled at each other as they continued on through the woods. Dawn decided that this was nature at its finest.

Back under the pine tree near the stream, the girls had quenched their thirst and eaten their meal. Then Stella told Dawn, "It's safe for us to talk, now." They were grateful for the chance because they were both full of questions. Stella wanted to know about Night Hawk and Rae, about all of their families, and whether Dawn had heard from Stella's two brothers, Rob and Jewell. But her biggest question was, "What is your family thinking, letting you come here?"

"It was with the help of Night Hawk that I got here," Dawn explained. "At first my family was upset, but now they're just proud of me, and worried, of course. Rae wanted to come with me, but one of us had to stay behind to be there for our families. Besides, she is very busy helping the Railroad there in Indiana. "No, we've not heard from your brothers. Night Hawk told me he saw them about six months ago and they were just fine. He said that Rob was as tall as he was and Jewell was growing just as fast. When he talked to them, they seemed happy.

"Now it's my turn to ask questions," Dawn said. "Have you seen or heard anything from Beth or Zane?"

"I've not seen Beth, but I hear she's been very busy helping the Railroad. I was told she almost got caught once a few months back. As usual she talked her way out of trouble. You know Beth. She can make you believe anything she tells you. As for Zane, I see him about once a month. In fact, we're on our way to his camp now."

"Oh, oh!" Dawn was so happy. "I can't believe my luck! First I find you, or you find me, whichever, and now you're taking me to see Zane! I'll have to say an extra prayer tonight thanking God for all my good luck. But I really want to help you, so please tell me what I can do."

"Having you along with me will be a great help. Now we can take turns sleeping and hiding our trails. I know it's a lot to learn, but I'll teach you as we go," Stella explained. "Right now I think we need to get on our way, especially if we want to reach Zane's camp in a few days."

"How long will that take us?" Dawn wanted to know. "I'm really anxious to see him and see what he has to say about me joining you."

"Close to ten, maybe twelve days," Stella told Dawn. "And I can tell you right now, he'll be as surprised as I was."

"That long? Then let's get going." Dawn got up and started walking. Then she stopped, "Uh, by the way, which way do we go?"

Stella looked at Dawn and laughed, "I can see I've got a lot to teach you. If you remember, we just came down that mountainside to reach the stream. Now we'll need to go up on the other side."

The girls crossed the Smokey Mountains avoiding all the towns and settlements along the way. They didn't want anyone to see them. It seemed to Dawn that everything Stella did was a secret.

The girls were both wearing black men's pants and dark blue men's shirts, making it harder for them to be seen in the woods or recognized when they were spotted. They also each wore a pair of high-topped boots. Night Hawk had explained to Dawn that the boots were best to protect her from snakes. It had taken her days to get used to wearing them, and in the beginning she had had blisters on top of blisters. Now she decided that they were more comfortable than the shoes she usually wore back home. To complete their disguises, both girls had bound their busts and tied their hair up in scarves to wear under big brimmed black hats. With a layer of dirt smeared on their faces, no one could tell they weren't boys.

Dawn soon learned that the backpack Stella wore was full of all kinds of things, including her cup and plate, a change of clothes, a pair of binoculars, a medicine bag, and maps of Kentucky, Tennessee, North and South Carolina and Georgia. She also wore a rope as a belt around her waist where she had strapped on a gun and holster as well as a dangerous looking knife. Dawn was glad Night Hawk had helped her put together a backpack of her own, but it didn't take her long to realize she was going to need a few more things to survive out here in the woods. For instance, she, too, had a gun but no knife.

One morning before the girls started traveling for the day, Stella informed Dawn that they would reach the foothills of the mountains before night fall. Dawn told Stella, "Thank goodness! I'll sure be glad. These mountains were really hard on a body."

For the most part, the girl's march was uninterrupted. But one day around noon as they began hiking down the side of a mountain, Stella suddenly held up her hand and put a finger to her lips. Then she pointed ahead of them. Dawn was surprised at what she saw. Daisy had told her about a group of old men who wore ragged clothes and traveled all over the mountains playing hillbilly music. They called themselves the Bubba Brothers, which was funny because none of them were brothers. Dawn could see that each one of these men had a musical instrument slung on his back. It looked to her like they had guitars, banjos and fiddles. Daisy had also told her that they could make music by hitting two spoons together, blowing into empty moonshine jugs or rubbing a washboard with a stick or their hands. The men carried a few jugs of moonshine with them, and in fact, a lot of people paid them with moonshine. They had no families, so they just lived off the land and stayed wherever they wanted for as long as they wanted. To Dawn and Stella, these men made quite a sight. The girls looked at one another and shook their heads.

When the Bubba Brothers were out of hearing distance, Dawn told Stella who they were and what Daisy had told her about them. "Well, one thing is for sure," Stella said. "They sure were old and dressed in rags. Bet none of them has taken a bath in months, maybe years. I could smell them from here."

"Let's hope that is the last of our excitement for the day," Dawn said.

✶✶✶✶✶✶✶✶✶✶✶✶✶✶✶✶✶✶✶✶

The girls were dirty, tired and hungry when, after traveling for a total of thirteen days, they found Zane's camp. Dusk was just beginning when they saw the camp fires. Stella asked Dawn, "Want to play a trick on Zane?"

Dawn nodded her head and whispered, "Always. What do you have in mind?"

Stella grinned and motioned for Dawn to follow her. She walked right into the camp with her head held high like she owned the place. Dawn followed, keeping her eyes on the ground. As they entered the camp, a sentry stopped them. When he recognized Stella he just smiled, "Evening, Smoky. Corporal Brown is in the major's tent. They've been expecting you any day now. They'll be happy to see you're OK."

"Thank you. I'm glad to be here safe and sound, myself," Stella told the private. Then she led the way to Major Odell's tent, which wasn't difficult to find because it was the largest tent in the camp. Another sentry was posted in front of the major's tent, and again the soldier recognized Stella. When he saw her coming he tapped on the tent pole and informed Odell, "Mr. Smoky is here, sir. He's got a boy with him this time." Zane jumped up to open the tent flap and greet Stella. He wondered who the boy was with her. She had never brought any of the runaways into camp before. "Stella, come in," the major called from inside the tent. "We've been worried about you. We expected to see you a couple of days ago."

"Well, you see Major, I had this new boy with me and he wanted to see the trails, so it took me a little longer to get back," Stella explained. All this time Dawn stood just inside the tent with her head down so Zane couldn't see her face.

"Come in, boy, come in. Have a seat. J.B., go and see if you can find our guests something to eat," Major Odell instructed. "I'm sure cook can come up with a few leftovers, especially since we all knew Smoky was due any time. He's been cooking extra for her for the last few days just in case she showed up."

"Yes, sir. I'll see to it right away," J.B. replied.

Once J.B. had left to carry out his orders, Zane looked at Stella and asked, "Aren't you going to introduce us to your new friend?"

Stella looked first at the major then at Zane. "Major, I would like for you to meet a friend of mine from Indiana."

Zane had been studying the newcomer, but when he heard this, his attention snapped back to Stella. Then he started looking back and forth from one traveler to the other. "What do you mean, from Indiana?" he wanted to know.

"Well, you see, this boy is a girl and her name is Dawn

Jefferson, now known as Indiana." As Stella said this, Dawn looked up at Zane with a big smile on her face. She removed her hat and scarf and started laughing.

Zane rushed over to scoop her up in a huge hug. He was so glad to see Dawn but was wondering why and how she had come here to Georgia. But there would be time in his tent later to ask these questions. Just then J.B. was returning with the food. He stopped dead in his tracks when he saw Dawn, his mouth hanging open. He just couldn't believe this boy was a girl.

Zane laughed. "J.B., put the food on the table; these girls are starving. By the way, this here girl is the friend from Indiana that I've been telling you about," Zane told his partner.

"What do you mean, Zane Brown? You've been talking to this man about me?" Dawn looked at J.B. "Just remember, you can't believe half of what this boy says. That is, unless he told you how I can out-fish, out-shoot and out-ride him," she told him as they stared at one another.

J.B. looked at Zane, "I can see now that this girl has got your number. Sounds like she knows you pretty good."

"Hey, you two, now just a minute. I feel like I'm at home where it was all girls giving me a hard time," Zane told them with a chuckle.

While the others were going at it, Stella looked at the major. She just shook her head, sat down at the camp table and started eating. When Dawn saw her do that, it didn't take long for her to join in. "Well, gentlemen, it looks like the ladies are a bit hungry," Major Odell said to Zane and J.B. "I suggest we leave them to enjoy their meal. It might be nice if you put some water on the camp fire to heat. I'm sure these young ladies would enjoy a hot bath."

When they were alone again, Dawn licked her fingers and said, "This sure is good. Wonder what it is."

Stella just laughed. "We probably don't want to know. I suggest we eat and enjoy it while we can. We'll be off on another mission in a few days."

Dawn stopped chewing, "That soon? I can hardly wait!"

When they finished eating, the girls met up with Zane and he showed them to a tent set up next to his and J.B.'s. J.B. had started a small camp fire in front of the tents and a large pot of water was heating there just for them. After Stella and Dawn finished enjoying the hot bath they joined the boys around the fire. The four of them were still sitting there hours later.

Zane had to know how everyone was at home, especially his father and Rae. And he was really curious about what Dawn was doing in Georgia and how she had found Stella. After Dawn had satisfied Zane's mind that she knew what she was doing here, she told him all about things at home, including Abby, whom Zane knew nothing about. When she was finished, Zane started to tell the girls about their new assignment.

"Wait," Stella said. "Before you tell us about the future, bring us up-to-date on the latest war news."

"OK," Zane agreed. "Where do I start? Our lawmakers in

Washington, D.C. have been busy passing new laws. One of them gives farmers the right to homestead, meaning they can receive 160 acres of land in the west for as little as $26 to $34 an acre. I'm sure when this war is over a lot of people will be heading west to take advantage of this new law.

"On a more serious note, a lot of battles, big and small, have been taking place both in the north and south," he told her. "There have been reports of more fighting in the western states, like Texas and Arkansas. Just think, not only are the Texans fighting feds, but Mexicans and Indians as well. I sure wouldn't want to be in Texas right now. There was a really big battle at Shiloh, Tennessee on April 6th and 7th in '62. I'm not sure either side won that battle. They say the Union casualties numbered around 13,000 and the Confederate army lost 11,000. That's the first battle to lose so many. Then there was the evacuation of Confederate troops from Nashville, Tennessee. The Union army destroyed their railroad tracks. That really put a hardship on the South since this was how they were receiving produce from the west as well as one of the main ways to ship army supplies to their troops. There's been a lot more going on all around us. Right now, both armies are winning some and losing some. Who knows who will be the winner in the end? Probably no one," Zane finished with a sigh.

"Sounds like we all have our work cut out for us," Stella said. "Guess it's time to learn about our future. So tell us, what is this new assignment you have for us?"

CHAPTER TWENTY

Beth's in Trouble

Zane took a deep breath. "Beth is in big trouble, but she doesn't know about it, or at least she didn't. She really needs our help and Major Odell is sending us to Savannah to help her," he explained. "Someone has been spying on her and reported that she is helping runaways. She and her whole family are all being watched. We need to get to Beth as soon as we can to warn her. While you two were eating, the major told us that if you want to go with us he would have no problem with that. What do you say? Want to go along?"

"Of course!" Stella exclaimed. "When do we leave?"

"Night after tomorrow. The major feels you girls need to rest before we leave," Zane explained.

"Nonsense. We don't have time to waste," Dawn said. "We'll be ready at first light tomorrow morning, right, Stella?"

"That's right, so let's get to bed now. We'll need to get up bright and early and head south."

So early the next morning, even before the rest of the camp was up, the four were on their way to Savannah. They only had the boys' horses, so Stella rode behind Zane and Dawn behind J.B. While traveling, they decided on a plan. When they were about three miles west of the city, Zane changed his old clothes and straw hat for a Confederate Army uniform. He tied his arm in a sling so that he would look like he had been injured. Before he rode off, he told the others he would be back in a few hours.

Zane rode into Savannah and past the Jefferson House. He tied Puddles to a hitching block down the street then walked back to the house. He opened the garden gate and went around the house to the kitchen door. Gertrud, the cook, was just coming outside. Recognizing him despite the uniform she said, "Oh, Mister Zane, what's you doing here at this back door?"

"I'm looking for Beth. Is she here, Gertrud?"

"No, sir, she be at Rivers View. She went home three days ago. Sorry, Mr. Zane."

"Thank you, Gertrud. Please keep my being here a secret. Don't tell anyone you saw me."

"Why, Mr. Zane, my lips are sealed." Gertrud gave Zane a hug. "Now, you be careful, you hear me, Mr. Zane?"

"I will, Gertrud." Zane tipped his hat to her and went back out the garden gate and down the street to where he had left Puddles. After taking the time to ride through most of the town, he made his way back to the others, checking all the time to make sure he wasn't being followed.

"Looks like we're going to Rivers View. Beth went home three days ago," he reported to Dawn, Stella and J.B. The three rejoined Zane on the horses and they all rode off.

Late the next night after dark, Zane slipped into the kitchen at Rivers View. He had changed back into his old clothes, so it took Dilly a few minutes to realize who it was standing in her kitchen. "Mr. Zane, is that you? I's see it is. Bless my soul, you scared this old woman half to death. What's you doing, coming in the back door, anyway? Miss Beth didn't tell us you was a coming." Dilly had a habit of talking a lot.

"Miss Beth didn't know I was coming. I want to surprise her. Is she the only one at home?" Zane needed to know.

"Yes, sir, the rest they all stay in Savannah. She be eaten her supper in her Pa's office cause she been taking care of the plantation for months now. I tell you, Mr. Zane, that young thing is plum worn out, she is."

"Dilly, do me a favor and go get her for me. Don't tell her I'm here. Just tell her you need to show her something in the kitchen that can't wait."

A few minutes later Beth walked through the kitchen door. She was in for a surprise because standing there in front of her was Zane. "Oh, Zane, I'm so glad to see you. Are you safe?"

"If you're so glad to see me, then come here and give me a hug." Zane was remaining in a dark corner of the kitchen so that if anyone was outside they couldn't see him through the windows. Beth gladly went to him and after they held each other for a few minutes, he said to her, "We need to talk. But first I have another surprise for you."

Zane slipped out the kitchen door, closing it silently behind him. He was gone so long that Beth began to think she had been dreaming. But no, it hadn't been a dream. She could hear him coming up the back steps. When he came into the room, he walked around and extinguished all the lanterns except for one that he turned down low. Then he disappeared onto the porch for a moment and was followed in by three more people.

"Zane, what is going on?" Beth wanted to know.

Zane picked up the one lantern that he hadn't blown out and whispered, "Let's all go into the pantry."

Beth didn't know what to think, so she just did as Zane asked. Once he had shut the door behind them, he turned up the wick of the lantern and held it high. When Beth turned around, there stood Dawn, Stella and J.B.

"Dawn! Stella!" Beth rushed to give her friends a hug. "Oh, it's so great to see you! But someone needs to explain what's going on here. And for heaven's sake, what are we doing hiding in the pantry?" she wanted to know.

Zane reached out and took Beth's hands in his. "Beth, you're in danger and we've come to help you."

"Danger? What kind of danger?" Beth asked.

"Someone suspects that you've been helping runaways and they're watching you and your family."

"My family? Are they OK? Oh, Zane, what am I going to do?" Beth was beginning to feel panicky.

"You have to stop now before it's too late," Zane explained.

"But, Zane, you don't understand. I've got a group of six hidden in the woods right now just waiting for me to help them."

J.B. put his fingers to his lips, signaling for everyone to be quite. Whispering, he told them, "I hear footsteps coming across the kitchen."

The footsteps stopped right outside the pantry door, and Beth almost squealed in terror. Then they heard Momma Jo, "You all come out of that pantry. I want to see who is in there." Sighing with relief, Beth opened the door, and Momma Jo told her, "I done had Honey go up to your room, Miss Beth, and close the curtains so no one can see in. Now all of you get on up them back stairs. We'll be bringing you some supper up in a few minutes. I done sent Dilly out to the stables to fetch Bow and Sunny. Something tells Momma Jo you gonna be needing them two."

Beth squeezed Momma Jo's hand, "Thank you, Momma Jo. Whatever would I do without you?" The little group left the hot, crowded pantry and followed Beth up the servant's stairs to her bedroom. The first thing they all did when they reached Beth's room was find a place to sit down. Everyone's legs were just a little shaky. Beth and Zane sat on the edge of her bed, Stella pulled up a small stool, Dawn moved a rocker over close and J.B. sat on the rug next her.

Then, Zane realized that Beth and J.B. had not been introduced. "Beth, this is my partner, J.B., that I was telling you about on my last visit."

Beth got up to shake J.B.'s hand. "It's a pleasure to meet you, regardless of the circumstances," she said before returning to sit on her bed.

Before Zane could get back to explaining more to Beth there was a knock on the bedroom door. Opening it slowly, Bow stuck his head in the room and almost fell in when Sunny gave him a push. He whirled around, but before he could retort, Momma Jo was right behind him saying, "You boys get yourselves in that room and help Honey and me with this food. I figure these people be starving."

In most places in the south, food was getting scarce. But so far they had plenty at Rivers View. They had been able to sustain their gardens and keep their livestock hidden from looters. Honey cleared off the window seat and Momma Jo and Dilly set up a modest buffet for the young folks. There was some cold fried chicken, boiled eggs, biscuits and cold sweet potatoes. Dilly told them, "I be back in awhile with some hot fried apple pies for you all."

"Mmm, this is so good. However did you fix all this so fast?" Stella asked Dilly before she left the room.

"Well, honey, we had just finished supper when Zane popped into my kitchen and scared me to death, he did," Dilly told her.

No one had to be told to eat because they were all very hungry. But as soon as J.B. put down his plate, Beth said, "Now, I need some answers. What makes you think someone is watching me and my family? And how did you find out about this spy? And above all this, what am I going to do about that party that's waiting for me in the woods?"

"To answer your first two questions, a Union spy in Savannah sent us a message that you were being watched. As for the ones in hiding, you'll just have to tell us where they are and we'll take it from there," Zane told her.

"Do any of you know how to help these people?" Beth asked, looking around the room.

"I believe Stella and I can be of help there," Dawn answered her. "That's what Stella's been doing for months."

"I don't think I can tell you how to find them. You see, there are two groups in two different places. I'll have to take you there," Beth told them.

"No, Miss Beth you'll not do that," Bow informed her. "I'll take 'em, right, Mr. Zane?"

"But Bow, if someone is watching the house you'll soon be missed. Then they'll suspect you and start hunting you. I would not allow that to happen," Beth told Bow.

"I have an idea," Dawn explained. "Bow and I are so near the same size we could trade places. I know how to handle horses and do farm work as well as most. I'll stay here and help Sunny, and Bow can go help the others. Then when your people are at the next safe house, me and Bow will just trade back. What do you guys think?"

"Dawn, I always knew you were clever. I say you and Sunny should head on back to the barn and we'll be on our way shortly," Zane said, patting Dawn on the back.

"How we gonna trade back?" Bow wanted to know.

Zane looked at Bow, "What do you think, four days there and back?"

"That should be about right, five at the most."

Zane asked Beth, "Do you still have your racehorses? And do you and the boys still exercise them every day?"

"Yes to both questions. But why do you ask?"

"I'm thinking that for the next few days you need to go a different route every day. On the fourth day, take the trail behind the house and somewhere along the way we'll meet up and make the trade. We'll watch to make sure you're not being followed. If for some reason we don't make it that day, then on the fifth day go down the front lane and take the main road toward town. Again, the same plan. Sound alright to the rest of you?" Zane asked.

Everyone nodded their heads in agreement. Soon after that Momma Jo, Dilly and Honey cleaned up the supper mess and left the room. Dawn and Sunny soon followed. J.B. looked at Stella and Bow and they all headed for the kitchen, leaving Beth and Zane alone. They turned to look at each other. Beth couldn't help herself and tears began to run down her cheeks. Zane wiped them away with his fingers and then wrapped his arms around her. Finally, Beth stopped crying. "At least I don't have to worry about my family, now that I have had time to think about all of this. Rosa Mae is living in Atlanta with her husband's family, Father and Robert both joined the army a few months ago, and who in their right mind would suspect Mother?"

"You'll be OK now, too, if you stop helping and do as I say. After all, President Lincoln has declared that all slaves are free. Promise me you'll stop. It would ease my mind so to have your promise," Zane told Beth. They were still sitting on the side of her bed holding hands.

"I promise," was all Beth could say for the lump in her throat. When Zane got up to go, Beth jumped up to throw her arms around his neck and give him a big kiss. "Now you promise me that I'll see you in four or five days, Zane Avery Brown."

"I'll do my best."As he walked out the door he looked over his shoulder and said, "I love you, Beth Taylor." Then he left the room, closing the door behind him.

CHAPTER TWENTY-ONE

Helping Beth's Runaways

Zane, J.B., Stella and Bow traveled the rest of the night. When they arrived at the place where the first group was hidden in an old abandoned barn, Bow went into the hiding place first. He had helped Beth when she had hidden the fugitives, so he knew the runaways would trust him. He explained to them that Beth wasn't coming but that they would be safe with the people he had brought with him. Then he motioned Zane and the others in to meet the slaves. They had decided that Stella and J.B. would take this group to the safe house. Bow had given them directions to get there. In the meantime, he and Zane would split off and help the second group. Everyone would rest together during this first day. Dilly had sent two large sacks of food, so everyone ate well. Then the four guides each found a place to rest, leaving the runaways to be on watch. The two groups would go their separate ways at nightfall and meet again at the safe house in two days if all went well.

Right after dusk the two parties went their separate ways. Stella and J.B. had an uneventful trip and delivered their group to the safe house before daylight the next morning.

Zane and Bow weren't so lucky. They hadn't traveled three miles when they heard a horse's neigh. Both of them stopped dead in their tracks. Zane ran behind a large bush with Bow right behind him. Just seconds later, a Confederate patrol of a dozen men went riding by. When they had ridden out of hearing distance, both Zane and Bow let out long sighs. Neither one had realized he had been holding his breath. Then just before they reached the second group it started to rain, making the ground slippery. They had planned to get the second group and make it to the safe house before dawn, but they could see that wasn't going to happen. When they reached the group they had to wait another day, so it was the next night before they met Stella and J.B. at the safe house.

Because of the one day delay, it was the fifth day before they made it back to Rivers View. They saw Beth, Dawn and Sunny as they were riding down the main road. When Stella, J.B. and Bow met them, Zane was nowhere in sight. Beth didn't know that he had been trailing behind them in the woods for the last hour just to make sure no one was following them. Dawn had seen him, but hadn't given him away.

"Where is Zane? Is he alright? Somebody tell me now before I scream." Beth was so scared she was about to cry.

"Why, Beth, I think you really do care," Zane said as he walked out of the bushes behind her. He reached up and took hold of her horse's reins, "But I think we need to get off the road before someone comes along." Beth just sat there on her horse and stared at him. She was so happy to see that all her friends were OK. She didn't know what to say, except a silent prayer of thanks.

As soon as they were safely off the road, Sunny told them, "Bow, I mean, Dawn and I brought a picnic if anyone is hungry."

Dawn laughed, "Everyone knows that Zane is always hungry."

Beth led the way through the woods to a small stream and an open grassy spot for a picnic. J.B., Bow and Sunny took the horses down to the stream to water them and then hobbled them on a nearby grassy hill. Dawn and Stella spread out a couple of old quilts while Beth and Zane began unloading the two wicker baskets. Dilly had out done herself again. She had sent slices of country ham and fried chicken. She knew that chicken was one of Zane's favorites. To go with it she had sent pickled okra, cornbread, cracklings, green beans and a big bowl of her famous potato salad. And for everyone's sweet tooth she had packed a whole applesauce cake.

After everyone finished eating, Dawn, with J.B.'s help, carried the dishes to the stream and rinsed them off as best they could. The others repacked everything else. By the time Dawn and J.B. got back, Beth and Zane had disappeared. No one was going to bother them. They all knew the couple just needed some time to themselves. Who knew when they might get a chance to see each other again?

The others were content to just sit and enjoy the peace and quiet. They told Dawn all about the last few days and assured her that the runaways were safely on their way north. Then Stella asked Dawn, "How were your days on a plantation?"

"I wish I could have gone with you guys, but it was fun pretending to be someone else for a little while. I did learn that all the slaves and house servants are gone. Sunny, Bow, Momma Jo, Honey and Dilly are all the servants that are left. But Beth doesn't think of them as servants anymore. To her, they are all just friends, one big happy family, trying to stay alive and keep the plantation together. They all, including Beth, work outdoors and in the house as well. Her mother won't leave Savannah. She says she doesn't feel safe at Rivers View with Eugene and Robert both gone off to war. And she may be right. They've had trouble with looters a few times, so Beth's had all the valuables hidden in the woods. They even have to hide the horses, chickens and cow to keep the looters from stealing them. Beth told me that they have to worry as much about the Confederate troops as the Union ones."

"Sounds like things are getting pretty bad down here," Stella observed.

The girls were both quite for awhile thinking about what had just been said. When Dawn looked up and saw that the men had all gone to sleep, she caught Stella's eye and nodded toward the water. They both got up and walked downstream until they found a small spot covered in pine needles near an old pine tree. On the other side of the stream was a pair of brown squirrels. They were chasing each other up and down trees as fast as they could go, chattering all the time. The girls stood there watching them until one of the squirrels saw them and they both scurried off.

On the way to the stream they had passed a wild rose bush and each picked a pink rose. The roses smelled so good and the sweet smell brought back memories of home. Dawn sat beside the water remembering her Granny's rose garden. She sure would miss her Granny Bella when she got home. Beth had told her how Granny had died right after she had left home.

Even though it was late fall the weather was warm that day, so the girls sat down on the bank, took off their boots and socks, rolled up their pant legs and dangled their feet in the cool water.

"I think being a boy has its advantages, don't you?" Dawn asked Stella.

"Why would you think that? Just because pants make it easier to ride a horse, run, jump over logs, climb a tree if you need to, are a lot cooler in the summer and warmer in the winter? Yes, I'll have to agree with you girl, that I will." "Still," Dawn said, "I'll be glad to get home and wear a dress again. Well, some of the time, anyway." At that they both laughed until their sides were hurting.

Once they had regained control of themselves they both leaned back on their elbows and started looking at the fluffy white clouds overhead. "Look at that one," Stella said. "It reminds me of a snowman, makes me think about the winters I spent up north with my brothers."

"There's one over there that kind of looks like a fat pig, don't you think?" Dawn asked. While they laid there watching the clouds, a shadow flew over them. They soon discovered that the shadow belonged to a very large red tailed hawk. He was swooping down toward the opposite side of the stream. Then just as quickly as he went down he was back up in the air. "Look!" Dawn told Stella. "He's got a black snake in his beak, and he's coming right back over the top of us."

Stella rolled over on her stomach and covered her head with her hands. "Tell me when he's gone. You know how I hate snakes!"

Dawn was laughing so hard her sides were hurting again. "He's gone, Stella. Besides, I think the snake was already dead."

"Don't you be laughing at me, Miss Dawn Jefferson. You know you're just as scared of snakes as I am."

"I know I am. But it was amazing to see how that hawk grabbed that snake and flew off with him."

"Hey, you two! We were wondering where you had went off to. Then I heard you laughing. We followed that sound right to you. It was a happy sound, not one I've heard much of lately," Bow told them. He and Sunny sat down next to Stella and put their feet in the stream. They didn't have to worry about socks or shoes, they weren't wearing any.

Dawn got up and picked up her socks and boots. "I'm going to see if there's any chicken left," she said and walked off.

"I believe she was in a hurry," Sunny said as she disappeared down the trail. "I hope we didn't run her off."

"No, I think she just saw a chance to be with J.B.," Stella explained.

"You don't mean Dawn and J.B.? Well ain't that nice,"

Bow said with a big smile on his face. "Miss Stella, can I ask you a question?" he said more seriously.

"Sure, what is it, Bow?"

"I been helping Miss Beth with runaways for months now. And Miss Beth and her family, they real good to all of us blacks. They treat us like family. The ones of us that are still here will stay here. The other night when we had to sit the storm out, I asked Mr. Zane about you and Dawn. He told me how you and your family had run away from a plantation in Kentucky, and how your parents died on the way. Then he told me he and his three friends found you and your two brothers and how with the help of an Indian they got you all north. Weren't you all scared to even try such a trip?"

"Scared? We were all scared to death. That first day that we all hid out, I was so scared my teeth wouldn't quit chattering. But our Ma, she started humming to us and we all went right off to sleep. The next thing we know it was nighttime and time to move on."

"But, Stella, what's it feel like to be free?"

"It's hard to explain, Bow. But you don't have no one telling you what you have to do and when. You can learn to read and write. You can even have yourself your very own last name. White folk have rules and laws that everyone has to obey, but they're not like the rules the masters have. Being free makes you feel good and happy and proud of yourself."

"Maybe after this war I'll try this freedom thing myself. But right now, Miss Beth, she need me and the others to help her, so guess I'll just wait a spell. What's you think, we should get back? It gonna be dark before long?"

By the time they got back to the picnic area, Dawn and J.B. had picked up everything so Sunny went to retrieve the horses. Beth and Zane had returned and they all knew it was time to go back to reality. Everyone said their good-byes and Beth, Bow and Sunny headed back to Rivers View while the others just disappeared into the woods.

CHAPTER TWENTY-TWO

A Lady Spy

The group took their time getting back to camp. Before they had left to carry out this mission, the major told them he would be moving the camp to the northwest region of Georgia. He had given them details of where to find it. When they finally arrived at camp they learned that there had been a battle the day before. The company had lost a few more troopers but had successfully pushed the Rebels back south.

Now that there weren't as many runaways to help, Dawn and Stella went to work helping in the camp. They cared for the sick and wounded and sometimes even helped the cook. They were getting a little bored when one day Zane found them and told them that the major wanted to see them. When they got to Major Odell's tent, he had a new mission for all of them. "I need the two of you to do me a very large favor. We have a lady spy in Atlanta who has been compromised. She goes by the name of Mrs. Heart. We need to get her out of Georgia and back north right away."

"How can we help?" Dawn asked.

"I need for the two of you to go to Atlanta and act as her maids. Zane and J.B. will escort you there and help you however much they can. Then they'll escort all of you north to the Kentucky state line, where someone will meet you and take the lady the rest of the way to Kentucky. It will take a few weeks to complete this mission. In fact, I don't expect you back until after the first of the new year. Are you two up for this?" he asked.

"Yes, sir," both girls said together.

"Very good. You need to leave at first light."

As they left the major's tent the girls were so excited they were almost jumping up and down. "We're out of here! I was afraid we would be stuck here for the rest of the war. And who knows how long that will be," Dawn said as they walked back to their tent to get ready for this new adventure.

"I can't wait to get out of here. I think this might be a long night," Stella replied.

✳✳✳✳✳✳✳✳✳✳✳✳✳✳✳✳✳✳✳✳

Because they were traveling through enemy territory, the rescuers had decided that it would be safest to travel at night, staying deep in the woods and avoiding all towns. Thus, it took them four days to reach Atlanta. They made camp five miles from the city. The next morning, dressed again as a Confederate soldier, Zane rode into town. He soon located the house he was looking for. He rode slowly past it then around the block to check out the rear of the property. He knew he couldn't approach the house until late that night, so he decided to explore the rest of the city for other possible escape routes. On his tour he had passed a nice café and decided to have some dinner. After that he checked into a small hotel located on the edge of the city about three blocks from Mrs. Heart's house. He planned on walking there that night.

Once in the room he decided not to get undressed but to just rest for a while. He was hoping to take a little catnap. After all, it had been a long time since he had slept in a real bed. But the moment he closed his eyes all he could think about was Beth. He was still worried about her. He felt she would be fairly safe from Confederate troops, but what would happen if and when Union troops passed her way? Despite his worrying he soon drifted off to sleep, but his mind was still on Beth. He began dreaming of the last time they were together.

When they had left the others after the picnic, they had walked about half a mile upstream until they had come across a green mossy place under a beautiful weeping willow tree. The moss was soft and cool and had beckoned to them to have a seat. This is where they had spent the next two hours. There was an old log close to the willow's trunk, so together they rolled up the old quilt Zane had brought and placed it on top of the log for a pillow to rest their heads on. Then they both sat leaning back on the old log with Beth's head on Zane's shoulder and his arm around her neck. Duke sniffed around for awhile then found a sunny spot where he laid down and went to sleep. Zane and Beth sat there for a long time listening to the stream as it ran over a small waterfall created by some vines and tree roots that had grown across the creek. It was a long time before they had felt the need to talk, and when they did they only wanted to talk about happy times. They had talked of the summer they had met in Indiana and of all the fun and adventure they and their friends had shared. They had had a good laugh when Beth asked Zane if he remembered the family of skunks they had almost tripped over. The most memorable recollection was of when they had found Stella and her brothers. For the first time in months they both enjoyed the peace and quiet for a few stolen minutes they would never forget.

Then Beth had asked, "What about the future, Zane? What's going to happen?"

"I have no idea, but when this war is over we'll find a way to be together. I promise." Zane knew in his heart that somehow they would be together. They just had to be.

Zane woke with a start. He opened his eyes and looked around, taking him a few seconds to remember where he was. He looked out the one window and saw that it was dark outside. He got up and lit a candle to check his watch for the time. He had slept for hours, it was almost time for him to make contact with Mrs. Heart; Heart being her code name.

Dressed all in black, Zane left the hotel by the back stairs. He walked the three blocks to her house. When he reached the house it was dark, not a light showing in any of the windows. The houses on both sides were also dark. Zane walked around the house checking until he found an unlocked window. He climbed in letting his eyes adjust to the dark room. He then went upstairs where the bedrooms were. He thought that the room at the front looked like it was the largest. So this most likely would be Mrs. Heart's bedroom. He crept down the hall to the door. When he tried the door knob he found it was unlocked. Very quietly he slipped into the room. This is when he heard the sound of a pistol being cocked. He froze in his steps.

"I don't know who's out there, but if you so much as breathe hard, they'll be digging a six-foot hole for you."

"Now who are you? And what are you doing sneaking around in my house?"

"Sorry ma'am I didn't aim to scare you. My name is Indiana. Major Odell sent me. I'm looking for a Mrs. Heart."

"Well I'll be, it's about time. I've been waiting for you for days. I'm going to light a lamp so we can see," Mrs. Heart told Zane. "By the way, I'm Mrs. Heart."

After she lit the lamp, Mrs. Heart, who Zane found out later was actually Ethel Smith, slipped on her dressing gown and motioned for Zane to have a seat in one of the matching winged back chairs that were setting in front of the fireplace. There was still a fire burning, so Zane walked over and warmed his hands, the night had turned chilly and the fire felt good. They both knew they needed to stay away from the windows.

Zane had expected to find a much younger woman. Mrs. Heart had to be in her late sixties. This could make their mission a lot harder. He soon found out her age was not going to be a problem.

Zane explained the plan of how they were going to get

her out of Atlanta. This only took a few minutes and he was ready to head back to the hotel. He had noticed a lot of guards all around the city when he had taken his ride earlier. He didn't want to run into any of them and cause them to be suspicious. So he had decided to spend the night at the hotel and head back to camp the next morning.

Just before Mrs. Heart let Zane out the back door he remembered to ask, "How many servants will you be taking with you, Mrs. Heart?"

Mrs. Heart looked at him and smiled, "Why, not a one young man."

"Surely there's a maid or a house boy." Zane knew all southern ladies had a personal servant or two.

"There was until last week," Mrs. Heart explained. "I sent her and my house boy north with a group of runaways. I've been taking care of myself waiting for you or someone to show up to get me ever since. And let me tell you, it's been a long week," she said with a chuckle.

Before leaving the house Zane had latched and locked the window he had found unlocked earlier.

When he got back to his hotel room he stretched out on the bed. He wasn't sleepy so he decided to do some major thinking. He laid his head on his crossed arms and stared up at the ceiling.

He wanted to think a bit more about Mrs. Heart. The Major had told them she was his wife's aunt. Zane smiled, thinking more like a great-aunt. She was spry enough, and it looked like she knew what to do with a gun. He hoped they could get her back up North safe.

Early the next morning Zane rode out to where he had left the others. He explained how Mrs. Heart was a little petite, grey headed lady. And she was very anxious to leave Atlanta behind her.

"Sounds like we've got our work cut out for us," J.B. said.

Stella shook her head, "I agree."

"I'm taking J.B. back to town with me to act as my servant. I've been able to purchase a small wagon from the local stable. So we'll be picking Mrs. Heart up tonight just as soon as her neighborhood is dark. I went out before day light this morning and I found a place we can sneak through the guards. Hopefully, we'll be back here by midnight. We'll stop only long enough for Dawn to jump in the back of the wagon. If we're stopped and questioned I'm Mrs. Hearts nephew come to escort her home to tend a dying sister. Dawn is her personal maid and Stella is her servant boy."

"I know," Dawn sighed. "I'll need to put on a dress and act shy, while Stella has all the fun. Oh well, guess one has to do what they can for the cause."

By the time Dawn finished her little speech everyone was laughing at her.

True to his word just as the moon reached high in the sky Dawn and Stella heard horses coming down the road, so far so good. But their luck was not going to last for long. They had decided to go west toward Alabama and then head north. They knew there weren't as many troops in Alabama as in

Georgia.

They hoped to find a small Inn about twenty miles from Atlanta. They had planned to make a quick rest stop there. When they reached the spot where the Inn was suppose to be they found that it had burnt down. J.B. inspected the ashes and reported that the ashes were cold so it had been days since the fire.

Everyone looked at Zane, he knew Mrs. Heart was tired and needed to rest. Now they would have to make a new plan.

Zane called Dawn over too the side, "Can you make her some kind of bed in the back of the wagon?"

"I'll manage some way," Dawn told him. "I'll get Stella to help me."

At least they could be grateful, the well and the out house were still intact.

The next morning, just as the sun was coming up and they were getting ready to leave, they heard a number of horses coming from the East.

"Well, this could be do or die," J.B. said as he took his horse and rifle and went into the woods.

Sure enough it was a Confederate patrol a small patrol of six men. They looked ruff, especially the leader. When the patrol saw the wagon they all pulled their guns. The leader and one man rode on in.

"What we got here," he asked. Taking aim and spitting a large plug of tobacco on the ground, just in front of Stella.

Zane, still dressed as a Confederate soldier, told him their story. Hoping they would believe him.

"Private," the leader told the man that was with him. "I think we'll just check that wagon for contraband before we let these people pass." All this time the other four rebels were holding guns on them.

The private opened all Mrs. Heart's trunks and baskets. All the time Mrs. Heart was fuming, that stupid man was throwing all her things on the ground. She looked as calm as the sea on a windless day. That is until he started throwing her underwear around and making a joke about the size of each piece.

That's when she jumped up off the log she had been seating on and started toward the wagon. Stella and Dawn were both standing behind her. Stella reached out and caught her by the arm. When Mrs. Heart turned to look at the girls, Stella ever so slowly shook her head and Dawn looked down at the log. Mrs. Heart just shut her eyes and with a grunt sat back down on the log.

After the Rebs had left Stella and Dawn started to laugh. Stella told Zane, "When he got to her underwear it was all Dawn and I could do to keep Mrs. Heart from taking her umbrella to that private.

Later after all her things were re-packed she told the girls, I don't know how but I surly hope those two pay for what they just did. I surly do."

J.B. stayed where he was to make sure the patrol didn't follow the wagon. About an hour later he caught up with the rest of the group.

"At first I thought we might have a problem. But after a few times of passing a jug around they headed North," J.B. reported.

After this the group made good time the rest of the day. They were only a few miles from the state line when they stopped for the night. This time they stopped in a small town. They knew Mrs. Heart needed a bed for the night. There was one small hotel with a one room dinning room. They felt they were lucky to find this. Dawn, being Mrs. Heart servant was allowed to stay in the same room as Mrs. Heart. Zane had decided to stay in the barn with Stella and J.B. This way if there was trouble they wouldn't all be in one place.

That night Zane accompanied Mrs. Heart to dinner in the dinning room. The rest of the group, being black had to eat outside.

After leaving the next morning, they traveled north then east again. It took them several days to reach Lexington, Kentucky, were Mrs. Heart's family was waiting for her.

Kentucky was a confederate state, but Mrs. Hearts home was far enough from Lexington she had assured them she would be safe.

The group had decided to take her all the way. They all liked her very much and wanted to make sure she got home safe and sound.

They arrived in Lexington on a chilly morning early in December. It had taken them a lot longer to make this trip then they had planned. They had stopped in as many small towns as they felt were safe so Mrs. Heart could rest.

The night before they reached Mrs. Heart's home she over heard the group talking. They thought she was asleep. But she was almost home and so anxious she just couldn't sleep. They had put up in a small road side Inn for the night. Mrs. Heart had a room on the ground floor, at the back of the Inn. When she went to her window she could see the young people were all still up. They had built a camp fire and were setting around it drinking coffee and talking. They all had such serious looks on their faces. Mrs. Heart felt like she just had to know what their problem was. She had become very fond of these young people. So she pulled a chair over to the window, and opened it just enough so she could listen to them talk.

"It's too late for us to go back across the mountains. We'll have to wait until spring now," Zane was explaining.

"What will we do in the mean time?" Dawn wanted to know.

"We have no place to stay and very little money left to buy food. And definitely not enough to rent a place," Stella added.

"Looks to me like we'll just have to hope we can find us some work or some Union camp," J.B told them.

Before they could say anything else they heard Mrs. Heart's window being raised.

"Y'all come over here, please," Mrs. Heart said.

They all looked at each other, then got up and walked over to her window.

"Mrs. Heart, are you OK?" Stella wanted to know.

"I'm fine child. I didn't mean to ease drop but you all looked so serious. I think I have the answer to your problem.

I actually don't live in Lexington. I own a horse farm outside of the city. Well, it used to be a horse farm. I'm not sure what's left of it now. I am sure it is going to need lots of work. So, if you could, I would appreciate it if you all could stay with me there and help me get my place back together, at least until spring. You'll have a roof over your heads and food to eat. And we can all spend Christmas together."

Zane answered for all of them, "We would love to help you Mrs. Heart. And thank you."

"That's wonderful news. I've been wondering how I was going to get my place back in order. So, I thank all of you.

"Before we get to Lexington I need to tell you a secret. My name is not Mrs. Heart but Ethel Smith. Mrs. Heart was my code name. I don't plan to ever use that name again," she said with a laugh. "It would please me so if all of you would call me Ethel. I feel like all of you are a part of my family."

"We all feel the same about you. But, I think we'll just call you Miss Ethel," Dawn told her.

The next day when they arrived at Miss Ethel's farm they were all in for a very big surprise. Miss Ethel's farm was closer to a plantation then a farm. When they started up the drive it looked deserted. But as they rode up the drive they could see smoke coming from a chimney in the back of the house.

J.B. rode ahead to check things out, he found a young black boy digging turnips in a small backyard garden. When he told the boy that Mrs. Smith was coming up the drive, the boy ran to the house. Yelling, "Mrs. Smith be home, Mrs. Smith be coming home."

By the time they reached the house the front porch was full of people, including Mrs. Odell the Majors wife.

Later in the day Zane and J.B. rode into Lexington to find a telegraph office. They needed to send a message to Major Odell. He would want to know that they had delivered their package. They had met his wife and she was OK. Also, they wouldn't be able to get back to camp until spring.

CHAPTER TWENTY-THREE

The Trip Back to Camp

Spring 1863

In January, the big news was that on January the first President Lincoln had signed a document "The Emancipation Proclamation." A document that proclaimed that all slaves held in rebellious areas were "then, thenceforward, and forever free." Although the proclamation actually freed no slaves at the time, it accomplished humanitarian and political purposes. Everyone knew this would ultimately free all slaves.

This document swayed England to support the Union in the war. England, also did not like the idea of slavery.

This document caused a lot of unrest in both the North and South. Many politicians both North and South felt the President was over stepping his bounds.

It seemed to make the Southern states that much madder and more determined that no one was going to tell them what to do.

In the North, people became more determined to free all

slaves and to make the South pay for all the trouble they were causing.

People were still angry over this when the group left Kentucky in late February. They had received a telegram form the Major telling them that he was moving his camp ten miles West of Jackson Mississippi. He was going to need their help, as soon as, they could get back to camp.

It took the group nine weeks to reach this new camp. The weather had been the worst in years. It seemed like it snowed every day.

There were both Confederate and Union troops everywhere. They had almost ridden into rebel camps a number of times. There were times when they even had to split up to be less noticeable.

To make things worse three weeks out, Dawn tripped over a tree stump and pulled a muscle in her right leg.

This meant they had to find a place to hole up for a few days. It just happened that Stella had been in this area before. "If, I remember right there was a deserted cabin a ways back in these woods. I think it is two maybe three miles from here. I'll take J.B. and we'll go for a look. Be back as quick as we can," Stella said.

"Guess that means I'm going for a walk," J.B. said as he started following Stella.

It was really getting cold and starting to get dark, when two hours later they returned.

"We were getting worried about you two," Zane told them.

"Sorry, about taking so long," J.B. told him. "We had a hard time finding the cabin and then we checked the surrounding area. Doesn't look like any ones been there in years. It's not in the best of condition, but it's got a good roof and a standing fireplace. We should be OK for a few days."

"Of course we had to chase a family of raccoons out and God only knows what else is living in there. But, as J.B. said, we'll have a roof over our heads and a fire to keep us warm," Stella added.

"I'm so cold and hungry that little cabin sounds like a castle to me," Dawn told them. By this time they were all laughing at her. They seemed to laugh at Dawn a lot.

J.B. reached down and picked Dawn up. "I think I'll just carry this one. I don't think she needs to ride a horse."

"Why, J.B. how gallant of you," Stella told him.

When they walked into the clearing in front of the cabin, Dawn looked at J.B., "Your right its no castle but it will do for a few days."

There were two windows in the front both had no kind of covering over them. What at one time had been a porch was gone and the outhouse looked like something had turned it over.

"Before you ask," J.B. told her, "We checked the well and the water is fine and there are plenty of downed trees for fire wood."

The next morning Zane and J.B. went off hunting and came back with a deer and some wild turnips and onions.

Stella made some stew for supper that night. She had found a pecan tree in the woods in back of the house, as well as a persimmon tree. She took the persimmons and made a pudding. She had also found some sassafras roots from which she made some hot tea. That was the best meal they had had since leaving Kentucky.

They had hoped Dawn would be ready to move in a few days. But, it took her almost two weeks to heal enough to walk on her own.

****

It was almost four weeks later before they found their camp. They were in for a big surprise. Major Odell's camp was larger than before, a lot more troopers and tents. When they were escorted to the Major's tent, he explained all of this to them, after they had told him about the last few months.

"It seems that we are now, not only a dispatch camp, but also we now have been joined by a fighting troop. There is a battle of wills going on at Vicksburg, and we all are to become a part of this."

"Why, Vicksburg, sir?" Zane asked.

"It seems that the rebels have been using Vicksburg as a port to help smuggle goods up and down the Mississippi River. The town has been surrounded for weeks now, completely cut off from the rest of the world. They tell me the people are out of food and are starting to eat their horses and in some cases even rats. All farmers have been stopped from entering the city, by road or by boats. Many families have dug out cave-like dwellings in the side of hills. They are living in these caves to get away from the shelling that is going on both night and day."

"Most of these people still believe the Confederate army is going to save them. They are a proud group of people and are not going down with out a fight."

"How awful," Dawn said in disgust.

"Sir, how long has this been going on?" Zane asked.

"Well let's see, it's the middle of May, about five weeks give or take a day or two," the Major told them.

"I can't imagine what those poor souls are going through, especially the children. They must be scared to death, as well as hungry. How much longer do you think they can hold out?" Stella wanted to know.

"Our spies tell us their starting to weaken. In fact there have been a few families to dessert the town in the last few days," the Major told them.

"Well, sir," Zane asked, "how can we help? None of us has ever done any fighting. But we all know how to use a rifle and a shot gun."

"It looks like we need people to run messages from camp to camp, someone that can be trusted and knows how to get around in the woods. So, it's been decided that you four are the best in our area. So are you all up to this assignment?" he asked.

After looking at the others, Zane told the Major, "Yes, sir, what do we do first?"

You'll need to work in teams of two, I'll let you decide who's is on which team," the Major told them.

"That won't be hard to decide. Stella and I'll work as a team and Dawn and J.B. on the other. That is if that's OK with all of you," Zane asked. He knew this would be all right, knowing Dawn and J.B. would want to be together.

"Sounds like a plan to me," J.B. replied, winking at Dawn. Both girls answered by nodding their heads.

"When do we get started?" Dawn wanted to know.

"I have two very important messages that need to be delivered tonight. So, if you'll be rested enough I'll send both teams out tonight."

So, for the next few days that is what the four did. They had a few close calls, because there were a few Confederate troops still in the area.

But, the major had been right. On May twenty-second Vicksburg surrendered.

After that event, the whole camp was moved back to Georgia. When they arrived at the new camp site they received a message telling of another large battle in Gettysburg, Pennsylvania in July. It had lasted for thirteen days. There had been thousands of casualties on both sides, over forty thousand wounded or missing. Both sides were claiming victory. But, with so many lost who could say for sure.

For the next few months the pairs ran messages from camp to camp. Many times they almost stumbled into the enemy. The summer was as hot and humid as the last winter had been cold. The war was getting more furious. Both sides were ready to end the war, but neither were ready to give up. There were battles every where, neither side wanting to lose;

after all their pride was important. During this time many lost their lives or were maimed for life. Many lost legs, arms, their sight, and some even their minds.

Up to that time the hospital had used only male nurses. These men were now needed for other duties, mostly on the fighting lines. As much as many thought it was wrong, women became nurses. In fact there had already been many women working as nurses, dressed as boys.

The leader of this movement for women to work in the hospitals was a Massachusetts born school teacher, a Miss Clara Barton. Small of build and somewhat timid she knew what she needed to do to help her country. So, she started by volunteering to organize the gathering of supplies and nursing services. It was later learned that in 1864 she went with the Union army to Richmond Virginia. After that she was credited with starting the American Red Cross.

By December of 1863 the fighting had slowed down again. It was very hard to move troops, camps and artillery in the winter.

CHAPTER TWENTY-FOUR

Christmas at Rivers View

Winter 1863

Knowing their camp was not likely to move until early spring, Zane went to the Major to ask permission for the group to go to Rivers View to check on Beth. As soon as, they were given the OK they headed south. They knew it was going to be a hard and dangerous trip. Zane was determined to go and the rest of the group didn't want him going by himself.

Again because of the dangers it took them a lot longer to reach their destination. It was the week before Christmas when they finally reached Rivers View.

They had sat in the woods for a long time watching the house to make sure they would be safe. At first they thought no one was there. No smoke was coming from the chimneys and they hadn't seen any movement around the barn. Then they saw Honey stick her head out of the summer kitchen, looking around then making a dash for the house.

"Well, someone's here, but something is not right," J.B.

commented. J.B. commented.

"Your right and I've got to find out what's happening," Zane told them.

"Tell us what you want us to do," Dawn asked.

"Guess I'll have to wait until dark. Then I'm going in. You'll need to wait here just in case I need help."

So, as soon as, it got dark Zane was on his way. Staying in the shadows of the building, trees and house hoping no one would see him. He was grateful this was a cloudy night and the clouds were hiding the moon. When Zane had last been here they had agreed on a secret knock. He didn't want to scare Dilly again. Zane used this knock and the back door opened at once.

When he had slipped in the door his first question was, "Where is Beth?"

"Oh! Mr. Zane I be so glad to see you. Miss Denise is very ill and Miss Beth she gone to Savannah. She hope to bring her momma home. But she be gone for over a week. I is really worried about those ladies," Dilly told him.

Zane wanted to know, "Is the house still being watched?"

"I 'speck not, if them spies are still around they surely followed Miss Beth to town," Dilly answered.

Zane slipped back out the door to go get the others. When they were all safe in the house Zane told them what Dilly had just told him.

"What we gonna do, Mr. Zane?" Dilly wanted to know. All the time wiping tears from her face with her apron.

"We'll give her one more day. If she's not here by dark tomorrow night I'm going to Savannah," Zane told her.

"Zane, are you crazy man? Stop and think how dangerous that's going to be. Do you really think Beth would want you to put yourself in that kind of danger?" J.B. asked him.

"I know, but I have to make sure Beth's OK. I couldn't live with myself if anything happens to her," was all Zane could say.

By this time Sunny had come to the house. Bow had gone with Beth to Savannah. Dilly and Honey fixed them all some supper. When they had finished eating, they all wondered off to the library where Sunny had built a fire for them. There each found a place to rest and wait. Momma Jo had brought quilts down stairs for each of them.

"You all look plum tuckered out. You gets you selves a good night rest and we talk some more in the morning.

✳✳✳✳✳✳✳✳✳✳✳✳✳✳✳✳✳✳✳✳

Beth would be so glad to get home. Her mother was so ill. The doctor had told her it was depression. Her mother hadn't heard from Eugene or Robert in months. She had just worried herself into this state of mind. The doctor had no idea how to help her.

Beth had insisted on taking Denise home to Rivers View. It was almost Christmas and they always spent Christmas at Rivers View. Beth was determined this year wasn't going to be any different. They had been traveling for days. The trains were so full of soldiers they had to wait for a train twice. She was so glad Bow was with her she just didn't know how she would have made it this far without him. Finally they had reached Metter where they had left an old wagon and mule at the livery stable. Beth was so glad that they were still there. She had been so afraid that someone would steal one or both.

When Bow pulled up at the train station with both, Beth almost fainted she was so relieved.

"Mother, only a few more miles and we'll be home," Beth reassured her mother.

Denise looked up at Beth with tears running down her face, "How will Eugene and Robert find me? I told them I would wait in Savannah for them?"

"They'll find you Mother I promise."

Zane had pulled up a chair to the front window so he could watch the drive for Beth. But because he had not slept the last two nights he had fallen into a sound sleep.

He was awakened by voices on the front porch. When he looked out the window and saw Beth he started shouting for the others to come quick. They had all went to the kitchen so as not to wake Zane.

All this noise scared Denise and she started crying. Beth was crying also, not because she was scared but because she was so happy to see Zane and her friends.

J.B. went to help Bow get Denise in the house, out of the cold. When they got to the stairway Bow picked Denise up and carried her up the stairs. Honey leading the way, she ran ahead to turn down the bed, leaving Denise in Momma Jo's and Honey's care Bow and J.B. went back down stairs to the library where the others were.

Beth was explaining about her mother's illness and the long trip home. All this time Zane had been holding her hands; they were so cold. He was rubbing them to help warm them up. He was so relieved to see her and to know she was safe.

Later, everyone except Denise and Momma Jo were in the kitchen eating supper. Dilly with the help of Dawn and Stella had but together a small feast. They had fried chicken, black eyed peas, boiled potatoes, corn bread with honey and peach pie. Dilly had used dried peaches to make the pies.

After everyone had finished eating Beth wanted to know why they were all here, and what they had been up to since she had last seen them.

They each took turns telling her about their many adventures, and how they couldn't keep Zane away any longer.

While the others were helping to clean the kitchen Zane and Beth wandered off to the library for a few minutes alone. No one was going to bother them, but they didn't know that, then.

When they reached the library, Zane closed the door behind them. When he turned around Beth was standing there with her arms open waiting for him. They hugged for a long time. Then Zane did something he had wanted to do for a very long time. He took Beth's face in his hands and bent down and kissed her. She was so happy she kissed him back.

"Oh, Zane I love you so much. I've been so worried about you. And I've kept my promise to not help any more run-a -ways."

Zane laughed at her last statement, "That's only because they don't need your help anymore, my dear."

Together they moved a sofa in front of the fire place and sat there for hours just holding hands. It was hours later when Beth awoke to find Zane still asleep. She sat there for a long time just looking at him. Then she laid her head back on his shoulder and went back to sleep. When they awoke the next morning someone had been in and added wood to the fire and put a quilt over them.

The next morning Bow and Sunny came stomping up the front steeps carrying a Yule log for the fire place. Then everyone bundled up and went to the woods to cut a Christmas tree. That night they decorated it with wild berries and home made ornaments. The girls had taken scraps of material and cut out all kinds of ornaments to hang on the tree. The men had tied pine cones together to make a garland to go around the tree. Usually there were candles to light the tree, but not this year. There was even an angel for the top. Beth told them the story of how she and Rosa Mae had made the angel when they were little girls.

Momma Jo had helped them cut it out of some old white muslin. They had used wire to shape the wings and had stuffed the head with cotton and had painted on the face. For hair, Beth had cut just enough off the end of her own hair to cover the back of the angels head.

Meanwhile, the men had all gone hunting and found a

wild turkey for Christmas dinner. Dilly had stuffed the turkey with corn bread stuffing. With the help of Stella and Dawn they had managed to also have wild rice with pecans, baked sweet potatoes, turnips, lima beans and hominy. And, for a surprise Stella had baked two pecan pies. Bow and Sunny had supplied the pecans from the ten pecan trees in the near by woods.

Together they had all sat around the dining room table and enjoyed their meal. At first the servants felt awkward setting at the dining room table. They had never sat in a dining room to eat before. Beth had insisted that they were all one big family now, and she wouldn't have them eat anywhere else. It only took a few minutes until everyone felt like this was where they had always eaten.

Soon everyone was talking and laughing and having a good time. Even Denise accepted them all eating together. Afterwards, everyone, even the men, helped clean up the mess. Zane and Bow washed the dishes, J.B. and Sunny dried. The girls were in charge of putting everything away. They had sent Momma Jo and Honey upstairs to keep Denise company, at least until she went to sleep.

Poor Dilly was beside herself. She was told to take a seat and prop her feet up. Her only job was to supervise. She had never in her whole life seen anything like what these young people were doing, especially the white ones.

After all this activity, they were ready to retire to the Library where there was a nice fire burning in the fireplace. That was the best time to sit around the Christmas tree and sing a few Christmas carols. The group spent a quiet but happy Christmas and New Years together. There were no presents; no one needed any. Just being together and knowing that they were all safe was presents enough. Just one more thing could have made it a perfect Christmas. They all wished Rae might be there with them.

Right after New Years Day it was time for the group to be off. They had to get back to camp. Saying goodbye was even harder this time than the last.

They were all grateful that Denise seemed to be doing a lot better.

CHAPTER TWENTY-FIVE

The End of the War Is Near

1864

By the time the group headed back to camp it was 1864. Each was hoping that this year would see an end to this terrible war. They all wanted to get back to their families and get on with their lives.

By the time they reached camp the troops were starting to move again.

In April they were told that a General Sherman and his troops were on the move. At first, no one was for sure where he was headed. But by the first of May everyone knew. General Sherman had declared that he was headed for the sea. He was going through Atlanta and Savannah to get there.

They would destroy whatever got in the way. And destroy it all, they did. They destroyed railroad tracks, telegraph lines and any thing they thought the Confederate army could use. But the worst thing was the destroying of dozens of plantations. They looted and then burned them to the ground, leaving the elderly, women and children with nothing.

When they reached Atlanta the Rebels fought stubbornly to defend their city. But it was not to be. On September second President Lincoln was waiting in the telegraph office in Washington D.C. when General Sherman sent a telegraph letting the President know, "Atlanta is ours and fairly won."

Once inside Atlanta General Sherman ordered that the railroad station and tracks be destroyed. He was not taking any chances that once they left the city the Rebels would sneak back in and use these. There were fires set all over town. It didn't take long for these fires to spread and soon there was almost nothing left of Atlanta.

After leaving Atlanta, General Sherman and his troops headed for Savannah.

The road they were taking would put them only a few miles from Rivers View. Zane knew this and was very worried about Beth and her family.

He went to the Major and asked him if there was anything he could do to help Beth?

Major Odell knew who Beth was and how she had helped many runaways. He also knew how important she was to Zane and his friends.

The Major looked at Zane and started scratching his nose. "Um, according to the dispatch I just received it should take General Sherman a good week, maybe two, to reach that area. I can't send you and Stella, because you're already assigned to another mission. But, I can send Dawn and J.B. with a message, explaining the situation and the facts and request that they pass her plantation by. I can't promise anything but we'll try to do our best."

"Thank you sir; that's all I can ask for," Zane told the Major.

'Three days later Dawn and J.B. delivered the message to General Sherman. They had been told not to wait for an answer. They were needed back at camp, as soon as possible. They weren't even told what was in the message. They had no idea until Zane told them a few days later.

After reading the message, General Sherman sent a corporal and three privates to Rivers View. They were to assure this Miss Beth that they would not be visiting her home.

Sunny was walking across the yard when he saw the Yankees coming up the drive. Oh, no please not Rivers View he thought to himself, as he started running to the house to warn the others.

He stuck his head in the summer kitchen and then ran straight to the library where Beth and Denise were. Telling everyone, "The Yankees are coming up the drive."

Beth closed her eyes and took a deep breath. She had been dreading this. She had prayed that there was some way that her home could be spared. Now the only thing she could think of was that it was River Views time to be put to the torch.

When the corporal and the three privates rode up to the veranda he was met by all the residents.

The corporal and one private stepped down from their horses, both removing their hats.

"I'm looking for a Miss Beth Taylor. Would you be her?" the corporal asked.

Beth stepped forward, "Yes, I'm Beth Taylor."

"I have a message here from General Sherman." Reaching into his jacket pocket he pulled out a sealed envelope and handed it to Beth.

Beth held the envelope for a few seconds before she opened it. She didn't think they sent messages to warn you that they were going to burn down your home.

After opening the envelope and reading the message Beth had to sit down. She walked half way up the stairs and sat down, reading it again.

Miss Taylor,

I have received a request from a Major Odell. He has told me how much help you have been to the Underground Railroad. He and four of your friends have asked that we spare your home.

I am glad to tell you that we will not be invading your plantation,

With your permission I've sent two privates to camp on your property. They will ensure you and your family's safety.

On behalf of all the U. S. Army I would like to say Thank You, for your help in the past.

May God keep you safe through the rest of this war.

Sincerely,

General William Sherman

Beth was still in a daze when Momma Jo sat down beside her. "Child, the corporal is asking you a question."

"I'm sorry corporal. What was the question?"

"Is it alright to leave the privates?"

"Yes, we would appreciate their presence very much. I would like to offer the hospitality for them to take their meals with us here in the house."

"On behalf of the privates, I thank you. I know they will enjoy that very much. Now I will leave you in their hands. They will know how to contact me if you require any assistance in the future."

The corporal and his private mounted their horses. They turned their horses around and rode back down the drive. When they reached halfway the two privates that were staying dismounted and started setting up their camp.

Beth turned around and saw the look on everyone's face. They were all still scared and had no idea what was happening. Beth explained part of what the message had said. She couldn't say anything about the Underground Railroad part in front of her mother. Nevertheless, they were all so relieved. Denise started crying and the rest started cheering.

The corporal, hearing this rode off with a smile. Miss Beth seemed like a very nice young lady. He was glad for her family.

✳✳✳✳✳✳✳✳✳✳✳✳✳✳✳✳✳✳✳✳

One day, a few weeks later, Dawn and J.B. returned to camp after a two day mission. When they walked into camp everyone was cheering. President Lincoln had been re-elected on November the eighth.

On December the tenth General Sherman and his army reached the vicinity of Savannah, causing many of its citizens to evacuate the city. Rumor had it that many had escaped to South Carolina.

It was also reported that the Confederate troops left their camp fires burning, after spiking their cannons and leaving the city behind them. They had even set their navy yard and vessels on fire to prevent the Union Army from capturing them.

On December the twenty-second General Sherman once again, sent the President a telegraph. He was offering Savannah with its twenty-five thousand bales of cotton as a Christmas present.

General Sherman gave the order that the city was to be spared the torch. For their own safety and that of their families many of the citizens decided to be hospitable to the Union troops and especially General Sherman. Word was passed from camp to camp that a Mr. Charles Green had offered his home to General Sherman to use for his headquarters and living space. From there he could control a large area of Georgia. The Union troops were all laughing. It sounded like the rebels were coming around, thanks to General Sherman and his march across Georgia.

A month after the surrender, a fire did break out in an ammunition depot. The depot was located downtown, the fire spread causing more than one hundred buildings and homes to be lost.

The news papers reported that there were rumors that the loyal Confederates, in Savannah, knew that this was the end. So, they had decided to destroy the depot so the Union Army couldn't use it.

CHAPTER TWENTY-SIX

Zane Gets In Trouble

Fall 1864

Zane was really worried about Beth. He had no idea if she still had a home or not. Had the message the Major sent done any good, since most of the fighting in this area seemed to be over. Most of their work was done. Word had it that there were still a few battles in the South and East of where they were camped. He, again, went to ask permission for this group to go to Rivers View.

The Major knew how worried all the friends had been so he was prepared for this request. Before Zane could open his mouth Major Odell looked at him and smiled, "Go, man and take your friends. I'll see you back here in a few weeks, that is, if there is still a war on. You might do a little spying on the way. Bring me back a report of what you see."

"Thank you, sir," was all Zane said as he backed out of the Major's tent.

They had traveled for two days when they decided to split up. They knew that the closer they got to Savannah there would be more chances of running into enemy troops.

Zane was riding down a small dirt trail just off the side of the main road hoping no one would see him, when out of the bushes jumped a renegade group of rebels. One look told Zane that they were deserters.

As they surrounded him, the leader, who still wore his army jacket with sergeant stripes; picked up a stick and started poking Zane and Puddles. "Well looky what's we got ourselves boys. I think he's a Yankee. Am I right boy?"

Zane just looked at this man and didn't say a thing. At the same time they recognized each other. This sergeant was the same man and patrol that had stopped the group when they were escorting Mrs. Heart from Atlanta. Zane knew he was in a lot of trouble. He could tell by this man's face. He was out for revenge. He could also tell right away that they all had been drinking.

"Now, here boys," the sergeant told his companions, "is the same boy that helped that old lady spy escape. Remember how much trouble that cost us, cause we let her slip through our fingers?"

"Are you sure, sergeant?" one of the deserters asked.

"Of course I'm sure. Now I'm a thinking this boy owes us. How about you boys? What say we have us a little fun?"

"Sounds good to us, what's you got in mind, Sergeant?" one of the deserters asked.

"First let's get him off that fancy horse. I been looking to replace my own since the army took mine. And I think we had better get ourselves off this trail and a little deeper into the woods. Wouldn't want nobody to spoil our fun, now would we?"

At first Zane tried to fight them off, but soon found that there was no way he could take all three of them. The sergeant was short and heavy set. But the other two were tall and lean and looked like seasoned fighters. So they soon had him gagged and tied. Then they dragged him deeper into the woods, with the sergeant now riding Puddles.

When they had gone about half a mile the sergeant found a small clearing and called a halt. "This looks like a good place to me. Tie that boy up to that tree over there."

While his men were doing his bidding he found himself a tree stump to sit on and pulled a bottle of whiskey out of his jacket pocket. After he took a drink he passed the bottle to his men.

"Well, boys I'm thinking we got us a spy here a Yankee spy at that. And you know how I feel about spies. I say we make him suffer a lot, but just a little at a time."

Both of the sergeant's men laughed. And the sergeant took another drink and again passed the bottle around.

Zane knew this was going to be a long day. He knew at this point all he could do was pray and hope the others found him, and soon.

✳✳✳✳✳✳✳✳✳✳✳✳✳✳✳✳✳✳✳

The group was to meet up by midnight; when Zane didn't show up everyone started to worry. "We'll wait till morning, then we'll backtrack and find him," J.B. told the girls.

When Zane hadn't shown up by daylight the group was on their way back to where they had last seen Zane. They reached this spot by late morning. Right away J.B. started following Zane's trail. It didn't take him long until he found where there had been a scuffle. There were signs where someone had been dragged off into the woods. J.B., as well as the girls, knew that the someone was Zane.

They all knew that they would have to travel with care. They had no idea what they were going to find. It didn't take J.B. long until he could tell they were tracking three men and a horse. One was being dragged, he was sure this had to be Zane.

They hadn't rode very far when they found the make shift- camp. But, it was what they saw that made all of them very angry and sick.

There on the ground were three rebel deserters. It didn't take long to figure out that they were all passed out. They were all on their backs and snoring so loudly that it sounded like a family of bears. Stella pointed to two empty whiskey bottles that were left on the ground.

It was the sight of Zane tied to a tree that made them so angry. They weren't sure if he was alive or dead.

Very quietly J.B. motioned to the girls. He pulled the rope he wore from around his waist, and headed for the unconscious Sergeant. Both girls did the same, each heading for a different man. As soon as, all three had been tied up they all ran to Zane. Right away they knew he was alive but in really bad shape.

J.B. cut him down from the tree and the girls lowered him

to the ground.

Dawn looked at the others, "They've used him for fun. What kind of animals are these?"

"I'll say just about as bad as they get," Stella answered.

Zane was unconscious. He couldn't have seen them or talked anyway. Both eyes were black and blue and swollen shut. His lips were busted open and swollen as well. He had been beaten really bad. His back was a mass of welts where he had been beaten with a stick, which Dawn found on the ground laying next to the sergeant. One leg was broken and both hands were swollen. They couldn't tell if his hands or fingers were broken or not because of the swelling.

They did what they could to make him comfortable until they could get him to a doctor. Dawn and Stella had treated his wounds as best they could, knowing that whatever they did might not be enough to save him.

While J.B. made a stretcher to tie behind Puddles, the girls went to work on the deserters. They dragged each to a different tree and tied each so they couldn't see the others. Then, they gagged them with their own dirty socks. It would be a long time before they got away, if ever.

Then they went to help J.B. First they covered the stretcher with dry pine needles. Stella had found some Spanish moss hanging from some nearby trees. They all knew that many people in the South used this moss to stuff their mattresses with. She and Dawn gathered as much as they could find. They covered the pine needles with the moss, hoping this would help cushion the stretcher. They covered all this with their army blankets and then as carefully as possible put

Zane on top. They laid him on his stomach, because his back was so torn up. Stella and Dawn again cleaned his wounds as best they could. They then covered his back with one of J.B.'s clean shirts and a blanket. J.B. led Puddles. The girls followed so they could keep an eye on Zane. The other three horses had been tied together and whoever was leading Puddles also had to lead the other horses.

They soon decided that this ride was too rough on Zane, so they all took turns, one leading Puddles and the other two carrying the other end of the stretcher.

They had remembered passing a Union camp a few miles back. So this is where they headed. When they reached this camp they went straight to the hospital tent.

The doctor took one look at Zane and shook his head. "What ever happened to this man," he wanted to know? All this time he was motioning for the orderlies to put Zane on an examining table. After the doctor had done all he could for Zane he told J.B. and the girls, "The best thing for this young man is to get him home. His physical wounds should heal in time. But it will take a lot of time and care to heal his mind. Let's just hope he's strong enough to overcome the odds."

J.B. went straight to the telegraph tent and sent a message to the Major, requesting for all of them to be released from further duty so they could take Zane home.

An hour later they received a return message from the Major. "Take the boy home. All of you are released of duty. God bless all of you. And thank all of you for what you have done for your country."

The doctor suggested they wait a couple of days. He was giving Zane small doses of laudanum to ease his pain and to help him sleep. The doctor instructed the girls on how much and how often to administer the drugs, on their trip home. He told them that rest was the best medicine he could prescribe.

It took a month to get Zane home. It would have taken twice as long if Dawn hadn't accidentally run into Night Hawk in Nashville, Tennessee. She had been at the river front with J.B. looking for a way to get up river instead of across land. They knew this would be easier on Zane and a lot faster. They would have to stable their horses and come back for them later.

Dawn couldn't believe her eyes when she saw this Indian talking to a trader.

"J.B., I know that Indian; it's Night Hawk. You know we've told you about him many times. I think our prayers have been answered.

"Night Hawk, Night Hawk, it's me Dawn," she was yelling as she ran down the wharf. She threw her arms around his neck and gave him a great big hug.

Night Hawk was so surprised to see her, he just danced around with her in his arms. His Little One would be so glad to see Dawn and know she was alright. Now if he just knew about Zane.

When Dawn could stop hugging him and could talk without crying she introduced him to J.B. and told him why they were in Nashville.

"Take me to Zane. I want to see him for myself. And yes we'll get him home just as soon as we can," Night Hawk told her.

Night Hawk and J.B. soon found an old raft that nobody claimed. They fixed it up and soon had Zane, Dawn and J.B. aboard. Stella was going to ride with Night Hawk in his canoe.

Night Hawk had a friend from his tribe with him. This friend volunteered to take care of their horses and bring them to Indiana.

With Night Hawk as their guide they made good time on the river. By this time most of the swelling had gone down in Zane's face and hands and his leg was healing. They were no longer giving him anything for his pain. He hardly talked to any of them. He just sat and stared into space. They were so afraid that he might never be the same.

Stella had explained to Night Hawk how they had found Zane and how much better he now was. The doctor said, "it would take longer for his mind to heal than the rest of his body."

They were all surprised and so happy that by the time they reached the Wabash River at Mt. Vernon, Zane was a lot better. He was talking more and even started to help pole the raft.

They all were feeling better because they knew they were almost home.

CHAPTER TWENTY-SEVEN

Rae's Special Journey

1865

It was now late August. Dawn, Stella and Zane had all made it home safe and sound. Well not everyone was sound. Zane still had bad dreams about the time he was captured and almost killed. Thanks to his friends he was home now. His leg and hands had healed. The leg only bothered him when it rained. The scars on his back had healed, but not his mind. There were nights when he still had bad dreams.

No one had heard from Beth and her family in almost a year. He had wanted to contact her before he left Georgia, but he was just too weak.

J.B. had finally convinced him that he needed to go home to heal. They would find Beth, as soon as he was strong enough. Well he was strong enough now and the war was over. He had decided to head back to Georgia on the first of September. He had to find Beth if it took him the rest of his life.

On their trip home Night Hawk had told them, "I took

all of you South. Now I'm taking all of you North to your homes. Besides bringing all of you home at the same time will make my Little One very, very happy. And I wish to make her happy."

The trip took a week longer than usual because they had to stop for Zane to rest. The first few days they really weren't sure if Zane was going to live or not. They were afraid he had given up. But, Night Hawk had his medicine bag with him and Stella also knew a lot about healing. So together they doctored Zane all the way home. Now he was feeling strong and healthy again, thanks to all his friends help.

Rae had been so happy when Grant rode over to tell her that the gang was home. He told her and her family about Zane, but that he was getting better now and was going to be OK.

Thomas sent Alan over to Dawn's farm to get her family, so that they could all go to Grants.

Within an hour they were all together. Everyone was hugging each other with big tears of happiness running down their cheeks, even the men.

Bessie was with them but not Gerald. He had been gone for almost two years. Bessie hadn't heard from him in six months. The last letter she had received was dated December 1864. She now had a little three year old girl, Holly and an eighteen month baby boy Hayward. Gerald had never seen his son. She prayed every night that Gerald would be home soon. She missed him so much.

Grampa Teddy had stayed at home. He was just not well enough to travel, even a short distance. Dawn was anxious to get home and see Grampa as well as to introduce him to J.B. She had already told her folks that she and J.B. were getting married before the summer was over. Were they ever surprised.

Thomas had looked J.B. up and down, "Guess you look good enough for our daughter. So, if that's what our Dawn wants; that's what she'll get." Then he reached out to shake J.Bs hand. J.B. reached out and took Thomas's hand, "Thank you sir. She's a hand full but I promise to take good care of her." Everyone started laughing, even Dawn.

Rae was so glad to see all her friends, especially Night Hawk. It was all she could do to keep from running to him and throwing her arms around his neck. When she looked in his eyes she could tell he felt the same. She had been so worried. They had not seen each other in almost four months. Night Hawk just moved his lips, and told her later. Rae just blinked her eyes and nodded with a big smile on her face.

Stella was anxious to go home to Illinois. She had really missed her brothers and her new family. It was decided that Night Hawk would leave to take her home early the next morning. Rae wanted her to spend that night with her. She wanted to talk to Stella. She needed her help.

Rae had stayed at home while all the others had been off on a long adventure. Now she was ready for her own adventure.

Early the next morning J.B. went with Night Hawk to the river to help him uncover his canoe. Were they ever in for a surprise. Waiting for them was not just Stella but also Rae. Night Hawk and Rae had talked the night before about their own future. But in the end they just didn't know what to do. After talking to Stella, Rae had made up her mind. She had left a note for her family.

I know this is no surprise but Night Hawk and I are in love. I don't know how our being together is going to work but I have to find out. I have decided to go with him to take Stella home. He knows my family and now I need to know his. I don't know if they will accept me or not but I have to find out. Night Hawk does not know of my plan to join him and Stella today. It will be a surprise for him. I hope you understand what I am doing and will wish us the best. We will be home in a few weeks.

> Love you all,
> Your daughter
> Rae

Night Hawk smiled at Stella, "I see you have a few extra things to take home with you?"

"Actually none of these extra bags are mine, they belong to Rae. "

"Does this mean what I think it means?" Night Hawk questioned Rae.

"Yes, I've left my family a note. I told them I would be home in a few weeks. Now it is our turn."

Night Hawk went to Rae and put his arms around her and

kissed her forehead. He then shook hands and thanked J.B. for his help. Looking at Stella he said," My Little One has spoken so I guess it's off we go."

"But, Rae," J.B. said, "What ever will I tell Dawn? You know she won't get married until you get back."

Night Hawk looked at Rae, "Tell her I will have my Little One back in three weeks."

When Rae and Night Hawk returned in three weeks there would be a big surprise waiting for them, and everyone else.

✽✽✽✽✽✽✽✽✽✽✽✽✽✽✽✽✽✽✽✽

Rae and Night Hawk did a lot of talking on their trip. Night Hawk told Rae about his family and friends at his camp. He described how it was to live in a tepee and cook all their meals around a camp fire. The women took care of everything that had to do with the camp and the man's responsibility was to do all the hunting and to protect their families at all times.

Rae asked, "Do the women ever get to go fishing or hunting? Please, tell me yes."

She was really surprised when Night Hawk told her, "only when we're away from the others."

"I hope we're away from the others a lot," Rae told him.

Night Hawk just laughed at her, "We will try as often as we can."

While they were having this discussion Rae was watching

the river bank.

"Oh, look at all those trees that have fallen down? Was that caused by the flood last year, in February? There are dozens of them just lying every where."

"Yes, and wait until we round the curve ahead of us. You will see where a whole farm was washed away, the house, barn and all the out buildings. I understand that this was one of the worst floods anyone remembers on the Wabash, Ohio and Mississippi rivers. Hundreds lost their homes and many small towns were washed away."

"How awful that had to have been. We were so lucky to be far enough from the river to not have lost anything," Rae said just shaking her head in wonder.

A week later when Rae and Night Hawk arrived at his village everyone had stopped and stared at them. Night Hawk led Rae straight to Lone Star's tepee. Lone Star had heard all the excitement so he had come out of his tepee to see what was happening. When he saw his brother with Rae he was very pleased. When they were close enough the two brothers put their hands on each others shoulders, both smiling.

"I have been waiting for this day for many moons, my brother. To know you are safe and you have brought our little sister for a visit." Lone Star walked over to Rae and they shared a hug.

Whispering in her ear, Lone Star asked "Want to help me pull a joke on my brother?"

Rae nodded her head and whispered, "Oh, yes."

Little Dove had followed her husband out of their tepee.

She didn't know what to make of her husband hugging a white girl. There had been very few whites in their village and never a female.

"Come Little Dove meet our sister. I have told you about our friends in Indiana. This is Rae. We must have a feast to welcome Night Hawk home and to make our little sister welcome."

All the time Lone Star was talking he had his back to Night Hawk. He was having a hard time not laughing.

Then Lone Star took Rae's hand and started to lead her into his tepee. It was then that Little Dove remembered, Rae's red hair and Night Hawks vision. Yes she remembered now. So she decided to have a little fun at Night Hawks expense.

"Yes, yes, I remember now you told me how she was just like a little sister to you and Night Hawk." Little Dove started to follow Lone Star and Rae into their tepee

Rae was looking at Night Hawk, like she didn't know what to do or say.

"Stop," Night Hawk shouted. "Enough; Little One has come here with me not as my sister, but to be my bride. We wish to be married in my village in two days, so stop this little sister stuff."

Rae, Lone Star and Little Dove started laughing.

"Oh, so you think to make fun of my love, two days Lone Star, two days." And he stomped off to find his mother.

By this time everyone, except Night Hawk was laughing.

In two days the tribe had organized a feast fit for a king.

Little Dove and her mother-in-law, Moon Beam, had helped Rae to erect and supply the bride tepee.

On the night before her wedding, Rae asked Little Dove, "What am I going to wear? I want Night Hawk to be proud of me. But, I didn't bring a thing to wear for a wedding."

"I have thought of that also," Little Dove told her. You and I are almost the same size. How would you like to wear my wedding dress?"

"Oh! Are you sure? Night Hawk told me about your wedding and how beautiful you and your dress were."

"I must remember to thank him," Little Dove said. Then she went over to a wicker trunk and pulled out her wedding dress. When she held it up in front of Rae all Rae could do was cry. "Are you sure, really sure about me wearing your dress?"

"Yes, Little One, I am sure," Little Dove knew she had made a wise decision.

"Please, can we not tell Night Hawk? I want it to be a surprise for him."

"It will be our little secret, until tomorrow," Little Dove agreed.

When Rae awoke the next morning, even before she opened her eyes she was smiling. Today was the day she and Night Hawk were to be married. She was a little sad that her family and friends were not with them. But, she and Night Hawk had decided they would have another wedding just for them when they got home.

"Wake up sleepy one," Little Dove said to Rae. "We have

much to do before your wedding." And much to do there was. Rae would never have dreamed what all there was to do. When she and Little Dove left the tepee to go to the creek to bathe, they were followed by all of Night Hawks female family, that being his mother, sisters and cousins. When they reached the creek they all took off all their cloths and waded into the water. Rae didn't know what to think of this. She, Dawn and Beth had gone swimming before, but never without any clothes.

"Come, Little One," Stormy, her future sister-in-law said. We will help you bathe and get you ready for your wedding."

Well, Bessie had always said, when in Rome do as the Romans do. Rae decided this must be her Rome.

When Rae got in the water all the ladies started to help her take a bath. Some were soaping her back some even wanted to help her wash her front. This is where Rae put up her hands, looking at Little Dove shaking her head.

Little Dove looked at the other women. "I think we need to help Rae wash her beautiful red hair instead." Little Dove had to hide her smile Rae was blushing so much she was red from her head to her toes.

When the ladies thought Rae was clean enough they helped her out of the creek. By this time Rae felt like she must be dreaming. She was led over to a grassy spot that was bright and sunny.

"Now we will dry your hair. Then we will go back to our tepee and finish getting you ready," Little Dove explained. Moon Beam started drying Rae's hair, using a soft beaver skin.

"Why a beaver skin," Rae wanted to know?

"The oil in the skin will make your hair shinny, you will see," Moon Beam told her.

When Rae's hair was dry, she was wrapped in a large buffalo hide. All the women surrounded her as they walked back to the tepee. Only Rae and Little Dove entered the tepee. The others rushed off to get ready themselves.

Little Dove had explained to Rae that when she stepped out of the tepee that Lone Star would be waiting for her, he would escort her to Night Hawk.

When Rae saw the look on Night Hawks face she knew all she had been through that morning had been worth it. He looked at her with such worship on his face that her knees almost gave way. Lone Star felt her almost stop.

He whispered in her ear, "Come Little One, my brother waits for you."

Rae took a deep breath and smiled and told Lone Star, "I'm ready to join with Night Hawk."

If Night Hawk thought Rae was beautiful, Rae also thought how handsome her soon to be husband looked. He stood there in front of her in white leggings with fringe down the legs. He wore a matching vest with fringe all around the bottom. On his head he wore a beaded head band with an eagle feather. Around his arms were beaded arm bands to match the head band. Just looking at him was like looking at a prince. Rae couldn't believe this man was really going to be her husband.

When Rae had reached Night Hawk's side he had reached out and taken her hands from Lone Star. He then turned so they were facing each other for a few seconds. Night Hawk winked at her and smiled. Then they turned and there in front of Rae was a short and very thin man. He also looked to be very old. Little Dove had told Rae this would be the Shaman, who was the tribes medicine man and religious leader, Big Bear. Big Bear reached out and placed a hand on each of their heads. He bowed his head and said a few words, first in their tribal language and then in English so Rae could understand. He than took a small bundle of dried wheat and touched each on both of their shoulders. Chatting words for all to hear. When Rae asked Night Hawk about this later he had told her the wheat symbolized a blessing for little ones. The Shaman then gave his blessing, to all the tribes as well as to the newly married couple. When Rae and Night Hawk turned around, everyone in the tribe had made a tunnel by clasping their hands over their heads. As the couple walked through this tunnel everyone cheered. Rae could feel the love from these people, who were now her people. She just knew she was going to be loved by her new family, as well as, by Night Hawk.

Waiting at the end of the tunnel were two drummers. They started beating their drums, leading the way to the wedding feast. Some of the drums were round and some were long; they had all been made out of tree stumps and limbs. They had used rawhide strings to tie different kinds of animal skins over the ends and were beating them with their hands or with drum sticks. The sticks, Rae noticed were made from animal bones and small tree limbs. One end of each stick was also covered with some kind of animal skin. Some still had the fur and some were just the dried skin, thus making the different sounds.

The ladies of the tribe had prepared a large feast for the bride and groom. Everyone from the tribe was excited about this feast. The men had been hunting and there were three deer roasting over an open pit. The ladies had been preparing food since yesterday. There were corn cakes, roasted corn, turnips, potatoes boiled with wild onions, wild greens, slices of watermelon, and okra in a tomato sauce. When everyone was full, they brought out desserts, fried apples, peaches and pears and all kinds of nuts.

"I'll never be able to move," Rae told Night Hawk.

"Yes you will, Little One. Now is the time for me to teach you the way Indians dance. We will have lots of fun," Rae's new husband told her.

"You lead and I'll follow," Rae told him. There was much dancing, young and old, all having a good time.

The drums, as well as flutes were played for the dancing. The flutes were made from hollowed out tree limbs with different size holes down one side. Sometimes the music was really fast and sometimes so slow that it could almost put one in a trance.

There were times when only the women danced around the camp fire and other times only the men. It seemed that the favorite dance was when they made two circles. The dance would start with the women on the inside circle and the men on the outside. Night Hawk explained to Rae this symbolized that it was the men of the tribes' duty to protect their women and children.

Just as Rae thought she couldn't take one more step Night Hawk reached for her hand. When she looked at him he had his fingers to his lips. He told her in a very low voice. "It is time for us to leave."

Rae followed him, both walked at a slow pace so as not to attract attention. When they reached the edge of the camp they started running. Rae knew that they were headed for the bridal tepee.

Little Dove and Moon Beam had helped Rae erect the tepee. They had explained to her that usually the bride and her family provided all the supplies for the tepee. But, since Rae had no family here, except them, they would see that she had all the supplies she and Night Hawk would need.

When the couple reached the bride's tepee Night Hawk had a surprise for Rae. There, tied to a tree was an Appaloosa mare. When Rae saw the mare she looked at Night Hawk, he smiled down at her and nodded his head. "Yes Little One this is your wedding gift from me. You can name her any thing you want." Rae just couldn't believe this beautiful creature was hers. She walked up and started petting the mare's nose. It was as soft as velvet. That's when Rae decided to call her Velvet. "But how will we get her home," Rae wanted to know?

"We will worry about that later, Little One. Now it is time for us to enjoy the very fine tepee you have put together for us. "

There they stayed for a week, it was their private time. This was a very special time to get to know each other before they had to make the trip back to Indiana. When they went back to camp, it was to tell everyone thank you and goodbye for now.

CHAPTER TWENTY-EIGHT

The Beginning of the Rest of Their Lives

"**J**.B. where are they? He promised they would be back in three weeks. Their three weeks are up today and our wedding is in two days. She just has to be here. I can't get married without Rae." Dawn was asking this all the time while pacing the river bank.

J.B. didn't have an answer. He looked at Zane who just shrugged his shoulders.

Dawn, J.B. and Zane gathered at the river, in the same spot where Night Hawk always hid his canoe.

"Let's take a walk," J.B. said taking Dawns hand. Maybe we can find those wild flowers you've been looking for. You know the ones, for your bouquet?"

When they returned Zane was sound asleep. "I guess sitting there in the sun and listening to the water lapping on the bank was just too much for him," J.B. said with a smile.

"He always could sleep anywhere and anytime," Dawn told J.B.

"I remember when we had been walking for two days,

non stop. We had an important message to deliver so we had to hurry. Then all of a sudden Zane stopped looked around and told me, 'This is the place.'"

I asked him, "'What place?'"

"The 'place' where we're going to stop and rest," he told me and he took off his back pack, laid right down beside a tree using his pack for a pillow and went right off to sleep. An hour later he was shaking me awake, and off we went again."

"Would you two stop talking about me? Who could sleep with you two around? You sound like a couple of old hens," Zane told them as he was sitting up and stretching.

"I was just resting my eyes. Waiting for you two to get back from your walk."

"Uh, Dawn just in case you've not noticed there's a canoe coming up river. Looks like an Indian and a white girl, headed this way. The way that white girl is waving her arms it looks like that Indian is having a hard time keeping that canoe from turning over. Do you think that might be Night Hawk and Rae?" Zane asked Dawn.

"You know I think Zane might be right," J.B. said.

By this time Dawn was waving back and crying tears of joy. Rae was back. Her best friend had kept her promise. Now her own wedding would be complete.

The minute the canoe touched the bank Rae was out and on the run to meet Dawn.

"Oh, Rae we've all been so worried. I was so afraid that you weren't going to get home in time for our wedding in two days. But, now you have and I can see you're safe and, Rae you look different. You have a twinkle in your eyes and such a smile. What have you two been up to," Dawn stopped talking and just looked at Rae?

Zane and J.B. had helped Night Hawk to secure his canoe and carry their belonging up the bank.

"Lets all sit down and we will tell you," Rae suggested.

They found a shady spot under an old pecan tree. When everyone except Night Hawk was sitting down, Rae explained how she and Night Hawk were married. Night Hawk was standing behind Rae. When the others all looked at him he just smiled and nodded his head.

"But, how, when, Oh, Rae you must tell me everything. Your family, what ever are they going to say?"

Rae looked at Dawn with a question on her face.

"No, not that you married Night Hawk. We all were expecting that. But you went off and got married without any of them there."

"I guess we'll just have to find out when I get home. Besides, Night Hawk and I plan to also be married by a minister, as soon as, it can be arranged. Of course we'll have to wait until after your wedding. But soon real soon," Rae answered.

Dawn looked at J.B. they both smiled at each other. J.B. stood up and looked at Rae and Night Hawk. "Dawn and I would be honored if you would share our wedding day. A double wedding sounds like a double good time to us."

Rae looked up at Night Hawk and he just winked at her,

"Why not, friends to the end."

Zane had been listening to the others talk. All this talk of love and weddings was making him miss Beth even more. So, he decided it was time for him to head home. Before he left, he shook Night Hawk's hand, congratulating him and Rae and wishing them all the luck in the world. He told Night Hawk, "You'll need lots of luck with this one. And you Missy, I'm glad for both of you." He than gave Rae a brotherly hug. "I'm heading for home. You love birds don't need me. I'll see you all at your weddings. Who would have ever thought you two country mice would ever get married," Zane said chuckling as he walked away.

On the walk from the river to the Edgewood Farm, Rae and Dawn talked all the way. Rae wanted to know all about Dawn's wedding plans. And Dawn was happy to tell her.

Dawn wanted to know when and where Rae had gotten married and all about her special day.

Night Hawk and J.B. just walked behind them carrying Rae's bags and shaking their heads smiling at each other.

"That woman, she loves to talk, J.B. commented.

When they got in site of the farm, Rae told Dawn, "We'll be over in the morning to help with what ever needs to be done."

It was at this time that Rae's brothers Lee now twelve and Alan now fourteen looked up from their work in the garden. They were picking tomatoes for their Mom to can the next day.

"Look," Lee said pointing up the lane. "There comes Rae

and Night Hawk. I'll go find Mother, and you go find Father." They both ran off in different directions. By the time the newly weds reached the front yard everyone was waiting for them.

Anna had been so worried about Rae. Now she was so happy to see that she was safe and home again. But, one look at Rae's face, and like Dawn she knew Rae had changed.

"You come here right now young lady and tell me what you've been up to. And don't even try to deny what ever it is, remember I'm your mother and mothers can tell when you've done something. And you know you never were any good at hiding secrets." Rae looked at Night Hawk. She couldn't wait another minute to tell her family, "Night Hawk and I are married."

"You what," Andrew asked? "Don't get me wrong we knew this was going to happen and we're happy for both of you. But, how could you do this without us being with you?"

"I'm sorry," Rae told her parents. "When we got to Night Hawks village we just knew that it was the right time. And before you ask we've already made plans to be married by a minister."

"In fact Dawn and J.B. have asked us to share their wedding day."

"That's in two days, well actually now a day and a half," Anna told her daughter.

"All I need to worry about is a dress. Dawn says everything else is already done. So, Mother I was wondering if I could still wear your wedding dress. You know that's what I have always wanted to do?"

Anna reached out and grabbed Rae's hand, "Yes, Yes oh Andrew just think our Rae is getting married in my dress in, oh my, less than two days."

"Come girl, we need to hurry. We may need to alter the dress, then it will need to be aired out and pressed. This is so exciting."

Andrew, Night Hawk and the boys were all laughing so hard that they could hardly stand up. They were all bent over at the waist except Alan, who was down on all fours. He really couldn't stand up.

"Women," Andrew said. "The idea of a wedding just sends them off in a tizzy."

✳✳✳✳✳✳✳✳✳✳✳✳✳✳✳✳✳✳✳✳

The next morning just as the family was finishing breakfast they could hear horses coming up the lane.

"Who, could that be this early," Andrew asked? All the while he was getting up from the table to go see.

Everyone else was just a curious. So they had all followed Andrew to the front porch.

There on the other side of the picket fence was a rather dilapidated carriage and a grey mare that looked like she had seen better days.

A lady, with her back to them, was helping a man out of the carriage. The man looked rather old. His hair was long, past the collar of his jacket, it was grey and dirty looking.

His face was covered with a long beard which was also grey. When he stepped down from the carriage the lady handed him a pair of crutches.

This is when the lady turned around. Rae's, mouth feel open. "Beth is that you? Oh! It really is you. But who is this man with you?"

Bessie had just now joined the family on the porch. Right away she knew who the man was. "Miss Rae, that's my Gerald." Bessie ran down the steps with her arms above her head, until she reached Gerald. Then she threw her arms around his neck and started weeping. When she looked up Gerald was crying with her.

Beth explained that she and Gerald had run into each other in Lexington, both trying to get to Indiana. They had traveled the rest of the way together. She also told them that Bow was on his way to find Stella. What a surprise that was.

Rae walked out to meet Beth. "We're so glad that you're here. We have lots and lots to tell each other but that can wait. You both look worn out and I bet you've not eaten a decent meal in days?"

"You're right Rae, we could both use food, a bath and some rest. But first I have one question?"

"The answer is yes. He's home and worried about you. He had a bad time at the last but I'll let him tell you about that. Would you like for the boys to go and bring him here for you?"

Beth looked at Lee and Alan. "Would you boys mind? Please, don't tell him I'm here just tell him Rae needs him, I want to surprise him."

Beth hadn't needed to ask. Both boys were already running to the barn to get their horses. A few seconds later they went barreling out of the barn door. Neither one had taken the time to put on a saddle. They were in a race to see who could get to Zane first.

Anna looked around her, "Guess we had better hurry; those boys will be back with Zane in no time."

Andrew was already helping Gerald, his best friend, up the front steps.

Anna and Bessie started fussing over Beth and Gerald. There was enough food left from breakfast so it didn't take long to feed them.

While they were eating Rae had put kettles on the stove to heat water so Beth could take a quick bath. As soon as she got the kettles on, she motioned to Night Hawk to follow her to the back porch. "Will you please go to Dawn's and tell her Beth is here. I know she'll want to come over right a way."

"I'm on my way Little One." Saying that he was out the door and running to Dawns.

All the time Gerald was eating, his daughter and son just sat on the other side of the table staring at him. Hayward had never seen his father and Holly didn't remember him. She had been just a baby when he had gone off to war.

When Gerald had finished eating, Andrew told Anna. "I'm going to use the carriage to take Gerald and Bessie home."

He turned to Bessie, "Get the children; I'm taking you all home. You're to stay there until you get this man of yours up on his feet."

"Thank, you Andrew. Did you hear that, Gerald; we're going home." Home would be their own cabin a half mile from the main house. Andrew and Gerald, with the help of neighbors, had built it five years ago just before Bessie and Gerald were married.

While Beth was eating, Andrew had taken Beth's luggage up to Rae's room. As soon as Beth had finished eating, Rae helped her undress and step into the copper tub.

"You won't have time to take a good soak. I'm guessing you have about fifteen minutes. That is, unless you want Zane to catch you in your birthday suit."

"Rae, I want to surprise him not shock him," Beth said giggling.

The girls were just coming down the stairs when they heard voices in the yard. Rae stepped out on the front porch just as Zane jumped off his horse.

Zane looked Rae up and down. "Well, I'll be, you look fine to me. The boys said to hurry that you needed me right now. So what's so important that you would take me away from chopping fire wood?"

Rae wanted to stall for just a few minutes, hoping Dawn would show up.

"Gerald's home; he's hurt and looks like an old man but, he seems to be OK."

"I'm real glad to hear that Rae, but you didn't need to

scare me half to death just to tell me that."

Zane looked up and saw Night Hawk, Dawn and J.B. coming out of the woods. They had taken a short cut through the woods and were riding horses now.

"I guess you sent for Dawn as well, properly scaring her as well," Zane said shaking his head.

"Maybe, maybe not," Rae told him.

"Rae what's this all about? You're up to something, and it's not about Gerald?"

"Smarty pants, we never could fool you, at least not for very long. So turn around and close your eyes and count to ten."

Zane knew better than to argue with Rae. He knew she wouldn't budge until he did what she asked.

The minute Zane turned around Rae opened the screen door and Beth stepped out on the porch. There in front of her was her Zane.

By the time Zane stopped counting everyone had moved in close to see what his reaction was going to be.

"I've counted to ten and I'm turning around." He didn't even make it half way around before he saw Beth.

The looks on both of their faces was a combination of happiness, joy, surprise and most of all love.

Later when there was a lull in the conversations J.B. stood up and cleared his throat, "I have an announcement to make." Everyone stopped talking and looked at him. Even Dawn wondered what he was up to.

"As you all know Dawn and I, as well as Rae and Night Hawk are getting married tomorrow. I know Dawn will agree with me. I say we make it a triple wedding. What do you say Zane?"

Zane looked at Beth and they both answered "yes," at the same time.

"I can't think of anything more fitting than all of us getting married on the same day. Can anyone else," Rae asked?

CHAPTER TWENTY-NINE

The Weddings

Zane had taken Beth back to his farm to let his father know about their plans. Everyone planned to be at Dawn's house early the next morning to help with the rest of the preparations for the weddings. Dawn could hardly wait to tell her folks that it was now going to be a triple wedding. But all the couples had decided they needed to get together later that same evening. There were a lot of things they wanted to share and a lot of questions to be answered as well as asked.

Later that evening, they all met at Rae's farm, it being in the middle. Even though it was late August, Night Hawk had built a small fire for them to sit around.

"A camp fire always helps me to relax," Dawn had told Night Hawk as she thanked him for the fire.

So when the others arrived there were three logs around the fire. One for each couple to lean back on and relax, as well as three quilts that Anna had provided. There was also a big pot of hot coffee and apple cinnamon cookies to eat. At first they all just sat and watched the fire and the stars over head. It was a beautiful clear night. There was a full moon and the sky was full of stars. J.B. was really interested in the stars and the constellations. He started pointing out a few of them. Night Hawk pointed out the Big Bear. Rae laughed and asked him, "Is that where Big Bear, your Shaman got his name?"

"Very smart, Little One," Night Hawk replied.

All three couples were holding hands and thinking about the next day.

Rae was the first to speak. She knew Beth had told Anna about her family in Georgia, but she hadn't been there at the time. So, she wanted to know how they all were.

"Beth, please tell us about your family. Are they all OK?"

"You'll be sad to know we lost Momma Jo right after Christmas this year. One morning she just didn't wake up. Mother's doing better now that father is home. Even though he lost half of his left arm, he seems to be adjusting. We still haven't heard from Robert. But, his friends think he was killed in a battle in Texas. And, of course, I told you that Bow was on his way to Illinois to find Stella and her brothers. This news didn't surprise me. But, just before we left home Sunny and Honey were married. They have decided to stay at River's View." While looking at Rae, "Now, we know what these travelers have been doing for the last four years. So Rae, tell us what you've been doing?"

Rae didn't feel like she had done much of anything, especially, nothing compared to what all the rest of the group had done.

"I've just been helping our families where I could, and teaching school in the winter months," Rae told them.

Dawn looked at Rae and just laughed, "That's not what my folks tell me. When Ma was sick Rae went over and took care of my family, doing all the cooking, and cleaning. She worked in the garden and even canned the vegetables and fruits. She helped Dad every year with his crops. She's even been taking the kids fishing and on picnics."

Zane spoke up then, "Dad tells me how much you helped him and Abby and the baby."

It was Night Hawks turn, "Besides all these good deeds she did more than her part helping to keep runaways safe until someone could get them further north."

Beth looked at Rae, "Now there Miss Rae, I would say you've been a very busy lady."

"Oh, my! I almost forgot I have a story to tell all of you," Dawn exclaimed. "You'll never guess who Stella and I met on one of our missions."

"Who was that?" Rae asked. "Was it someone famous?"

"Yes. To all of us she is and I believe in years to come she will be called a heroine," Dawn told Rae.

"Well tell us, girl," J.B. said.

"As I said, we were on a mission taking six runaways to a safe house in Tennessee. We hadn't been there long when what looked like a little old lady arrived. Our host told us she was there to conduct our group farther north. The lady introduced herself as Harriet Tubman! Stella and I just looked at each other. We both knew who Miss Tubman was. She was one of the most famous conductors in the Underground Railroad. We couldn't believe that she was standing in front of us.

"Stella found her voice first and introduced us as Indiana and Smokey." Then Miss Tubman told us that she had heard of both of us and what a wonderful job we were doing for both the Railroad as well as the army. Then she told us to be careful, so that we could get back to our families when the war was over. Soon after that everyone was sound asleep. The next thing I knew, Stella was shaking me and saying that everyone was gone. I sat up and looked around. She was right. We hadn't even heard them leave. We hurried and gathered our things and left the secret room we had spent the night in. When we reached the barnyard our host reached into his pants pocket and pulled out a note and handed it to Stella. It said, "Thank you both for all your hard work. May God bless you both. Harriet Tubman."

"That sends chills down my arms," Beth told Dawn. "What happened to the note? I hope you kept it."

"Stella has it. She wanted to share it with her brothers."

"I saw a Wanted poster on Miss Tubman. I believe it was on one of my trips to Savannah. There was a five hundred dollar reward for her capture dead or alive. The poster said she was a runaway as well as an abolitionist," Zane told the others.

"She must have done a lot of damage to the south to have a five hundred dollar reward on her head," Night Hawk said shaking his head.

"What a story to tell our grandchildren," J.B. told Dawn

giving her a big hug.

"And your friends? But enough of the past. What do all of you plan to do after tomorrow?" Rae asked to change the subject.

Zane spoke up first. "Beth and I have decided to go back to Georgia. Now that the war is over it should be safe. It sounds like her family will need lots of help. And Beth assures me that her family will accept me even if I am a Yankee. We've talked to Dad and Abby and they agree with us."

J.B. said, "Guess it's our turn. Dawn and I are going to stay right here in Indiana. Her family also needs help and I like this country life. We've talked to her parents and we're going to build a house close to the apple orchard. A small house to start with, but plenty of space to add on as we start filling it with little ones."

Dawn smacked J.B. on the arm but was laughing with the others.

"Does anyone know what Stella's plans are?" Beth wanted to know.

Night Hawk answered her, "When we took her home, she said she wanted to find a place for herself and her brothers of their own. I wasn't sure how she would do that, but now that Bow is looking for her she might just get her wish."

"How about you two," Zane asked Rae and Night Hawk.

"Rae and I have decided to leave also, at least for now. We've decided to go to Oklahoma. There are lots of whites and Indians in that area. We've been told that there is plenty of open range and land for the taking. We think it will be a good place to raise horses and cows. We know things are not going to be easy at first, but we hope it will. Our plan is to come back in a couple of years, maybe even live close by."

"I say we make a promise," J.B. told everyone. "That everyone will be here at this spot in two years. No matter if it's to visit or stay."

"Let's do it," Zane said in agreement.

A little later Zane headed for home, Dawn and J.B. to her family's place. Beth intended to spend the night in Rae's bedroom. Rae and Night Hawk were occupying the barn loft since this is where they had been staying since they had gotten home.

✳✳✳✳✳✳✳✳✳✳✳✳✳✳✳✳✳✳✳✳

The next day dawned bright and sunny. It promised to be a nice but cool day for early September. The sky was full of white fluffy clouds. Everyone was to meet at Dawn's at eight o'clock to help finish things up. The weddings were to be at two. They figured the girls would need at least an hour to change into their wedding finery.

Dawn's mother had helped Dawn sew a beautiful pale yellow muslin dress. Dawn had wanted it to be pretty but not fancy. She had made a ruffle for the scooped neck. It had short sleeves and a full gathered skirt. It was buttoned down the front with white pearl buttons. She had chosen a bright yellow satin ribbon for the waist, tying it in a bow at the back. She and her sisters Bree and Doris had gone out this morning to pick daisies for her bouquet and the girls had made a wreath for her hair.

Dawn was wearing a pair of earrings that Grampa Teddy had given her. They had been Granny Bella's favorite pair. Thomas had made them for his mother as a gift. Thomas had found a marbleized stone on a creek bank a few years ago. The rock had shades of purple, red, white and blue running all through it. He had carved a pair of birds out of this rock and gave them to his mother for a Christmas present. Dawn knew she would treasure them forever. Now they were actually a gift from her father, Granny and now Grampa.

Rae's mother's dress had required very little in alternations. They had to let the hem out since Rae was a little taller than Anna. The dress was pale blue cotton trimmed in dark blue eyelet lace. There was lace around the hem and the three-quarter length sleeves. Rae had decided on a narrow white satin ribbon for her waist, also ending in a bow at the back, the streamers going all the way to the hem. She had used a matching white ribbon to pull her curly red hair back from her face. Anna had given her Grandmother Becca's gold heart shaped locket and matching earrings. Lee and Alan had gone to the woods and picked some Queen Ann's lace and black-eyed Susan for Rae's bouquet. The bouquet was tied together with dark blue satin ribbon.

They had all wondered what Beth would wear. Only Anna knew Beth's secret. And she wasn't telling anyone else. All anyone knew was that Beth and Anna had been up most of the night working on something.

Beth had brought her mothers wedding gown with her

all the way from Georgia. She knew that when she got to Indiana she would be getting married. So she had planned ahead.

She and Anna had removed most of the lace off of the silver taffeta gown. The gown had originally been covered in lace but now there was only lace around the short puffy sleeves and the front of the neck. The skirt had been bell shaped which normally required a number of petticoats. But again they had taken enough of the fullness out so that Beth only needed one petticoat. For her hair she wore her Aunt Anna's lace veil over her long blond hair. The veil was waist length and made of Chantilly lace. Rae had decided not to wear a veil, thinking it was a little to fancy for her dress and the way she wanted to wear her hair. Beth was wearing a necklace of white pearls and matching earrings. Her mother had given these to her just before she left home. They had belonged to Eugene's mother. Zane had told her not to worry about flowers. He would be providing those. And was Beth surprised later when he showed up with a bouquet of wild red roses and Queen Ann's lace. They were all tied together with a red satin ribbon. Beth found out later that the ribbon had belonged to Zane's mother.

It was to be an outdoor wedding. So at the proper time each girl marched out of the house, Dawn with Thomas, Rae with Andrew and since Beth's father was not here she had asked Grant to do the honors.

Each groom, dressed in dark blue pants and white shirts, met their bride half way to where the minister stood. There really wasn't a need for the sun today. The smile on all six of their faces was enough to light up the country side for miles.

They all said their vows together. Then it was time to give the brides there wedding rings. First it was Zane's turn. He presented Beth with a plain solid gold band. His father had given it to him the night before. It had been his grandmothers and his mothers. Next Night Hawk gave Rae a ring he had made out of very small Indian beads. The band was pale blue with a yellow star in the middle. Then it was J.B.s turn. Dawn had no idea where he would get a ring from. When he reached into his pocket and pulled out a ring she was surprised. He placed a gold band with a small pearl on the top, on her finger. Dawn started to cry, she knew this ring had belonged to her Granny Bella. She would have to give Grampa Teddy an extra hug for sharing this with her and J.B.

Then, it came time for the grooms to kiss their brides and new partner for life. There were a lot of hurrahs and clapping from the guests.

Doris had played the violin for the wedding march and she and Thomas played a special, right after the vows were said.

As usual all the women had brought food to help feed everyone. So there was lots of food. When J.B. saw all the food he rubbed his stomach. He looked at Dawn and told her, "Um, I think I'll have to get married more often."

"Don't even think about it. This is your one and only wedding." The others overheard them and just had to laugh.

Anna, Dolly and Abby had been up since early that morning cooking as well. Even though Bessie had been told to stay at home, she had shown up to help. When Anna asked her what she was doing. Bessie told her," You don't think I'm going to miss out on our girls weddings do you?"

The tables were full of everyone's favorites. There were platters of fried chicken, a baked ham, stewed okra with tomatoes, green beans with lots of bacon for seasoning, corn on the cob, fresh baked bread, black eyed peas, fresh sliced tomatoes, stewed new potatoes, both sweet and dill pickles. For their sweet tooth there were fresh sliced peaches and watermelons.

Watermelon meant that before the day was over there would be a watermelon seed spitting contest. Alan had been last years neighborhood champion. He could spit a seed fourteen feet. All the other contestants knew they were up for some hard competition if they wanted to beat Alan.

Each couple had their own wedding cake. Abby had baked a two layer chocolate cake since chocolate was Zane's favorite. She had iced it with chocolate and had put sugared violets all around the tiers.

Anna and Bessie had baked a two tier white cake with white icing. They had topped it with the spun glass bride and groom from Anna's and Andrew's wedding cake.

Dolly had baked an apple sauce cake with white butter frosting. But, instead of tiers she had baked one large round and two small cakes, putting the smaller ones beside the larger one, not on top. She had laid daisies around the cakes. On top there was a wooden bride and groom that Thomas had carved.

All the cakes were so beautiful that no one in all the wedding parties had the heart to cut them. Not so for the younger people. It didn't take them long to decide which piece of cake they wanted and to dig into.

When the dinner was over, it was time for dancing. Thomas, with the help of some of the neighbors, would play until it was time for everyone to head for home. It was also a great time to catch up on the latest news.

The most important news that day was that the war was over. General Robert E. Lee had surrendered to General Ulysses S. Grant at Appomattox on April 13. 1865. And the most shocking news was that on April 26, 1865 an actor John Wilkes Booth had assassinated President Lincoln. The President and his wife were attending a play at the Ford Theater, in Washington D.C. It was months later and everyone was still talking about what a tragedy it had been. It was something people would talk about for years to come.

As the sun started to set everyone knew it was time to start for home. They all had chores to do and some of the neighbors had a long way to go to get home.

Early the next morning Rae and Night Hawk would be leaving on horse back for Oklahoma. Night Hawk had made plans with two of his cousins to meet them just east of St. Louis, Missouri. They would be bringing his horses Winds and Kalo, as well as, Velvet. They would also have a herd of horses that they were driving to Oklahoma. The two cousins were planning on traveling with them in order to make their home in Oklahoma, also. They were looking for a new start and hoped this would be the place to find one.

Zane and Beth planned to go by raft as far as Nashville, hoping the trains were back in operation by now. Otherwise, they would have to find another way to get to Georgia.

Rae had told Dawn and J.B. about the bride's tepee. Dawn had been so impressed with the idea. She had even committed on how great it would be to have a few days just by themselves. But, like the others she had made a special place for their very own wedding night in the barn loft.

Was she in for a big surprise. J.B. had asked Night Hawk for his help. They had sneaked off to the apple orchard the place they planned to build their new home. The two men had erected a tepee for Dawn's and J.B.'s wedding night. The day of the wedding while everyone else was partying Doris, Bree, Alan and Lee went to the loft and took the quilts, lantern and clothes that Dawn had put there and took them to the tepee. Dolly had also packed two baskets of food, enough to last the couple for three or four days.

After the guests had all left, Dawn started toward the barn. J.B. took Dawn's hand and told her, "Follow me, wife."

"Where are we going," Dawn wanted to know.

"Don't ask so many questions. Just trust me, I have a small surprise for you."

So, Dawn just kept quiet and followed her new husband. He had picked up a lantern to light there way. Dawn had no idea what this surprise could be.

But, when they came out of the woods, there in front of her was a tepee. The small lantern light burning inside, made it look like a fairy tale. Dawn just couldn't believe her eyes.

"You did this for me. Oh! J.B. this is the most wonderful surprise I've ever had." Dawn didn't ask about quilts or food or anything. She just knew everything had been taken care of.

When they went inside even J.B. was surprised. The brothers and sisters had made up a pallet for them. The sisters had picked wild flowers and spread them all over the place, as well as brought candles. The boys had gathered fire wood and had brought in fresh buckets of water from the near by creek.

The next four days were the happiest that both Dawn and J.B. had ever had.

✳✳✳✳✳✳✳✳✳✳✳✳✳✳✳✳✳✳✳✳

The girls had each written a letter to the other two girls. They had given the new husbands these letters, asking them to give them to their wives in a day or two.

Dear Friends,

You are both the greatest friends a person could ask for. I will always remember the summer that we spent together, including all the fun we have had. Because of that wonderful summer I met my Zane. I know we will all be happy now and have made the right choices. Our lives are going to be full of happiness and new adventures.

Dawn, I want to especially thank you for all you and J.B.

did to save Zane's life. We are both so grateful to you.

I know these next two years will be busy for all of us. I can hardly wait for August of 1867.

Best Friends Forever,

Beth and Zane Brown

Dear Friends,

Our lives are all so full of happiness now. I pray that they always stay that way. You have been the best friends in the world. We have had such adventures together. I'll never forget the day we found the family of skunks. I can still see Zane's face. And the first day Beth and I met. Who would have thought we would be such friends. And my dear Rae, I will miss you most of all. I know your love for Night Hawk is strong and the two of you will survive all the odds. We will be waiting for all of you to return to us in two years.

Best Friends Forever,

Dawn and J.B.

P.S. Does anybody know what J.B. stands for?

Rae's letter was a letter of both joy and sadness. She was so happy for all of them but sad they were going separate ways.

To our friends,

We have all grown up in the last five years. But, I hope that none of us ever get to old too have fun. I'm so looking forward to this new adventure with Night Hawk at my side. We know we will have problems. Not to worry, we'll be fine. We hope to start a horse ranch and raise racehorses, maybe a few head of cattle. I will miss all of you so very much. I can't wait until our reunion. I'll write with an address, as soon as we're settled. And one last secret that I've not told Night Hawk. I think I'm going to have a little Night Hawk in the spring. Just think of me as a mother.

> Best Friends Forever,
> Rae and Night Hawk

All three had signed their letters Best Friends Forever.

RECIPES

Here are some more recipes that the friends might have enjoyed. Try them and see what you think.

Dandelion Salad

2 cups dandelion greens	6 slices onion, in rings
6 slices bacon	¼ cup sugar
½ cup vinegar	½ tsp. salt

Pick and wash dandelions. Add onion rings. Fry bacon in skillet and add vinegar, sugar and salt. When hot, almost smoking, pour over dandelions and toss well.

Persimmon Bread Pudding

This pudding is usually a thick, cake-like consistency and is best if cut in squares. Serve warm with a sauce.

¼ cup butter, softened	½ tsp. ground ginger
½ cup granulated sugar	½ tsp. allspice
½ cup brown sugar	1 cup whole milk
3 eggs, beaten	1 cup persimmon pulp
1 tsp. vanilla	2 cups dried bread cubes
¼ tsp. salt	½ cup chopped nuts
½ tsp. baking soda	Nutmeg
1 tsp. cinnamon	

In large bowl, cream butter and sugars, blend in eggs, add vanilla. Mix in salt, soda and spices, alternately, stirring in milk, persimmon pulp, and bread cubes, mixing well. Add nuts. Pour batter into a buttered 8-inch square baking dish. Sprinkle with nutmeg. Cover and bake in a 350° oven 30-35 minutes. Remove cover and bake 15-20 more minutes. Pudding is done when a knife inserted in center comes out clean.

Orange Cake

History tells us that this was President Lincoln's favorite cake.

1 cup granulated sugar	2 cups flour
1 cup buttermilk	½ cup butter
½ cup chopped nuts your choice	1 egg
Rind of one orange, ground	1 tsp. soda
Juice from one orange	½ tsp. salt
2 tsp. sugar	

Cream sugar and butter. Add beaten egg and buttermilk. Mix a small amount of dry ingredients with orange rind and nut meats. Add rest of dry ingredients to creamed mixture then add fruit and nut mixture. Bake in 11 x 7 greased cake pan at 350° for 35 -40 minutes. Five minutes after removing cake from the oven spoon orange juice over the cake

Frosting for Orange Cake

1 Tb. butter	1 ½ Tb. Brown sugar
Sprinkle of salt	

Cook a few minutes then add:

2 Tb. cream	¾ cup powdered sugar

Mix and cook: 1 Tbls. butter until right consistency to spread on cake.

Oma's Pickled Okra

1 1/2 pounds fresh okra	2 cups water
3 dried red chili peppers	1 cup vinegar
3 tsps. dried dill	2 Tb salt

Divide the fresh okra evenly between 3 sterile (1 pint) jars. Place one dried chili pepper and one teaspoon of dill into each jar. In a small saucepan, combine the water, vinegar and salt. Bring to a rolling boil. Pour over the ingredients in the jars, and seal in a hot water bath for 10 minutes. Refrigerate jars after opening.

CPSIA information can be obtained at www.ICGtesting.com
Printed in the USA
LVOW05s1241151114

413870LV00014B/834/P